Paradise Pines Series

Night Angel

GAYLORD
PUBLIC LIBRARY
428 Main Avenue
Gaylord, MN 55334
(507) 237-2280

Paradise Pines Series
Night Angel
By

Paisley Kirkpatrick

Paradise Pines

Night Angel
Marriage Bargain
Forever After
Broken Promises
One Eyed Charlie

Desert Breeze Publishing, Inc.
27305 W. Live Oak Rd #424
Castaic, CA 91384

http://www.DesertBreezePublishing.com

Copyright © 2012 by Paisley Kirkpatrick
ISBN 10: 1-61252-795-7
ISBN 13: 978-1-61252-795-6

Published in the United States of America
Electronic Publish Date: August 2012
Print Publish Date: December 2013

Editor-In-Chief: Gail R. Delaney
Content Editor: Theresa Stillwagon
Marketing Director: Jenifer Ranieri
Cover Artist: Gwen Phifer

Cover Art Copyright by Desert Breeze Publishing, Inc © 2012

All rights reserved. No portion of this book may be reproduced or transmitted in any form or by any electronic or mechanical means, including photocopying, recording or by any information retrieval and storage system without permission of the publisher.

Names, characters and incidents depicted in this book are products of the author's imagination, or are used in a fictitious situation. Any resemblances to actual events, locations, organizations, incidents or persons – living or dead – are coincidental and beyond the intent of the author.

Dedication

Our daughter, Kellie Michelle Urso, taught me strength of character through grace and determination. I dedicate this book to her beauty and forever being a guiding light for me. I know she would have been proud and said, "Way to go, Mom."

Many thanks to my husband Ken, daughter Kristen and son-in-law Stanton Vedell who never gave up on me or my love of writing.

I send a special thank you to my mentor and dear friend, Karen Rose Smith, who told me to join Romance Writers of America and get into a local writing chapter. You were right. This is the right place for me.

What would I have done without my critique partners and friends who have shown me patience and encouragement through the years? You are the best. For my dear Carla Capshaw, a woman born with the patience of a saint, the endurance of a warrior and all the while still loving me no matter how frustrated you might have been, a special thank you for teaching me to write and expanding my world. Thank you dear Anne-Marie Carroll for pushing and prodding until I finally found the words right. Denise Pattison, another warrior, thanks for the polishing my work until it sparkled. To every one of my playmates in the Writers Playground, you are the best and never gave up on me either.

Sacramento Valley Rose RWA Chapter who gave me my first taste of being part of a special writing world, thank you. Nicole North for being one of my best teachers, I couldn't have done those emotional scenes without your guidance.

To the beautiful Scot with the cocky grin, thank you for providing the inspiration for my hero.

To my editor, Gail Delaney, thank you for taking a chance on me as a new author. Your patience won't be forgotten.

Chapter One

Sierra Mountain Range, California
April 1853

The stagecoach bumped to a stop in front of a four-story brick building. A tall, bearded man with dark hair curling at his collar stepped from its entrance when Amalie Renard looked out the little window. A large, white-haired dog scampered beside him in the fresh snow, barking with excitement.

"You're late, Lucas. It's past eight." His deep voice rolled with the hint of an accent. "I was gettin' worried. You run into trouble along the road?"

"The trouble's all yours now, Declan," the driver said. "Help me with these, will ya?"

Excited at ending her long journey, Amalie craned her neck and read a wood placard dangling on the ends of two snow-covered chains. A couple of gas lanterns lit the entrance to the Chaumers Hotel. She shivered and leaned back, tugging the cloak a little tighter.

Amalie's heavy cases and trunks thumped against the roof and rocked the stage a bit. Lucas handed them down one at a time. She tapped the toe of her boot on the wooden floor, more than ready to have the long, exhausting weeks of travel behind her.

The hotel owner peered into the coach and tipped his hat.

"What'd you do with the other passengers, Lucas?"

"There's just the one." Another case descended the coach's roof.

"You only have the one passenger?" Declan swept a hand toward the baggage. "Who've you got in there, a princess?"

"Yup. Princess High and Mighty. It's why we're late. She insisted I stop at darn near every bend in the road so she could stretch her royal legs."

Amalie stiffened at the driver's rude comments. If it wasn't for her tight corset, she'd resemble a dockside whore, weary and slumped over from the fatigue ravaging her body. What she wanted more than anything was to take her boots and corset off and slip between soft, warm blankets. She blew on her cold hands and rubbed them together. If there'd been a handle on the inside of the passenger door, she would have let herself out.

Except for the occasional word spoken between the hotelkeeper and her driver, silence enveloped the dark stretching around the coach. From what she'd heard about the place, she'd expected a robust community of noisy saloons and drunken miners. Maybe she hadn't made the right choice coming here after all.

Finally, the driver climbed off the coach and opened the door. Snowflakes covered his dark brown hat and across the shoulders of his leather coat. Realizing the uncouth driver meant for her to alight without the courtesy of his assistance, she leveled her gaze on the other man.

His welcoming smile warmed her. He tilted his head and offered her his hand. "Ma'am, Declan Grainger. Welcome to my establishment." His eyes sparkled and danced.

Her gaze fell to his full, firm lips. His whisper of an accent sent a delightful shiver through her. English? Irish? No, silky Scottish vowels had rolled over her. Annoyed by her body's heated reaction, she grabbed his outstretched hand and proceeded with great care onto the small coach step and then the boardwalk. She straightened her hat. "Amalie Renard." With practiced indifference, she nodded her thanks and swept past him into the dim hotel interior.

The tidy lobby took her by surprise. After the last couple of months traveling throughout the west, she'd expected something more rustic. The soothing scent of lemon polish and burning wood touched the air. A dark brown leather settee, several cushioned chairs, and a portrait of a young woman surrounded by hounds lent the space a homey air.

While Declan carried in her trunks, she warmed herself by the massive rock hearth at the end of the reception area. The heat thawed the achy tingling in her fingers and penetrated through her chilled bones. She turned as he placed the last of her luggage behind the check-in counter. He waved for her to join him.

Amalie removed her bonnet and slipped off her cloak before she proceeded to the caged area. "I'd like to go to my room now."

"Sorry. I wish I could help you, but it's most unfortunate my rooms are full."

"I thought--" She wanted to scream, or at least stamp her feet. Instead, she took a deep breath and calmed her temper. "I don't understand why you have no accommodations reserved for me?"

He motioned to the front window with his thumb. "It's snowing."

"Yes, I can see that, but what does the weather have to do with me?"

He shrugged one broad shoulder toward the empty cubbyholes behind him. "When we have unexpected snow late in the season, it's my practice to provide unprepared travelers shelter. I gave the last bed away about an hour ago, but under these circumstances I can offer you an empty settee and blankets for the night."

She studied the hotelkeeper a moment, trying to figure out what he was about. He seemed decent enough offering her the use of his lobby, but her intuition cautioned her. "I don't understand. Three days ago, Patrick Braddock told me I'd have accommodations at your hotel when I arrived."

He ran his fingers through his chaotic curls and straightened his position on the stool. "It's unfortunate he didn't say a word about you staying here to me. Your appearance was the first I knew of your arrival."

Her heart sank. Her sister's scoundrel of a brother-in-law had assured her Paradise Pines was a perfect place to put her poker-playing skills to good use. He'd better not have been lying about his job offer, too.

The impatient twist to the Scot's mouth drew her attention back to the problem at hand. She'd face that rat, Patrick, and his so-called promises tomorrow. Unless she wanted to sleep standing or fall into a heap from sheer tiredness, tonight's challenge must be dealt with first.

"Please, I'm so tired. Won't you check again?" A few tears streamed down her cheeks.

His gaze traveled over her face before his husky laughter filled the room. "Oh, you're good, lady."

A flush warmed her cheeks. The man was either more perceptive than she anticipated or her acting skills were failing her.

"Believe me, miss, I'm sorry I don't have anything available until tomorrow."

Pain lanced around her head. She rubbed her throbbing temple hoping to ease the headache away. "Why didn't you tell me you had no rooms before you unloaded my luggage?"

"At this late hour I doubt you'd find anywhere else to stay. Maude's boarding house is full, and I wouldn't send a dying dog to the other hotel." He pointed across the lobby. "I figured I could at least offer you a warm place by the fire to sleep tonight. Tomorrow you can move into a comfortable room."

She contemplated the settee, then the snow falling in earnest beyond the window.

He drummed his fingers in rapid cadence on the counter.

She glanced at her proposed bed again and shrugged.

"Is it such a difficult decision?" His deep frown emphasized his frustration.

"I suppose I don't have a choice. Unless, of course, you'd let me sleep in your bed."

Declan stilled. "Are you implying--"

"No, you misunderstand." His innuendo heated her flesh. "I don't want to sleep *with* you, just in your bed. Alone."

His irritating smile grew wider, exposing straight white teeth and a pair of dimples above the outline of his trimmed, dark beard.

"You appear to be a gentleman. I thought I'd ask."

"I can't fit on that settee, much less sleep on it."

"You've made your point, thank you. I accept your kind offer." Compared to weeks of sleeping on the ground with nothing but a blanket, his offer of the settee sounded a luxury.

"Good." He opened the registration book and pointed to the pen. "Please, sign in."

She dipped the tip of the pen into the ink bowl and signed her name.

"Lily Fox?" His eyes narrowed on her. "What kind of game are you playing?"

She checked the ledger and noted she'd signed her stage name by mistake. "I'm known as Lily Fox while I perform. Patrick has asked me to entertain on the stage in his saloon."

"An actress? Well, that explains everything."

Jutting her chin, she stared back at him. The first time she'd sung for the patrons at the renowned St. Louis gambling hall four years ago, she knew she'd discovered the perfect way of turning her bad luck to good. She'd grown accustomed to his kind of response to her profession, but nevertheless, the prejudice still pricked her ego.

"If you're a successful actress, why'd you come to this out-of-the-way mining community?"

Tired and hungry, she was in no mood to be questioned. "It's nothing you should concern yourself with."

He shrugged. "Hope you're not disappointed. I'm thinkin' your 'stage' is probably going to be a box."

"A box?" Her constricting chest robbed her of breath. After all the miserable cheats she'd dealt with in the past, Amalie could not believe she'd fallen for another one of Patrick Braddock's lies.

"My guess is Trick's isn't what you're used to. You might be happier someplace else with more action, like San Francisco."

Doggone right she would, but with dwindling funds and no immediate prospects to earn a living, she'd taken a chance on Patrick's offer. Three days ago they'd met at Sutter's Fort by accident. He'd assured her a woman of her skills would draw a crowd to his saloon. Apparently she'd acted naïve accepting Patrick's job offer in a mining town full of hard working men in need of entertainment. The unexpected opportunity had piqued her interest and seemed more than promising for a widow in need of building a solid life for herself.

"Yes, San Francisco would be a dream come true, but for a while I have no other choice but to try my luck here. You're sure Patrick's saloon has no stage?"

"Not unless he built it last night."

"Do you know Patrick well?" She stared at the man who studied her in the dim light.

"Aye, we both arrived here about four years ago. I'm more a friend of his brother, Ethan though. He's our local doctor."

Her heart sank. The situation worsened by the minute. "Patrick forgot to mention Ethan and my sister live in Paradise Pines."

"It's difficult to believe you and Marinda are sisters. If you'd be more comfortable staying at their home, I'd be happy to drive you. Their place isn't that far from here."

"I appreciate your kind offer, but doubt I'd be welcome." Shock loosened Amalie's tongue. "Other than both of us being blond, my sister and I have never had anything in common."

One dark eyebrow arched at her remark. "That's too bad."

Before she could rebuff his comment, her empty stomach erupted with a loud growl.

His chuckle rumbled from deep down in his throat. "May I assume you'd like something to eat?"

"I apologize for my stomach's lack of etiquette." She pressed her hands against her flushed cheeks and giggled. "Yes, food sounds wonderful."

"I'd be happy to warm up the leftover soup I have on the stove."

"Thank you." She studied the handsome Scot as he left the room. He was a charmer like her dead husband, a man whose quick smile had hid a sadistic monster. She'd stay cautious until she discovered Mr. Grainger's true character

*****

Declan jabbed at the embers in the wood stove and tossed a couple of small logs on the coals. He placed the kettle of soup left over from his supper onto the heat.

Amalie Renard puzzled him. She didn't fit the mold of any woman living in Paradise Pines. The haggard look on the faces of the miners' wives paled in comparison to the vibrant woman who lounged beside his fireplace. Her light golden hair glimmered in the flame's glow. If he were a betting man, he'd wager her sapphire eyes could pull a man into any web she chose to spin.

What was it about the woman he found so compelling? Granted, her looks were as tempting to him as honey to a freshly awakened bear, but beauty alone didn't usually draw him to a woman. From the short time he'd spent with her, it was more than obvious she knew how to use her considerable charms to her advantage.

While the soup warmed, he returned to the lobby with a pot of hot, black coffee and two cups.

"Nice dog." Amalie ran her hand through his pet's tangled hair. The dog's tail wagged.

He could have sworn he heard a low moan escape from the hound as her delicate hand stroked his ears. Declan expected the beautiful woman would have that kind of effect on any male she petted. Considering the way his body reacted to her nearness, he would certainly be no exception. Her presence made it painfully obvious he'd been missing something in his life.

"What's his name?"

"Bunny."

A teasing light glimmered in her eyes. To hide the visual sign of her having an effect on him, he slid his hands into his trouser pockets.

By the way she watched him from beneath her thick lashes, she appeared a bold female. An actress who'd already tried to work her wiles and discover the best way to manipulate him.

She leaned back against the chair and took a sip of coffee. "Didn't anyone tell you this is a dog, not a rabbit?"

"Aw, come on now, where's your sense of humor?" He patted the side of his leg. "Come here, Bunny." The dog didn't budge. "No?" He chortled. "I can't say as I blame you, boy."

He cast another glance at Amalie. Her heavy woolen skirt had hitched to expose one booted ankle in a promiscuous manner. The combination of her grace and boldness intrigued him. No doubt her presence would rattle his mountain community out of its complacency.

"Actually, his official name is Bunny Rabbit O'Hare."

Her mouth gaped before she started laughing. The rich, feminine sound was one he'd appreciate hearing again, and often.

"If you'll excuse me, I'll bring your supper." He took pleasure in the hearty aroma of the beef soup as he filled a bowl. He placed it on a tray along with a few slices of brown bread. Once he returned to the lobby, he set the meal on the small round table by her chair and retrieved a cloth napkin from a nearby cabinet drawer.

He wasn't ready to part company with her yet. He'd like to discover her reason for hiding behind all the bravado. He placed his chair in front of the fire. Bunny flopped to the floor beside him. "While you eat, I'll tell you a story about a young lass and a puppy."

"I must confess I'm intrigued."

After her aloof attitude up to this point, her interest was a pleasant surprise. He leaned back in the chair.

"When five-year-old Katherine lost her parents in a mudslide a couple of years ago, she needed someone to watch her until her uncle could travel from back east." He affectionately patted the dog on the back. "While Katherine stayed at the hotel, I gave her the job of caring for a puppy someone left in a box out front. She named him Bunny because of his white hair and pinkish nose. I didn't have the heart to tell her the name didn't fit."

Two men entered the lobby and stomped their feet on the entry rug. "Evening, Declan." They took off their snow-covered coats and hung them on hooks before they stepped up to the fire. Smiles curved their lips the moment they spied Amalie.

"Ma'am," Sammy Jones said.

Amalie nodded and bestowed them a quick smile.

His younger companion's eyes lit up. "You're the singer pictured on the poster at Trick's. Will you be stayin' a while to entertain us?"

"Maybe." She looked out from beneath those thick lashes, giving them a coy nod. Her gesture put a blush on the man's cheeks. "It depends on how gentlemen in this town appreciate a lady."

Declan expected an actress to take advantage of her talents for self-promotion, but after her sassy comment maybe he needed to give her unexpected arrival another thought. Patrick Braddock's irresponsible behavior wasn't always above board and he knew the man wouldn't hesitate to hire Amalie for more than a song in his saloon.

Declan rose to his feet. "That's enough. You two lads move along. You know where the bunkhouse is."

They tipped their hats and headed toward the courtyard door.

Her gaze met his. "Your behavior was rather rude, don't you think?"

"In case you're unaware, Mrs. Renard, I don't allow solicitation in my hotel."

Amalie squared her shoulders. "Solicitation?"

Deciding to ignore her until his temper cooled, he proceeded to the alcove behind the registration desk.

She rushed after him and grabbed his arm. "How dare you insinuate I have to stoop so low as to solicit men to make my way? I'll have you know--"

He raised his hand. "If I misjudged you, I'm sorry." He pulled a pile of folded bedding from a drawer under the counter and handed it to her. "If I find you've not been honest with me about why you're here, you'll no longer be welcome in my establishment."

Declan locked the hotel's entrance. "You best get some rest. The patrons rise early around here." He went through a door behind the counter and shut it with a firm click. Maybe she was on the up and up, and maybe she wasn't. For now he'd keep his eye on her behavior, at least in his hotel.

*****

Was there more to Declan Grainger than Amalie thought? One thing for sure, she'd best keep her past hidden until she found a permanent residence. He made a definite point about being a stickler for propriety. She'd only been having fun teasing the newcomers.

Amalie unfolded the sheet and tucked it and the blanket around the cushions. After a quick fluff of the pillow, she arranged herself on the settee and laid her head down. As tired as she was, sleep eluded her. After sliding off the narrow settee for the third time, she wrapped the blanket around her shoulders and curled up on the cushion of the tall chair next to the hearth.

A soft glow from two white glass chandeliers cast a warm ambiance over the lobby. Dark cherry wood covered the high ceiling and ran up the wide ornate staircase. His extensive collection of leather-bound books behind the counter, told her a lot about the man. He wasn't just a hotel manager, he was a scholar. The owner of the Chaumers Hotel provided a touch of class to this primitive mountain town.

A grandfather clock chimed the fourth hour of the morning as her eyelids drooped.

Something cool touched the tip of her nose. Thinking it was Bunny she adjusted her position on the chair and ignored the nuisance.

"Pretty lady?"

A man's deep voice broke through her sleep hazed mind. She opened her eyes and stared into two bloodshot brown eyes crowned by bushy grey brows. The man's filthy hand reached to touch her hair. A shriek tore out of her throat. "Don't touch me."

Horrified, she couldn't stop from watching little black fleas march across his scruffy leather coat.

Declan burst into the lobby carrying a rifle. "Harold, what in blazes are you doing to my guest?"

The confused man froze. The color drained from his face. "Nothin'. I... I... I was just looking."

Declan stashed the gun behind the counter. "You're in no danger, Mrs. Renard. Please keep the noise down."

"I am so sorry. I didn't mean to disturb anyone. He startled me."

Declan's gaze focused on the derelict. "What happened to the clothes I gave you last night?"

Harold straightened his stance. "I put them out back by the tub. Reckon you can loan them to somebody else who needs 'em more than me."

Declan faced her. "Will you be alright for a couple of minutes?"

She wrapped tighter in the blanket and nodded.

"Come on, Harold." Declan pointed to the dining room. "Let me get you some warm food before you're on your way."

It wasn't long before Declan returned with a cup of rich coffee. She relaxed against the back of the leather chair and sipped her hot drink. "Who was that?"

Drawing up another chair, he sat across from her and drank from his own cup before he answered. "If you plan on staying here, you're going to have to learn a bit of tolerance. Harold Eriksen was a respected cabinetmaker in Pennsylvania before he chose to make his fortune in the gold fields. He, as so many others who still reside in these mountains, didn't strike it rich."

"Forgive me for asking, but why do they stay?"

"Pride. They're too embarrassed to return home empty handed. Harold turned to the drink instead. It saddens my heart to see those poor lads search day after day and comin' back with nothing but broken dreams."

"You mean there are more men like him in this town?"

"You're not in civilization anymore. Most of them hit the bathhouse on occasion, but Harold's given up on personal grooming, too. That's why I made him bathe before he slept in one of my beds last night."

She plunked her cup down. Coffee sloshed onto the rock hearth. She quickly wiped up the mess with her napkin. "I'm a bit troubled. Will I be sleeping on the same mattress as some bug-infested drunk?"

"It's up to you where you stay," he said. "I assure you I don't let 'bug-infested drunks' stay inside my hotel. I have a bunkhouse out back for men without shelter. The settee you used last night was a lot more comfortable than one of the plank beds I threw together for the unfortunate."

He was right. She'd acted rudely after he'd been so kind to give her a place to sleep when he could have sent her on her way last night. She placed her hand on his arm before he could get up. "I'm sorry. I'm tired and I overreacted."

He rose from the chair and picked up her empty cup. Stopping at the kitchen doorway, he faced her again. "Ye be welcome to look elsewhere."

She glanced at the clock. Quarter to seven. Grubby and in desperate need of a change of clothes, she dropped back onto the chair and rubbed her aching brow.

Bunny observed her with soulful eyes. As she stroked the dog's head, she made a decision. She'd lived through worse. She'd survive this disappointment, too. When she became as famous in the theatre as Jenny Lind, she would own a beautiful place where she'd always have a room of her own to sleep.

The hotel sprang to life. Guests descended the stairs. Some headed into the dining area, others left the hotel. The constant opening and closing of the front door created a cool draft across the lobby floor. She pulled her stocking feet under her and snuggled deeper into the blanket. He stood at the base of the stairs and greeted each guest by name as they headed toward the dining area or left the building. The fire needed stoking again.

Not waiting for his help, she tucked the blanket tight around her and grabbed for a log.

"Let me get that." He brushed her out of the way and tossed wood over the coals before he used the bellows to kick up the flames.

"Thank you. I was a bit chilled."

"There's plenty more hot coffee on the stove. Once you're ready for breakfast, come on in and join us." He placed one last log onto the quickening flames before he proceeded down a nearby hallway.

The aroma of fried bacon sung a beguiling love song to her empty stomach. Her reflection in a tall mirror set back into an alcove along the hall stopped her. A street urchin stared back. A quick fluff up with her fingers brought a smidgen of order to the short curls. She took a handkerchief from her pocket and attempted to rub away the dark smudges from under her eyes. A deep sigh escaped her lips. Refreshing in her own room would have been nice before anyone saw her.

Patrons sat on benches at several long tables, positioned in front of windows in the cozy dining room. Her boots clacked against the hardwood floor on her way to an empty space at one of the tables. An adorable, curly headed little boy who ate with both hands caught her attention. His blond curls and rosy cheeks reminded her of the child she'd never hold again. She tamped down a swell of painful memories she'd worked hard to bury. With a slight nod at the boy's lucky mother, she took a seat on the bench next to Declan.

A young woman wearing a starched white apron placed a plate of bacon and scrambled eggs in front of her. Amalie took a piece of toast from a platter in the center of the table and spread butter on it.

Declan filled her cup with coffee. "By the time you finish breakfast your trunks and cases will be in your room, unless you'd rather not stay."

"I'll stay for a little while." She lifted a forkful of eggs to her lips.

"Rest assured, Mrs. Renard, you'll find no bugs in your bed. I'm having a bath set up in your room to compensate for your inconvenience last night. Thought I owed you that much at least."

"I don't know what to say." She returned to her breakfast.

"Thank you would be nice."

She was used to people who made promises and failed to follow through. She studied his face and the touch of mockery in his eyes. Still a little miffed by his attitude and insults last night, she decided to withhold her appreciation until she saw what accommodations he provided. "Your kindness has not gone unnoticed."

His chuckle resounded throughout the dining room. "You can't give even an inch, can you?"

She couldn't help but give a hint of a smile. "It's not my way."

Only time would tell if Declan Grainger was all talk, or if he deserved any real gratitude.

Chapter Two

Declan unlocked the door and motioned for her to enter. Amalie's heart lightened as she scanned the delightful hotel room. She couldn't resist running her fingers across the white quilted coverlet printed with small pink roses. A bit surprised at the luxury, she eyed the tall hotel keeper. "A brass bed with a feather mattress?"
"It suits your fancy, Mrs. Renard?"
"Oh, yes, very much so." Good luck had returned to her at last. She opened the carved doors to a large, oak armoire and found more than enough space to hang a good portion of the dresses packed in her many trunks stacked against the wall. A dainty vanity table with a scalloped mirror stood opposite the bed. "Are all your rooms as grand as this?"
"Not yet, but I'm workin' on it." A cocky grin tugged at his lips. "Am I to assume these accommodations are satisfactory?"
She returned his smile. "I haven't seen anything this nice since I left home."
Two young men entered carrying a copper tub. "Where do you want us to set it, ma'am?"
Amalie pointed to a spot where soft rays of sunlight filtered through the large window.
The tub thumped against the pinewood floor. They returned a few moments later balancing buckets of water across their shoulders.
"Is there anything else I can do for you?" Declan asked after his staff filled the tub and left.
Glancing longingly at the steaming water, she shook her head. "I'm looking forward to enjoying this bath."
"Alright then, you're all set. Should you require anything, you know where to find me." He moved into the hallway and tipped his head before walking away.
She shut the door and sashayed around the room, stripping off and dropping her clothes onto the floor in disarray. The room might not be as large as she'd have liked, but it was more than pleasant. Admittedly, the fancy brass bed had caught her by surprise. The accommodations were far beyond her expectations. She grabbed the bar of lavender soap off the vanity and sank into the inviting bathwater.

*****

A sharp rap on the door startled Amalie awake several hours later. She sat up and glanced around, taking a moment to regain her bearings. The long, dusty stagecoach ride yesterday must have worn her out more than she imagined.

"Who is it?"

No one answered. She checked her timepiece resting on the bedside table. It was almost five o'clock in the evening. Goodness, she'd slept most of the day away.

She slid from the deep feather mattress and opened the door. Nobody lingered in the hall, but a medium-sized wicker basket sat outside her door. She grabbed the container and took it to the table inside her room. Wafts of something inside smelled delicious. Persistent hunger pains grumbled in her belly. Under the blue cloth she found sliced brown bread, strawberry jam, and a pot of hot tea. How nice. It had been ages since anyone gave a thought for her comfort and her heart warmed at the handsome Scot's unexpected kindness.

She secured the sheer white curtain away from the glass with a pink hair ribbon. The view gave her a chance to survey the area behind the hotel while she ate. A thoroughfare ran between the hotel and a high rock embankment. Several large oak trees, dusted with snow, glistened as the last rays of the day's sun hit their bare branches. It would take a while for her to acclimate to the quiet nature of this mountain community, but she found it peaceful here.

After she'd eaten, curiosity drew her onto her private balcony encased in wrought iron. She tugged her wrap around her shoulders and rested her arms on the rail. From the third floor of the hotel, the town stretched out farther than she'd thought from the brief glance she'd had the night before.

On the hillside across from her, houses and a church nestled among oak and pine trees. She wondered if her sister and Ethan lived in one of the whitewashed homes. If the shocked expression on Patrick's face last week in Sacramento was any indication, she didn't anticipate a warm reception from Marinda.

A brisk wind whipped opened her cloak. Amalie returned inside and shut the door. She dropped onto the chair's soft cushion and stared at her unpacked luggage. What would she wear tonight? First impressions could make or break a performer.

Rummaging through the first trunk, nothing tweaked her fancy. She searched through several more cases, tossing the unsatisfactory garments across her bed. The black dress with rows of red crystal beads stitched around the neckline caught her eye. She stepped into her choice for tonight's performance and secured the buttons. The tight bodice on this one barely contained her ample bosom. She ran her finger over the length of lace. Madame Pouter's bold creation would cause quite a commotion.

The mirror on one of the closet doors was too short to see her reflection full length, but Amalie knew she looked good. She retrieved her hatbox from under the bed and lifted the false bottom. The black onyx necklace with matching earrings would enhance the comeliness of her costume. She draped her black velvet cape around her shoulders, picked up her beaded bag and left her room. Now that she knew Patrick's offer to perform at his place might be a sham, Amalie acting as Lily Fox lifted her chin and set out for combat.

Declan let out a low whistle as she sauntered up to the counter. "Patrick's in trouble, isn't he?"

She nodded curtly at him. "I'd say more than a little. If you'd be so kind, I'd appreciate directions to his saloon."

"If you can wait a moment, I'd be most pleased to escort you, my lady. Let me find George to man the counter and then we can leave." Declan returned a moment later with his black overcoat and hat.

She slipped her arm through the crook of his as they strode into the brisk evening air. Her high-heeled boots hit a slick section of ice on the boardwalk. Declan caught and held her against his broad chest before she spilled backwards. Their gazes locked for a long moment. He straightened and took a slight step back, but she saw the flicker of desire before he glanced away. This was not good. A man didn't fit into her plans unless she could use him to get what she wanted.

He rubbed his hand across his beard and squared his shoulders. "Shall we continue?"

"Yes, thank you."

A merry piano tune and garrulous laughter carried down the boardwalk as they neared Trick's. A burly man stumbled outside the saloon and nearly collided with them. The miner ripped off his weathered hat and bowed before her. "Evening, pretty lady." He grabbed the handle and swung open the door, giving her a deep bow in the process.

Amalie brushed past him. A gasp escaped her lips, then a smile. Patrick's place wasn't as abysmal as she anticipated. Dusty bearded men in miner's boots and faded shirts mingled with gamblers in fancy vests and frock coats. She moved further into the crowded room reeking of smoke and stale whiskey. The familiarity of being surrounded by the rowdiness of a saloon again tugged at her heart.

A fast-clipped tune resounded from a piano tucked in the back corner. A tawdry woman with a glass of ale in her hand lingered next to the upright. Amalie stopped cold at hearing a bawdy song burst out of her bright red lips. Declan hadn't exaggerated. The painted hussy stood on a wooden box.

Amalie scanned the expanse of card players for Patrick. She should have known better than to deal with that lying scoundrel. Betrayal surged through her. She would not put up with his tomfoolery. The man needed to be taught a thing or two -- the first lesson, not tangling with *Lily Fox.*

Different colored bottles of whiskey and beer reflected in the mirrors along the wall behind the long wooden bar. Perfect. That's where she'd start her evening.

She slipped off her cape and handed it to Declan. His appreciative gasp brought a smile to her lips. Having men ogle her appearance was hardly new. She'd learned early to use her looks to her advantage. The way Declan's eyes heated with appreciation when he cast a glance at the deep cut of her décolletage reminded her how good it felt to be a woman.

"Now you'll see who I really am."

Declan grabbed her arm. "Don't let them forget you're a lady, Amalie."

She cast him a wicked smile. "The name's Lily Fox. Believe me, honey, Lily's *no* lady."

She approached a couple of gamblers and leaned over slightly to give them full effect of her daring dress. "Would you mind helping me, gents? I have need of your table for a moment."

The men jumped to their feet in unison, their cards forgotten. Amalie took the nearest man's outstretched palm, stepped onto a chair, over their cards, and up onto the long wooden plank bar.

"Good evening, boys." She strutted along the length of wood, avoiding whiskey glasses and kicking away eager hands.

The saloon girl stopped caterwauling. The room went still. She had everyone's attention, just the way *Lily* liked it.

"Get down, young woman. This ain't no place for you to prance about," the barkeep snarled in outrage.

Ignoring the scowling face with the handlebar mustache, she kicked up her heels. Adding a dance step, she pranced back and forth the length of the makeshift stage. *Lily* reveled in the whistles and disregarded the uncouth remarks. She was in her element. "My name is Lily Fox, and I'm here to entertain you tonight."

With the flick of her hand, she caught the attention of the stunned piano player. "Play something quick and lively, will you, honey?" She glanced around the room of excited faces and turned on her brightest smile.

*****

Disgusted by her brazenness, Declan headed for the exit. A heartbeat from the door her voice froze him to the spot. Dumbfounded, he turned and sought out the glorious sound that poured over him. His body tingled with the awareness of Amalie's bold sensuality.

Sweat trickled down the side of his neck as she moved across the bar. Her sultry, come-hither glances made him burn with desire, but her voice reached deep inside him, touching a chord of awed amazement.

A woman of Amalie's talent needed her own stage, and he was the person to make sure she got it. Keeping her in Paradise Pines had become his first priority.

She finished the ballad and curtsied. As the hoots and hollers bounced off the rock walls, excitement flushed her radiant face. *Lily Fox* certainly knew how to control her audience.

She slipped off the bar. On her way through the poker tables and love struck miners, she continued the feather light steps of her flirtatious sashay.

Buck Thatcher snaked his arm about Amalie's waist and tugged her onto his lap. The ruthless gambler held out a gold nugget and leaned in to steal a kiss.

Declan snatched her off Buck's lap.

The music died away. Outrage crossed Amalie's face. She started to open her mouth.

"Not a word." Declan shoved her behind him. Ready to teach the slick poker player a lesson, he fisted his hands and cut Buck with a stern glance.

Chairs scraped across the wooden floor. Nearby card players grabbed their winnings and moved out of the way.

Buck nonchalantly pulled a cigar from his vest pocket, bit off the tip, and lit a match. As he puffed the stogie alight, the gambler's gaze never faltered from his. The man rose and tossed down the last of his whiskey. Buck moved past Declan, deliberately knocking against his shoulder. He crossed the saloon with an arrogant strut and strode out the door without a word.

Mad as hell, Declan wheeled around and glared into two flashing blue eyes. He should have known better than to push her further, but he knew Thatcher's reputation. "What do you think you're doing?"

Nobody could miss the woman's obvious indignation. He waited for the explosion. By the expressions on the faces around them, the patrons expected it too.

"You have some nerve, Mr. Grainger."

He grasped her hand and hauled her outside into the cold night air.

She poked him several times in the chest with her index finger. "No man owns me, including you. I am Lily Fox, and I take care of myself just fine without your meddling."

He was known for being a placid man, but the obstinate set to her lips nearly provoked him to violence. He ripped off his hat and shoved his fingers through his hair. "No, you're Amalie Renard, the most infuriating woman I've ever met." He'd never come this close to throttling a woman. What kind of witchery was she using to charge his emotions to such a state of turmoil?

With an air of confidence, she tipped her chin and whirled back inside the saloon.

He followed her, settled near the bar and fumed while watching the lady rouse the lust of every drunken, lonely man in the jam-packed room. She'd had a good point insisting he had no right to interfere. He fought the urge to protect.

Patrick Braddock strutted across the room and joined him. "It appears I've discovered a new goldmine."

Declan pulled his attention away from Amalie's antics on the bar. "What?"

Patrick nodded toward Amalie. "She's more brazen than I remembered, but it'll make her even more profitable."

"Don't count on it. She's more than a bit miffed with you right now."

"She just got here. What'd I do already to make her angry?"

"You mentioned a place for her to perform."

"Oh, that." Patrick shrugged. "Can't hold a man to anything he says when he's drunk. Besides I can't remember what I promised."

"She heard 'stage' and since you don't have one, she's out for your blood."

Amalie finished her song and curtsied. The crowd's cheering enthusiasm encouraged her to sing another song. She glanced around the room accepting the acclamations as her right. Her gaze locked with Patrick's. The atmosphere reminded Declan of the lull between lighting a fuse and the explosion.

Keeping her eyes focused on Patrick, the lady sauntered with an exaggerated sway of her hips toward the edge of her stage. Young Braddock put his hands around her narrow waist and lifted her down with an easy swoop. Unexpected jealousy wrenched Declan's gut. He rubbed the tense spot at the back of his neck. For God's sake, he was acting a besotted fool.

With her feet planted on the floor, Amalie moved back a pace and slapped Patrick hard across the cheek.

Declan snickered at Braddock's stunned amazement. If his dropped jaw was any indication, she might as well have kicked him in the groin.

"What was the slap for?" Patrick demanded with a sideways glance at his customers.

Amalie thrust her chin into the air and played the role of betrayed damsel with flair. A quick assessment of the room assured him he wasn't the only man she'd pulled under her enchanting spell. Everyone's eyes focused on her.

"I know you've never been known to keep a promise, Patrick Braddock, but I still trusted you to treat me with respect."

The saloon owner sputtered and rubbed his fingers across the already forming red welt. His face turned crimson. "So I jumped the gun a bit." He shrugged to the room at large and turned back to her. "I'll build the damn stage. There was no need if you weren't in Paradise Pines."

"Humph." She tapped her foot. "Liar."

The patrons returned to their cards. Someone ran the scale on a harmonica. "Come on Lily, sing another song."

"I'll be right there." Amalie gave Patrick a go-to-hell look and turned on her heel. Her short curls bobbed as she stopped and glanced back. "We're not finished, Mr. Braddock."

Declan watched Amalie wander away before turning to Patrick. He pointed upstairs toward his office. "We need to talk."

In the cluttered room at the top of the stairs, Patrick snatched a bottle of whiskey from the liquor cabinet. "Sure you don't want some?"

"You know I never took up the habit of the drink. Go easy on the stuff, will ya? I want to discuss an idea I have." Declan dropped onto a chair, waiting for Patrick's full attention. If he could pull off the sham, it would work toward his goal of reestablishing a productive way of life into Paradise Pines. Downtrodden residents desperately needed both work and their pride restored now that the dazzling lure of gold had dimmed. His town was dying from lethargy.

"You know I own the empty building next door."

"Right." Patrick swigged down the whiskey and reached for the bottle.

"I have a proposition. I'll build a stage. Turn the whole damned building into a theatre for Amalie as long as everyone thinks you're the owner. I dinna want my name connected with the project."

Patrick poured another drink and set the bottle down with a thud. "I don't understand, why the secrecy?"

Construction of the music hall would provide jobs for townsfolk. If he used Patrick as the apparent proprietor, it would give him more leeway to continue his benevolence under the guise of the Night Angel. "Not your concern. All you have to do is pass the word you'll open the theatre for Lily Fox. We can both get a share of the profits. What do you say?"

Patrick's eyes widened at the proposal. "It's a deal, but I think you're a fool. Why not let Amalie know it's you doing this for her?"

"Her potential is an untapped vein of gold. I want to give her a chance to perfect her talent, to hear her sing." He shifted uncomfortably in his chair. If truth be known, he'd do anything to keep her close until he figured out why she affected him like she did. Until he'd met her, he thought he knew what he wanted in a woman. Now he wasn't sure.

"What's going on between you and Amalie, Patrick?"

Patrick poured another drink before he relaxed. "She brought catastrophe to my family. It makes me furious Amalie won't admit it. She owes Marinda so much more than saying she's sorry."

Declan frowned. "Aren't you asking for more heartache by bringing the lady to Paradise Pines?"

"She owes me, too, and I intend to collect."

Declan leaned forward in his chair. "What are you talking about? What does Amalie owe you?"

"An apology, which I know I'll never get. I'll settle for cash or gold. Her type is a magnet for drawing men. This idea for the theatre is brilliant. I can taste the profits."

"You'd better ask Amalie if she's stayin' first. Settle it between you, and then I'll get started on the renovations."

Patrick rubbed his hand along his cheek and winced when he hit the sore spot where Amalie slapped him. "I'll speak to her later tonight."

Declan left through the rear door. The steep decline along the dirt path led him to the backside of his hotel. He entered through the kitchen and headed toward the storage room. He opened a significant part of his past with the turn of a key.

The faded blue cloth stretched across Judith's pedal organ lay covered with dust. He pulled the cover off and ran his fingers over the yellowed keys. He could almost hear his foster mother's voice singing those hymns she loved. Amalie's incredible voice stirred memories he'd kept locked away for the past four years.

"Are you here, Grainger?"

"I'll be right out."

Declan replaced the cloth and joined his friend in the hotel lobby. His heart quickened at the red stains on the front of the sheriff's white shirt. "What the hell happened, Matt?"

"It's not my blood. Somebody knocked Jess O'Reilly over the head and took the mine's cash bag."

"Is he alright?"

The sheriff nodded. "Just a scalp wound. Mad as hell, though."

"Damn. He's sure to get fired this time."

"Yup, I'm 'fraid so."

"How'd he get caught off guard again?"

"The thief shoved a gun in Jess's back in the alley next to the Wells Fargo building and whacked him over the head."

"You look as if you could use a stiff drink."

"I'd prefer coffee."

"Come on, I always have a pot on the stove." They strode into the dining room.

Minutes later, Declan handed the lawman a steaming cup and sat on the bench across from him. "This is the third robbery in the past month."

"Yes and whoever is doing it is clever. Have you seen anyone suspicious here at the hotel?"

"I can't think of anyone off hand, but I'll let you know if I see something that doesn't seem right."

"Thanks. I appreciate any help you can give me." Sheriff Stanton tossed down the last dregs, stood, and strode toward the door. "I've got to get movin'."

As Matt left, the clock struck ten. Declan called Bunny to his side, knelt, and rubbed the dog's ears. It was time to take care of business. "You guard the door, boy, until I get back."

The dog wagged his tail and positioned himself as lookout.

Inside his private quarters, Declan slid the bolt into place. He shoved the foot of his bed far enough to slide the lid off the tunnel.

Chapter Three

Declan rubbed his damp palms against the coarse fabric of his trousers. The claustrophobic panic plaguing him since childhood welled up, suffocating him again. Every time he entered the shaft, his boyhood memories of death and rotting flesh bore down on him. For years he'd fought his terror, but he couldn't banish the nightmare. It started the day he'd seen his father's lifeless body amongst the dead in the hold of the ship on their voyage from Glasgow to New York.

Breathless from his deep-rooted anxiety, Declan stepped off the ladder. He pulled a wooden match from his shirt pocket and scratched the tip against the slate wall. Once the lantern's wick ignited, the beam lessened his discomfort.

The yellow glow cast eerie shadows along the damp rock as he progressed through the narrow passageway to the prehistoric riverbed, now a mere creek. The large cavity held a stash of rusted shovels, picks, and ore carts abandoned by disillusioned gold miners. The space served as his storage area now.

Once he'd dressed in black garb, with the leather knife sheath secured at the right side of his shoulder, he fitted a black silk mantle over his head. Positioned so he could see through the small eye holes, he tied the covering firmly at the bottom of his jaw and picked up the black hat. The ridiculous silver fluff balls dangling from around the wide brim proved a perfect distraction to draw attention from his identity.

With a length of coiled rope draped over his shoulder, he grabbed the lantern and trekked along another tunnel toward the eastern end of town. At the entrance to the smaller, shorter shaft dug under Main Street, his stomach clenched. He ducked his head and traveled the rocky ground at a rapid pace until he reached the ladder at the end. He shoved the plank away and dragged in a deep, fresh breath, appreciating the night breeze cooling his sweaty face. Air filled his lungs, uncoiling the knot in his gut. He snuffed the light and eased himself onto the frozen ground. The three-quarter moon gave him enough illumination to find his way.

Buck Thatcher's concerted interest in Amalie at Trick's had made him more than uneasy. The feisty lady might think she could take care of herself, and maybe in most instances she was right, but he had no intention of letting her tangle with Buck. He'd heard the rumors. No woman should have to endure brutality.

His boots crunched along the crust of snow through a grove of fir trees. Before he stepped from the forest's cover, he stood still as stone and surveyed the area. This time of night he didn't often run into anyone, but it was no reason for lack of caution. He reached the narrow set of wooden stairs to the second floor of Maude's boarding house. The first room along the balcony appeared empty. He pulled back after seeing a golden glow coming from the second window. He chanced another glance. Buck lay stretched across the bed, snoring loud enough to cover any noise he might make. An empty bottle of whiskey lay on the pinewood floor next to the bed.

Declan dislodged the casing's brass lock with the tip of the smaller knife he kept in his boot. The window slid open for an easy entrance. With a quick eye, he perused the room for unexpected weapons, but saw no items to cause worry. The empty Wells Fargo bag tossed on top of a tall chest of drawers did catch his attention. A red haze clouded his vision. He wheeled around to stare at the scoundrel.

Declan stuffed the canvas carrier into his waistband and slammed his boot against the bed frame. "Get up you worthless piece of crap."

Buck's gaze locked on the Night Angel. "What the hell?" He jumped off the mattress and bolted for the door.

Declan knocked him to the floor with a powerful punch to his gut. He drew the sharp knife from his shoulder sheath and stuck its point against Buck's midsection.

"I shall run this blade into your belly, sir, if you do anything so foolish again." As the Night Angel, he'd programmed himself to speak without the slightest trace of accent.

Buck's eyes grew wide. "Who are you? What do you want?"

He grabbed the front of the gambler's shirt and pulled the thief upright. "This is *my* town. These are *my* people, and you dare steal from them."

Buck's lips curled back into a snarl. "You hide behind a mask and condemn me? Hah!"

Declan rolled his eyes. "I want the payroll you stole now. Or, if you prefer, I can slit your gut open and let you bleed to death while I look for it myself."

A modicum of fear radiated through Buck's steel gray eyes. He shoved his hand into his hip pocket and withdrew a few coins.

Declan gazed at the paltry amount of cash Buck had thrust into his outstretched palm. Molten rage coursed through him at the man's audacity. He rammed Buck against the bed frame. The jingle of coins caught his attention.

"You dare deceive me, you lying bastard?" Declan slid the tip of his knife across the bottom of Buck's leather vest pocket and watched a large number of gold coins tumble onto the mussed bedding.

He pulled the Wells Fargo bag from his waistband and tossed it at Buck. "Fill it."

Buck didn't move.

A downstairs clock chimed the midnight hour. His patience gone and about out of time Declan bound Buck's hands behind his back and filled the bag himself.

The incensed man fought against the restraints, spewing out a stream of colorful obscenities. "The money's mine."

"Not anymore." Declan slipped a handful of coins into his own pocket. He grabbed a discarded sock off the floor, shoved it between Buck's teeth, and secured it with the man's kerchief. He would have enjoyed toppling the thief down the stairs, but not wanting to wake the boardinghouse guests, he restrained himself and held tight onto the rope instead. Might as well have, considering how much noise Buck made with each boot stomp down the winding staircase in protest.

Maude opened her door a crack. The lantern cast a glow across her wrinkled face.

"Evening, Ma'am." Declan tipped his hat. "Sorry to have awakened you."

She grasped her blue crocheted shawl around her shoulders. Her eyes grew wide. He began to worry she might make a fuss until he noticed the wink and quickening of a smile.

"What are you doing here?"

"I'm taking the trash out, Ma'am. Would you please open the front door and then lock it again after we leave?"

Maude acknowledged him with a slight nod. She padded across the hardwood floor and unlocked the entrance.

"Thank you." He pulled the coins from his pocket and placed them in her hand before he propelled Buck outside.

"Bless you, Night Angel." Maude closed the door.

He waited until the lock clicked and then moved off the porch with Buck secured in front of him.

The insolent gambler gave him no choice but to drag him down the path and through town. A couple of miners walked along the boardwalk on the other side of the road.

He shoved the tip of his knife against Buck's neck. "Quiet!" he hissed at the snarling man. "Don't be foolish to think I won't end your life to save mine."

Once the area quieted, Declan tied his prisoner to the wrought iron rail around the bell tower. He removed his kerchief and secured it through the tie of the Wells Fargo bag. With the stolen payroll hung around Buck's neck, Declan tugged the bell's rope.

He hastened into the alley next to the Wells Fargo building and watched from behind a stack of boxes.

Matt opened the jailhouse door and walked toward the clanging bell. "Well, I'll be damned." He glanced up and down the street and shook his head.

"Hey, Roberts!"

His deputy stumbled outside, snapping his red suspenders over his shoulders.

Matt retrieved the moneybag. "If you can stay awake long enough, lock this scallywag up."

"Yessiree, Sheriff." Roberts unbound Buck's restraints and marched him to the jail.

The sheriff stopped a mere two feet from Declan's hiding place. Declan pulled farther into the shadows and held his breath.

"I know you're here somewhere, Night Angel." He held up the canvas bag. "Thank you for this. I'll see it's returned to the rightful owners first light of day." He turned to go, but stopped and peered over his shoulder. "A job well done, I might add."

Exhilaration pumped through Declan. He'd done a great night's work. A thief jailed. Money returned. Jess wouldn't lose his job for losing the money bag.

*****

Amalie narrowed her eyes at Patrick's unexpected offer. "Why should I have anything else to do with you after the continuous string of lies you've told me?"

Patrick shrugged. "I expected an independent woman such as you to jump at the opportunity. You lose the Benjamin family nerve you usually flaunt?"

She read the blatant challenge in his eyes. She had no intention of giving into his taunt. "You're a good one to talk."

She studied him closely. What was his latest ploy? Nobody got anything handed to them for no reason, especially from a man like Patrick Braddock. To have her own theatre had been her goal since she'd enjoyed overwhelming applause on the stage in St. Louis.

"I think you'd lie to get whatever you want and the hell with anyone else. You say you want to build a theatre -- for me -- the person you say you hate?" She let out a long, dramatic sigh. "Why?"

"Profits."

She chortled. "Now that's something I can believe."

Patrick pulled a chair next to hers. "Let's make a deal. You do this, and I'll forgive you for the hurt you caused Marinda."

A cold chill ran through her. Aw, the catch. "Forgive me for what?"

He leaned toward her in a most bothersome manner. "Are you aware Marinda almost died on the ship where Jonas Danforth held us captive? We wouldn't have been kidnapped if you'd lived up to the bargain you made with the madman. I heard you say you'd return those illegal bank notes he wrote as soon as he made arrangements to have your father released from jail."

Amalie didn't know what to say. With his biased attitude, Patrick wouldn't believe her explanation.

"Why'd you do it? Why'd you run out on your family? They already had more than enough to deal with."

Her first reaction was to burst out the truth, but she didn't respond. How would she convince Patrick her father had been the one who had set the tragic events in motion? Even she didn't understand what happened.

She swallowed her pride. "Leaving was a lot easier than I expected. I pride in my independence and never intended to make my home near family. How was I to know Danforth would hurt you and Marinda because he was angry with me for setting him up to lose in a poker game?"

"The man's a lying, thieving bastard, Amalie. You should have recognized his hostile arrogance by the belligerent way he acted after you confronted him over his marked cards."

Memory of the eventful night brought a smile to her lips. "He was certainly spittin' mad, wasn't he?"

Patrick guffawed. "I've never seen anything so grand as when you stood on the poker table and embarrassed him in front of his friends. Danforth's face was so red I thought he'd explode." He shook his head. "We made quite a team. Let's do it again. This is a gift I give you. Take my offer."

"If I accept, and I'm not saying I will, I'd want new costumes, control of the sets, and all else pertaining to Lily Fox's career."

"Are you crazy?" Patrick rose and moved behind his desk. "I don't have money to pay for what you demand plus renovations. Accept the offer before I change my mind. It's the theatre or nothing."

She wanted to accept his proposal, but didn't want to seem too eager. It would give her better leverage if he wasn't so cock sure of himself. She'd let him stew for a while.

"I need to think about it." She got up and headed for the door. "If you're playing me for a fool again, Patrick, I promise you'll live to regret it. *Lily Fox* doesn't take kindly to being hoodwinked, and this time I would not hesitate to ruin you."

The saloon was close to empty when she reached the bottom of the stairs. The barkeep tossed his broom behind the bar. "Let me escort you to the hotel, Miss Lily."

"Thank you, Joe. It's very sweet of you to offer."

The crisp night air tamped down her enthusiasm and heightened her misgivings about Patrick's motives. Joe tipped his hat at the hotel entrance and continued on his way.

An empty lobby greeted her. She knocked on the door of Declan's private quarters, but received no answer. Bunny lay on the floor, his tale wagged his excitement at her arrival. She knelt next to him and ran her hand along his back. "Where's your master, boy?"

Amalie slipped out of her boots and sat next to the dog. She leaned her head against the wall and ran her fingers through Bunny's hair as she reflected on those days just prior to leaving home. Patrick's words hit a nerve tonight. How did Marinda feel about her inadvertent involvement in their abduction? They'd worked together to free their father from jail. The effort had brought her and Marinda closer as sisters than they'd ever been. Thank God Marinda and Patrick survived the sinking cargo ship.

She sorted her thoughts. After Ethan took Marinda out of their father's cell and rushed her down the hallway, Papa had restrained Amalie a moment. He begged her to find a way to get him out of jail. Since she'd always wanted to be a real part of the family, she jumped at the chance to finally please her father. The pain struck deep when Papa failed to meet her as planned. She discovered too late Papa and her late husband Rupert were cut from the same dirty cloth.

Bunny's tail thumped against the floor. The dog stretched beside her and raised his head at the click of a lock. The door to Declan's private quarters opened. The man stepped past them and stopped behind the counter.

"Can we talk?" she asked.

Declan whirled around. Concern replaced shock. "Why are you on the floor? Are you hurt?"

Something was different. Something almost dangerous in the way he looked at her tonight. Tongue-tied, she couldn't speak. She shook her head without taking her gaze from his.

He reached toward her. She slipped her hand into his warm palm and let him help her to her feet.

*****

Declan stood face to face with Amalie. The fascinating woman possessed a vulnerability he'd not noticed before. Searching the depths of her dark blue eyes, a slow burn moved the length of him. He didn't hesitate. He rested his hands on her shoulders and leaned toward her until his lips caressed hers. Declan wanted her much more than he'd imagined possible. The thought brought him to his senses forcing him away from her.

She'd pursed her lips, poised ready for another kiss. What the hell. He ignored the loud blare of warning signals, slipped his arms around her waist, and pulled her back against him. His lips claimed hers. The eagerness in her response about drove him beyond the brink of sanity. Her arms wrapped around his neck. Desire rose in him to fever pitch. He deepened his kiss and plundered her mouth.

"Enough," he barely choked out, although his quickened breaths expressed something entirely different, "before we can't turn back." If he wasn't careful, their passion could easily push him beyond his boundaries. What kind of madness had overcome him?

He rested his forehead against hers. "Amalie, why are you here?"

"I... I... came to ask you a question."

She shivered in his arms. Not too steady, he grabbed a blanket from behind the counter. "Wrap yourself in this and wait for me over there." He motioned toward the two chairs by the hearth.

"Come, Bunny, let's get your walk over with."

He turned to Amalie. "I'll be right back."

The cold air slapped him in the face. He drew deep breaths in order to cool his over-stimulated body. What's the matter with you, Grainger? You're acting a horny rogue for God's sake.

Bunny scratched at the door and turned soulful eyes toward him. "You're right, it is cold out here."

He took one more deep breath before he stepped back into the cool lobby. While Amalie sat curled in the chair, he hunkered down and poked at the embers in the fireplace. "What did you want to talk about?"

"Patrick's offered to build a music hall for me."

He gazed over his shoulder, admiring her hair's golden glow, while he waited to hear more.

"It's an answer to my prayers, but I don't trust him. What do you think I should do?"

"Why come to me?"

"I have no one else to discuss this opportunity with. You seem honorable. A man of your word, and I haven't met many of them. If you'd made the offer, I wouldn't even question it."

Declan stared at her dumbfounded. "An honorable man? After what happened a moment ago, I'm surprised you don't consider me anything but a rogue."

Roses appeared on her cheeks. "I kissed you back."

Declan let out a low rumbling chuckle. "Yes, you did. A most delightful experience it was, too."

He continued to stand, taking the safe way out. He figured the more space he kept between them the better. His life would be hell if, like tonight, she continued to share her confidences with him.

"Would it help if I told you Patrick's already talked to me about the renovations?"

Her eyes widened. "Why would he talk to you?"

"I'm a master craftsman." He directed her attention to the lobby. "My foster father and I did all of this woodwork."

Her eyes widened. Her jaw dropped as she surveyed the room. "I had no idea."

He took the seat next to her. "You've been given an extraordinary gift. Don't waste it. This town needs you. Let me, along with the townsfolk build a place where your talent can excel. You belong on the stage, to sing in front of the masses, dignitaries, and ordinary folks like me."

Her eyes searched his. "After the scene you caused in front of the saloon tonight, I can hardly believe you approved of my performance."

"My 'so-called scene' had nothing to do with your talent. You tread on dangerous ground when you incited the crowd." He took both of her delicate hands. "I realize you've had no choice but to perform in saloons and you'd play poker with the devil himself if it got you what you want, but don't sell yourself short. You're too talented to prostitute yourself for a gold nugget."

Chapter Four

The Scot's insensitive words snapped across her back. Amalie jerked her hands from his grasp and moved behind the chair. She barely controlled the urge to slap his face. "That's the second time you've taken my character to task, Mr. Grainger. Prostitute myself indeed."

Declan got to his feet. Disgust exuded from his powerful gaze. "Woman, you take yourself far too seriously. I did not call you a prostitute. I said--" He stepped back, stared at his feet a moment before speaking again. "You have my apologies. I meant no insult to your character. Buck Thatcher is a dangerous man and must be taken seriously. You and I both know he wanted more than a kiss for the gold nugget."

"I didn't need you to swoop in and protect me. I am not some inexperienced schoolgirl."

He threw up his hands. "My mistake."

He gave her the most pitiful, insincere look she'd ever seen.

"I should have remembered you explained all of this with eloquence outside the saloon tonight, but I couldn't concentrate on your well-chosen words with you barely contained in your black dress."

She caught the mischievous tilt to his lips. She also noticed where his gaze settled. At any other time she'd appreciate the attention, but not under these circumstances. She pulled the soft woolen blanket tighter across her breasts. He baited her, but she couldn't let his comment go. The deliciously handsome man was far too sure of himself and needed to be put in his place.

"Lily Fox doesn't need or want your advice on how to handle Buck Thatcher. She's dealt with worse than the cocksure gambler."

"Not in my presence, you haven't." He moved with slow, but determined steps toward her. "Surely you can find it in your generous heart to take pity on this most humble of men?" He placed his hand over his heart and tapped his fingers. "An uncontrollable desire to protect a woman just bursts outta me when I see her in harm's way."

When he flashed a wide grin, she relaxed her stance. "Oh, you are a charmer, aren't you?"

His low rumbling chuckle shot through her. If she was as smart as she proclaimed, she'd flee from the man's hotel this very night. He was a lot more dangerous than Buck Thatcher ever could be. She feared her defenses might not be strong enough to protect her heart from his more than abundant charm.

He cocked his head to one side and gazed deep into her eyes. "Am I forgiven, then?"

"If I say yes, will you promise to restrain this supposed *uncontrollable desire* to meddle in my business?"

"I can promise to try, but meddling comes naturally to me."

Amalie grabbed the back of the chair. His spontaneous chuckle along with the devilish grin made her go all warm inside. The glint in his eyes nearly buckled her knees.

"Oh," she said, throwing her hands up in defense of her unbridled emotions. How is it possible this man could so easily turn her into the silly schoolgirl she just denied being? It was time to retreat.

"It's been a long day. Good night." Forgetting her shoes and key in her embarrassment, she rushed toward the stairs.

Declan grabbed her key off the board behind the counter and caught up to her at the first landing with her hotel key in one hand and boots in the other. "Please, let me see you to your room."

She stopped to catch her breath at the second corridor. They strolled down a carpeted hallway illuminated by gas lamps. His touch sent a warm tingle along her sensitive skin. Not good. Not good at all.

He unlocked the door and she started past him. "Wait," he wrapped his arm around her waist and tugged her behind him.

"What's wrong? What do you see?"

"Someone's vandalized the place. Let me check the room first."

She couldn't believe he was spouting orders again. It hadn't been five minutes since he'd promised not to act so bossy.

Declan lit the lamp on the vanity table. She glanced past him and couldn't understand what worried him. The room hadn't change a bit since she'd left earlier in the evening.

He moved around making certain the window latch and outside door were both secured, and then checked under the bed before motioning her to enter.

"What'd you expect to find? Buck Thatcher?"

His deep scowl silenced her.

"Look at the mess." He pointed at clothes tossed haphazardly around the room. "Someone has obviously broken in here and gone through all your possessions. He picked up a few scattered garments and hung them in the armoire. "I'm sorry. If you can live with the room like this tonight, I'll have someone come in and clean early tomorrow."

"It's only clothes. I tossed them on the bed and chair myself."

He reached for a blue taffeta gown at his feet. "Have you never thought a hanger might be a better place for this beautiful dress than the floor?"

"You're certainly bossy tonight." She shrugged. "I need a maid."

He handed her the gown and strode into the hall. "Come see me in the morning. I'll try to find someone who can be your maid while you stay at my hotel. Good night."

He mumbled a few incoherent words as he walked away. She closed the door and leaned against it, surveying the mess and trying to see the clutter from his point of view.

She pulled open the armoire and grabbed a handful of wooden hangers.

*****

Early the next morning, Declan grabbed a broom and stepped outside the hotel entrance. Bright sunlight greeted him. He stopped long enough to enjoy the warmth on his face. Spring was in the air today. Soon the redbud trees would burst into bloom and change the drab gray of the hills into a blush of dark pink.

Sweeping remnants of snow and mud off the boardwalk, he whistled in contentment. Several townsfolk tipped their hats as they strolled past him.

Sheriff Stanton approached at a fast pace. "Morning, Declan. Did you hear the Night Angel caught Jess's attacker last night?"

Declan stopped sweeping and stared at Matt in mock surprise. "Damn, what a stroke of good luck."

"Yep, of all things, I found Buck Thatcher tied to the bell tower with the Wells Fargo bag full of twenty and fifty dollar gold eagles hung around his neck."

Declan grinned and chuckled. "It sounds like the gentleman has a sense of humor. How'd you know it was the Night Angel?"

"Buck acted a damned fool. He wouldn't stop his rant about the black beast's unlawful attack on him. Personally, I think he's still a bit rattled from his close encounter with the dark mask."

"I dunno. Maybe it's the fact he got caught that's buggin' him, Matt." Declan raised his hand and shaded his eyes. "The gambler, you say? Never did figure him a thief."

"Beats all, doesn't it? He was slick the way he strutted around all fancy and thinking himself high and mighty. Rumor has it you confronted him at Trick's earlier in the evening."

"Nothing I couldn't handle." Declan pushed his broom back into action. "Jess going to keep his job then?"

"It looks that way."

"Good. You got time for some coffee? I have a pot on."

"Not this morning." Matt gave him a friendly pat on the back before he headed on his way.

Ethan Braddock strolled down the boardwalk on the other side of the road. Declan darted across Main Street, stepping over mud puddles and dodging around an overloaded lumber wagon to catch up with him.

"Good morning, Ethan. Do you have a moment?" Once he'd started his nighttime jaunts through the tunnels, Declan took Ethan into his confidence. From then on the two of them worked as a team helping the townsfolk.

"Morning. Gossip around town says you had a busy time last night."

Declan snorted. "Matt's probably told everybody by now," he said, glancing up and down the awakening street. People milled around. He needed privacy to let Ethan in on his plans. "Let's step into the bakery and have a cup of coffee. There are a few things you need to be aware of."

Ethan opened the bakery door and motioned Declan to enter ahead of him. "I heard a troubling rumor this morning. You haven't given my bitch of a sister-in-law a room in your hotel, have you?"

Declan turned and stared into the doctor's steely brown eyes. "It's not like you to be so judgmental."

"You're not answering my question. Is Amalie Renard staying at Chaumers or not?"

"Yes, I booked her into one of my rooms this morning." Declan paid the clerk for a plate of warm cinnamon rolls. He set them on the table while Ethan joined him with two cups of coffee. Settled, Ethan stirred a spoon of sugar into his cup. He didn't wait long to set the tone of their conversation.

"I'd hoped after Amalie ran off the last time she wreaked havoc on our lives we'd be rid of her for good." He set the spoon onto the tablecloth and stroked his beard. "My God, what does the shrew want now?"

"Seems to me you're overreacting. Patrick ran into her in Sacramento and invited her to sing at Trick's. Until I mentioned she might want to stay with you instead of the hotel, she didn't realize you lived here. Under the circumstances, I can't see where you'd get the idea her intentions are malicious."

"The boy's a damn fool. I thought he had more sense than to get involved with Amalie again." Ethan pulled off a section of a cinnamon roll and shoved it into his mouth. Washing it down with a gulp of coffee, he shook his head. "You have no idea what she is capable of. If you knew the true Amalie Renard, you'd not be so smitten."

"I do know. Patrick's filled me in. I still don't see a problem unless your wife objects to the theatre I plan to construct for her sister."

"A theatre?"

"My plan is to turn the abandoned building next to Patrick's saloon into a music hall. He's to be my front man."

Ethan gaped at him. "Why is my irresponsible brother fronting for you? Patrick will only complicate matters."

Declan glanced over his shoulder making sure the two miners who sat on the other side of the bakery couldn't overhear him. Their voices boomed in a loud discussion on an article in the newspaper.

"It's a perfect way to create jobs for the townsfolk. Patrick's help will take the focus off me," he said in a hushed tone.

"Amalie has already gotten to you, hasn't she?"

Declan grimaced at the shocked expression on his friend's face. "This isn't like you, Ethan. Before you say anything else, give me a chance to explain."

"Alright, but it had better be good."

Declan rested his elbows on the white cotton tablecloth and cupped his hands around the warm mug. "I heard her sing last night. She touched something inside me and I can't let it go."

Ethan's cup thumped hard against the table, coffee sloshed over the edge. "You have no idea what you've done." He grabbed a napkin and soaked up the mess.

"You promised to let me finish."

"Yes, I did, but I didn't say I'd keep my opinion to myself."

"Don't judge me. Up 'til now I thought I knew what I wanted in a woman, but now I'm not sure anymore. I want her in Paradise Pines where I can watch and listen to her perform."

"Take my advice and find some nice lady who'll keep your secrets, not Amalie Renard. She'll find out about your underground excursions and spill everything she knows to gain attention for herself."

Declan raked his fingers through his hair. "You may be right, but I'd like to think otherwise."

"Give her time, and I promise she'll show you her true character."

Insulted on Amalie's behalf, he squeezed his fingers tight around his cup. He understood Ethan's anger, but the uncontrollable protectiveness she complained about last night rose to fever pitch. "You're being a bit harsh, don't you think?"

"I've had my say." Ethan rose. "I'd appreciate it if you didn't tell my wife about her sister being in town. I'll try to find an easy way to break the news. It'll be a shock to both Marinda and her older sister Darrah. Amalie always causes some kind of crisis which, in turn, spills over onto them in one disastrous way or another."

He leaned down and gripped Declan's shoulder. "Good catch on retrieving the stolen cash bag last night, by the way. Trust what I have told you. I've been burned too many times by the scheming woman to not distrust her arrival under any circumstance." The doctor left the bakery and turned left past the window.

Declan walked back to the hotel deep in thought about Ethan's warning. Maybe his friend had good reason to dislike Amalie, but it didn't make any difference. The woman had wormed her way into his heart, and no matter what, he planned to build her the music hall.

He settled behind the lobby counter and started the hotel's bookwork. Glancing at the clock, he noted the morning hours had flown by. He tried to focus on the papers, but found concentration difficult.

He glanced up at Patrick's entry into the lobby.

"Sorry, I don't have an answer for you. I mentioned our theatre plans to Amalie, but she wouldn't commit herself."

"Don't worry about it. She spoke with me last night."

Patrick grabbed his arm. "You told her, then?"

"About the music hall being my venture?" He shook his head. "No, she still thinks you're the one who wants to build it for her." He set aside his bookwork and pulled a checkerboard from under the cabinet. "You got time for a game?"

"You bet. Set 'em up."

Declan dumped the box of checkers and placed them across the red and black squares. "If I was a betting man, I'd say she'll accept. We discussed the benefits and it's my opinion she felt better about her options by the time she went to her room."

"Did she mention the new costumes she expects?"

"Costumes?" He moved his red checker to a square close to one of Patrick's blacks. "No, but I wouldn't expect her to. She thinks I'm only the carpenter."

"She wants control of the sets, too," Patrick continued, as he concentrated on his next move.

Declan rubbed his brow, easing the building pressure. "I suppose this demanding nature is what your brother referred to as her 'true character' when I mentioned our plans?"

Patrick nodded. "I can't believe you told Ethan about our partnership."

"Relax, he's only concerned about Amalie being in town and why."

Patrick jumped his black checker over two of Declan's reds. He deposited them in the wooden bowl on the counter. "Are you playing checkers with me or not?"

Declan raised his brows and shrugged. "Sorry, I can't focus today."

"Afternoon, boys." Amalie moved into the lobby with the swish of her skirt. A little girl he hadn't seen before tugged at her hand.

"You're just the two gents I wanted to see."

"Afternoon," he and Patrick said in unison.

"I found Julia wandering the hallway. Do you know where this little girl belongs?"

The toddler moved behind Amalie's skirt. Her eyes widened. Declan knelt in front of her. "Can you show me where your mama is?"

Julia scrunched her nose and let out a wail. "I can't 'member which door. She lost me. I miss my mama. Where is she?"

Declan opened the register and ran his finger down the list of new guests until he found the one he needed. "Follow me. I believe she's Julia Ridley." The three headed up the staircase. At the second floor landing, Declan led them down the hall to the far end. He knocked on the entry to 5A.

Mrs. Ridley jerked the door open and dropped to her knees, wrapping a hug around her young daughter. "Oh, baby, you scared your mama. You know better than to leave the room without me."

Amalie touched the woman's shoulder. "No harm done."

The fretful mother grabbed Amalie's hand. "Thank you for your kindness. I was so worried when your knock woke me and I discovered my daughter gone."

Julia tugged at Amalie's skirt. When Amalie leaned down, the child wrapped her chubby arms around her neck and squeezed. She hugged the little girl back.

Amalie gazed at Mrs. Ridley. "You were lucky this time. Count it a blessing." She cupped Julia's dimpled cheek. "Don't worry your mama anymore, alright?"

A bleak expression crossed Amalie's face before she walked away from the room. He caught up with her at the top of the staircase. "I'm impressed how well you handled Julia and her mother."

"I adore little children."

"I wouldn't have guessed you'd have enough patience."

"There's a lot about me you don't know. The worse possible pain for a woman is the loss of a child."

He placed his hands lightly on her shoulders and turned her to look at him. "Have you lost a child, Amalie?"

The flicker of pain clouding her eyes stopped him cold.

"It's not something I discuss." She broke away and rushed down the stairs.

He found her at the registration desk talking with Patrick.

"You find a maid for me yet, Declan?"

"No, I've been busy," he shot back at her, miffed she could change moods without even the slightest hesitation. "I didn't see you up early putting an effort into finding one on your own."

Patrick looked between the two of them. "If you need a maid, check with Marinda. She knows everyone in town, and most likely could recommend someone for you."

"The day I contact my sister for anything will be the day angels find snowballs in hell." Amalie rubbed her hands together and gazed at the hearth. "Speaking of snowballs, this lobby is quite cold. Let's sit by the fire. Would you get me a cup of something hot, Declan?"

Patrick rolled his eyes behind her back.

"Join me in the dining room instead and you can have something to eat with your coffee. The room's warmer and it's been cleared of the breakfast crowd for a long time now."

Amalie ignored his gibe and led the way. She settled on a bench and Patrick dropped down beside her. "You make a decision about the music hall yet, Amalie? I'd like to get Declan started on renovations as soon as possible."

Declan handed her a hot mug and slid a plate of brown bread and strawberry jam across the table. She picked up a slice and covered it with the sweet fruit. "Thank you. I'll take the deal as long as you throw in new costumes, and we discuss what I want for my sets."

Before Patrick could open his mouth, Declan jumped in. "I'm fine with your ideas for backdrops. There are a lot of structural changes needing to be made first."

"Good, I'm glad you understand. Now about the costumes--"

Declan gave Patrick a quick nod.

"You have a deal," Patrick said. "We can check with Marinda about a good dressmaker."

"Why are you fixated on my sister? I won't ask her for help or agree to wear dresses made by some local dressmaker. I've discovered the Swedish singer Jenny Lind uses a seamstress who owns a shop near the

Grand Plaza in San Francisco. I won't settle for anything less."

Patrick rose off the bench and glared at her. "Don't push me too far. Construction hasn't started yet and you've already made me regret my offer."

She laid her fork on her plate and stared at Patrick. "Please sit. We're not finished."

"What do you want now?"

"Money." She lifted her cup and took a long sip, gazing at him from under her lashes. She waited to speak again until she had him dangling with dread at what her next well-chosen words might be.

Declan had to give her credit. She was good. He'd already experienced her tactics and had sympathy for Patrick.

"You've not mentioned my percentage or what I might expect for my performances in your saloon until the theatre's ready."

Patrick's jaw dropped. "Your *percentage* will be a salary, nothing more."

Declan nearly choked on his coffee at Patrick's damning words. When he noticed her thunderous expression, he bit back a comment.

Amalie leveled her gaze on Patrick. "It's always about money. My talent will put a large amount of cash in everyone's pockets, including mine. If I don't get my equal share of the profits, the deal's off." She rose, smoothed her skirt and strutted out of the room with her chin raised.

Patrick slumped. "That went well. Can this day get any worse?"

"Why'd you antagonize her?"

Amalie's raised voice in the lobby pushed Declan to his feet. He found her in an argument with a Mountain Review reporter. "What's going on in here? Are you bothering one of my guests, Eric?"

"No, I'd like an interview with Miss Fox. This morning I overheard you mention the music hall with Garland. This would be a great story for the Mountain Review and also promotion for her career."

Stunned at her behavior, Declan turned to Amalie. "You have a problem with this?"

"*Lily Fox* does not give interviews." She turned in a huff and headed toward the staircase.

Declan wanted to shake her for being insolent with the Mountain Review reporter. The savvy woman had to realize they'd need publicity to draw in customers.

"Patrick, escort Eric to the building, show him around, and give him what information he needs to write his article. I'll reason with Amalie."

"Sure. I need to get back to the saloon anyway. Good luck with Amalie."

After the two men left, Declan grabbed the master key and bounded up the stairs two at a time. Amalie didn't answer his knock. He banged louder. "I have a key. You might as well open the door."

She still didn't respond. He shoved his master key into the lock and pushed the door open. One of her bags lay open on the bed. "What are you doing?"

"What does it look like I'm doing? I'm packing."

"Why?"

"I've changed my mind. I will not stay in a place where I'm harassed."

He grabbed the bag and tossed it to the other side of the bed. "Don't be flippant with me, Amalie. Does the dream not live up to your expectations or is this an attempt to finagle something else with your dramatics?"

She leaned across the bed and pulled the container back. "I don't want to discuss it. Leave me alone."

"Is it the reporter?"

Her hands fumbled.

"If there's something you need to tell me, now would be the time."

"I can't." She dropped another empty case onto the bed.

He wanted to shake some sense into her. "You will not run this time."

"Why do you care? The music hall hasn't been started yet. You've lost nothing."

"You wee fool. We've all lost if you leave, especially you."

"Don't you think I know what Patrick's offer means? I've dreamed of nothing else since I was a child." She stopped long enough to regard him. Her eyes misted.

"Then why leave? Give the theatre a chance. Give me a chance."

She turned away and sank onto the bed. The vulnerability she tried to hide clenched his gut.

"There's nothing you or anyone else can do. I don't know what I was thinking when I agreed to the music hall. It's best I go now before it's too late."

Frustrated at her defeatist attitude, he wanted to strangle her. "It's too late for what?"

"It's easier to run than stay and deal with problems."

"You're a lot stronger than you realize. Isn't it time you stop running and for once stay and face your past? It can't possibly be as bad as you imagine."

With every item she tossed into the bag, his patience waned. He needed a way to get through to her. Before she could strap the bag closed, he seized her hand. "Amalie, nothing is worthwhile unless you take a risk."

Her gaze locked with his. "What if the risk is too great?"

"Is someone searching for you? Is that why you don't want your name in the newspaper?"

She went rigid.

"Talk to me." The vulnerability he'd seen earlier in her eyes now turned to fear. "Dear God," he whispered. "What have you gotten yourself into, woman?"

Chapter Five

Declan tightened his hold on Amalie's hand. "Come with me."

"No!" She looped her free arm around the bedpost. "You can't order me. I'm not your flunky."

He wagged his finger in her face. "Don't push me, Amalie. Start walking or I'll throw you over my shoulder and carry you."

She considered the ramifications of his threat, then straightened and composed herself. "I'll walk, thank you."

She hurried out the door ahead of him and marched stoically down to the lobby. Without a word, he guided her along the boardwalk past Trick's and stopped in front of a boarded up building. "What do you think?"

"This, this--" she stuttered, stamping her foot. "This is the reason you threatened to carry me down the street?"

"Now, if you please," he continued, ignoring her protests, "picture your name across the front of the renovated music hall -- 'Lily Fox Performs' or 'Starring Lily Fox' in big, bold letters."

"What?" She gaped at him.

"Come on, I know you have a vivid imagination."

She took another look at the facade. His ideas sounded too good to be true. She wanted the opportunity so much she could taste it.

Declan dropped an arm across her shoulder and pointed to the side of the double doors. "Over there we can have playbills with dates and times of performances."

She got caught up in his excitement. She'd worry about the bounty hunter tomorrow. It would be magnificent to have this. Her own theatre had been her dream all of her life. Her heart lurched with excitement.

"Black letters outlined in gold spelling out my name and maybe a picture of me in an exotic costume and outrageous hat." She giggled. Oh, this was fun.

"Excellent." He swung both doors wide open and lit a lantern. With her hand grasped securely in his, they maneuvered around a pile of discarded lumber and tools left in the middle of the room. Layers of brownish-red dust covered everything.

"We could put rows of seats along both sides of the room. An aisle can run along the edges and one through the middle." He glanced at her. "We must be careful in case of fire."

"Are fires common in Paradise Pines?"

"Unfortunately, fires are much too common." He pointed to the rafters. "Up there we can hang a candelabrum to cast a soft glow over the guests. If you prefer the musicians positioned behind you, I can round out the front of the stage or they could be positioned to the sides."

She placed her hand on his sleeve. "You can stop trying so hard, Declan. This is beyond my dreams."

"No retreat, then?"

Throwing caution to the wind, she shook her head. "I can't walk away, but you counted on me wavering when you brought me here."

Declan gave her a quick nod. "I hoped, but it's not always easy to figure you, my dear."

They moved up the narrow staircase which led to a loft. "I plan on building you a large dressing area up here and we can store instruments or whatever over there."

Amalie let out a couple of quick sneezes.

"Come." He opened a door at the back of the loft.

Outside she found a wide open dirt yard backed by a high rock wall and a six foot wooden fence along each side. The fresh air revived her spirit. "From the street you'd never know about this place."

He leaned against the fence. "We won't have anyone sneak in during a performance." His eyes sparkled with mischief. "It saves me from having to shoot them."

"You make an excellent point. My reputation might be ruined if you do." She returned inside and, once her eyes adjusted to the dim interior, took a critical examination. "The place is a filthy mess. You've got a lot of work to make it ready."

"The place has been boarded up for the past four years."

"What happened? Why wasn't it finished before now?"

"My foster mother had the same dream as you. Angus started the work, but when his beloved Judith died, the dream died with her. The dear man set his tools down, locked the front door, and let the building go. Judith's death broke his heart. My foster father never mentioned the job again."

"I'm sorry." She rested her hand on his arm. "We'll make two dreams come true then."

"Thank you. I'd like that." He led her downstairs and pulled a broom from a stack of tools against the wall. "You going to help or stand around all day caterwauling?"

She rolled her eyes. "You never let up, do you?"

"Not too long ago you demanded a percentage of the action. You should be eager to pitch in and help with some of the work until I hire a crew."

"I'd get my clothes dirty."

A wide grin spread across his face. "It's a bit late for your concern, I'm afraid." He pointed to the hem of her dark blue skirt. "You're already toting dust on your finery. You might as well get ta sweepin'."

When she accepted the broom thrust at her, he cupped her chin and ran his finger the length of her nose. "That settles it. Your face is smudged with dirt, too." He stepped back and gave her a once over. "I dunno, I think the smudge is sorta appealing on you."

"Declan, honey?" A sugar-sweet voice called from the street entry. "Can I come in?"

Amalie raised her brows. "Honey?" she mouthed.

He ignored her sarcastic remark. "Afternoon, Phoebe. What are you doing here?" He strode toward the petite redhead.

"Mother asked me to invite you to join us for supper this evening."

He grasped Phoebe's hand. Amalie nearly choked at the moonstruck expression on the prissy woman's face.

"Tell your mother thank you. I'd never turn down one of her meals."

"Wonderful. About six?"

He nodded and led her around the obstructions, closer to where Amalie stood.

The uninvited guest placed her hand through the crook of Declan's arm.

Amalie wanted to use the broom on her. Sweep her out of the music hall and out of Declan's life. What could he possibly have in common with the strumpet?

Phoebe looked her up and down. "Mother told me you're in search of a maid, honey, but I guess I'm too late. I can see you've already found one."

Declan's head whipped around in Amalie's direction. His frown warned her to let it pass, but it just wasn't in her. Amalie walked around a pile of rubbish and pushed her hand against his chest, moving him out of her path and away from Phoebe. "I'll take care of this, Declan, *honey*."

"Amalie!"

She stopped in front of Phoebe. "I'm the one who's in need of a maid." Ignoring Declan's warning, she circled the woman dressed in a simple blue cotton frock and snorted. "Don't bother to apply for the job. You don't live up to my stringent requirements."

Phoebe's mouth dropped open. She gazed at Declan.

"Phoebe, let me introduce Mrs. Renard. Renovations are in process to change the building into a music hall for her."

"Oh, I see." She ignored Amalie and peered around the interior.

"Amalie, meet Miss King. Her father's the preacher in Paradise Pines."

"Humph!" Amalie said. "Excuse me. Since I don't have a maid, I need to get back to work." She pushed the broom with a bit more enthusiasm than necessary, stirring up a nasty cloud of dust.

Declan strutted toward her after he escorted Miss King from the building. Amalie leaned on the broom handle, admiring his self-confidence. He was definitely a man who knew how to handle himself around a woman. "Are you going to be the main course this evening, or dessert?"

He stopped within inches of touching her. "You've got the wrong idea. It's only a sociable gesture from the preacher's wife. I've gotten supper invitations since they joined our community a couple of years ago."

"She's not your type."

"What type do you think suits me, hmmm?"

Amalie wanted to wipe the irritating grin off his face, but didn't know what to say. She really had no idea what kind of woman attracted him. "I'd say some old crone with a big wart on her nose."

A smug grin tugged at the corners of his mouth. "Nah, of late I'm more partial to petite, blond, blue-eyed vixens."

His hands cupped her cheeks. "Amalie," he barely spoke above a whisper. The touch of his warm lips pulled her into a place she'd never been before. Her knees wobbled. She dropped the broom and held onto his shoulders.

"Trust me to make everything alright. You have no reason to be jealous of Phoebe."

If only she dared to hope. If only--

His possessive lips claimed hers again. All coherent thoughts vanished. She moaned and cuddled closer to him, reveling in the unexpected attraction warming between them.

He wrapped his hands around her arms and broke away from their clutch. "Come on, we've done enough for one day." Declan propelled her to the door with his hand in the middle of her back. He locked up and escorted her back to the hotel. When they stepped inside the lobby, the desk clerk motioned toward a stocky woman in one of the chairs by the hearth.

Declan grinned. "Claire, you got my message." He sauntered toward her with his arms wide open. The older lady stepped into his hug, squealing in delight.

Claire followed Declan back across the room and stopped in front of Amalie. "Looks like I'm just in time, too. Are you responsible for this child's tousled appearance, Laddie?"

A glint of amusement lit up his eyes.

"Oh, don't you give Mama Claire your cocky grin, you handsome devil." She clucked at Declan.

"What'd you get yourself into, lass?"

Amalie sent Declan a flash of sweet revenge. "Sweeping." She brushed at the dirt on her dark skirt.

"Humph. A pretty lady like you shouldn't have ta be doing no cleanin'. No siree. You best let Mama Claire take care of you proper like."

"Don't worry." Declan wrapped his arm around Claire as he glanced at Amalie. "She mothers everyone. You'd do yourself a favor if you grab her as your maid."

"How do you know him?" Amalie asked Claire.

"His Mama Judith was my best friend for years. We met when the family hunted for a place ta stay in San Francisco." She gazed up at Declan. Pride radiated from her eyes. "The lad was a tall, lanky teenager who easily stole my heart."

She turned back to Amalie. "You best be careful because he can charm the freckles off your nose if you're not."

"Now Claire, don't you give my secrets away. Amalie can hold her own without more ammunition."

"Humph, don't you boss me around, or I'll box your ears." She tugged playfully at his beard. "About time you shave your scruffy face, my boy. Maybe I should take a razor to ya."

He chuckled and wrapped his arms around her in another hug. "What are you doin' later?"

"Ack, you best not tempt me." She affectionately pinched his cheek. "Get a tub up to this lassie's room. You should be ashamed of yourself treating a lady with disrespect. Of all the impudence, you push the limit."

"I'll have the bathtub and water sent to her room immediately. Excuse me, ladies."

Amalie stood dumbfounded at the exchange between these two who obviously cared about each other. She'd never had affection from her own mother and wondered what it would be like to experience it herself. The idea of Mama Claire as her maid pleased her. Pleased her a lot. "When can you start?"

"I can give you a few hours every day, starting right now." Claire pointed toward the stairs. "Lead the way."

After the boys filled the tub and left her room, Amalie sank into the blissfully warm water. The scent of lavender soothed her body. It hadn't been the sweeping, but the stress over whether she should stay or not that tensed her muscles. She still wasn't sure she'd made the right decision, but there was no turning back now.

Claire busied herself around the room sorting her clothes. When she finished, a pile of soiled garments mounded near the door.

"On my way out of the hotel I'll arrange to have the empty bags stored in the attic," Claire said, picking up the dirty clothes. "If you don't need me for anything else, I'll be saying good night."

Amalie took a quick perusal of the room. "You've done a remarkable job. Thank you. I'll see you tomorrow."

"You have a good evening." Claire smiled and closed the door behind her.

Amalie was pleased with Claire's choice of a scarlet dress with rows of delicate black lace around the bottom of a full skirt. She'd laid it on her bed ready to wear to Trick's tonight.

*****

Declan knocked on the preacher's door a few minutes after six. Maybe Amalie did have a point. He accepted the supper invitations as a convenience, with no consideration of their ramifications before now.

Phoebe opened the door. "Evening, Declan." She stepped to the side. "Please come in."

He was taken aback at the deep blue dress she wore. The bodice displayed a small, but adequate bosom he'd not been privy to before.

"Father waits in his study to talk to you in private before we dine."

He entered the room crowded with rows of books along all four walls a few minutes later. "Good evening, sir." He took the elderly gent's hand in a strong shake. "Your daughter said you wanted to speak with me."

"Yes, yes, please sit." He pointed to the chair across from his desk. "I'm quite disturbed by some news Phoebe shared with me this afternoon." He cleared his throat and leaned forward. "Was she right? Are you opening a music hall for a saloon singer?"

Hackles raised along the back of his neck. Phoebe's unexpected spite angered Declan. Maybe Amalie had been a bit rude, but Phoebe had taken her jealousy too far by tattling to her father.

"That's right. I'm responsible for the renovations. Patrick Braddock has hired Mrs. Renard to sing in his saloon until the hall is completed. Why do you ask?"

"I don't think it's proper for a young man who's courting the preacher's daughter to align himself with a strumpet. I must consider my daughter's reputation, and so should you."

Courting his daughter? Amalie a strumpet? It took all the control he could muster not to get up and walk out of the room. He pulled his temper under control. "I'm sorry you feel this way, but you're wrong about Mrs. Renard. She has a God-given talent and a voice blessed by angels. I wish you'd hold your opinion of her until you've had the pleasure of hearing her sing. She's a widow and needs the work at the saloon to support herself. I assure you, she is no strumpet."

"My daughter came home in high temper this afternoon. She implied differently. It's not like my girl to overreact to situations, so I must rely on her judgment."

"Phoebe's judgment is biased if she thinks I woo her. It's not true. I've never given your daughter reason to believe I have romantic intentions toward her." He stood and started to leave. Enough was enough. "I'm sorry you have such a low opinion of Amalie Renard, sir. My hope is you'll reconsider and give the lady a chance to demonstrate her remarkable talent. I am confident you won't be disappointed."

"Have her come to church and join the choir tomorrow morning at ten."

The preacher's words stopped him cold. "What?"

"If what you say is true, the Lord's house would be the proper place to hear her voice."

Declan angered at the slight curve to Reverend King's lips. He was certain the preacher didn't think Amalie would dare accept the challenge.

"If she lives up to my high praise, would you accept her as a decent woman and support the music hall?"

Reverend King rubbed his chin as he contemplated the question.

Phoebe opened the door and popped her head inside. "Supper's on the table and Mama said to tell you the food is no good cold."

The preacher patted Declan on the shoulder as they walked into the dining room. "I'll let you know my decision about supporting the music hall before you leave tonight."

Wonderful, he was being pulled down a slippery slope of his own making and worried where it would eventually end. As he tried to make polite conversation over dinner, he knew Amalie would never agree to the preacher's demand. She'd have to get up before noon.

Most of the time Mrs. King served a delicious meal, but tonight the baked fish and boiled potatoes could have been made from sawdust for all he knew. He couldn't get out of their place fast enough.

He returned to the hotel lobby two hours later. Amalie and Claire sat at the hearth with a drink in their hand. Amalie motioned him to join them.

He picked up the fireplace poker and jabbed at the coals. "I'm surprised to see you back here this evening, Claire."

"Ack, I am getting forgetful in my declining years. I came by this afternoon to borrow a book. With the unexpected turn of events, I forgot all about it."

He tossed another log on the fire. "You can borrow any book you choose. Please help yourself."

Amalie patted the older woman on the arm. "You were correct about Mama Claire being a perfect maid for me."

"I'm glad it worked out for both of you." He pulled a chair over and joined the ladies, but stared into the flames without saying a word.

Claire frowned at him. "You got something on your mind, Laddie? You don't look so good."

"Come on, out with it," Amalie said. "You've never struggled for words before. Did Miss King flip your world upside down during supper?"

He cast his gaze on Amalie. "No, but her father made derogatory comments about your job at Trick's."

Amalie's cheeks flushed. "Did he criticize my actions or take offense to my attitude with his precious daughter?"

"Both I suppose, but there's a way to fix the situation if you'll cooperate."

"Why don't you tell me why I'd *want* to cooperate?"

"He has a lot of influence around town and could do your career a lot of good."

"Or bad?"

"If you win him over, you'll gain a considerable part of Paradise Pines' population as well."

"He's right, Lass. The Reverend has more influence than I like ta see."

"I'll be honest," Declan said, leaning forward. "The preacher could make it very difficult for Patrick to open the music hall if he gets his hackles up. He's a dictatorial man who rules his congregation with an iron hand."

"Dare I ask what he expects from me?"

A lot rested on her reaction to what he'd done on her behalf. He could not allow her to miss a unique opportunity because of misplaced jealousy. "Dare is the word to remember, Amalie."

"What have you done?"

"Reverend King dared you to sing with the choir at church tomorrow morning, and I accepted for you."

Her eyes widened in shock. She jumped to her feet. "Why, I'd rather spit in that spiteful girl's face than sing in her father's church."

"Whoa, back up a minute." He reluctantly pulled his attention off her abundant breasts barely contained inside the black lace and gazed into her flashing blue eyes. "Phoebe didn't have anything to do with her father's challenge."

Amalie glanced at Mama Claire. "Are you going to help me here?"

"You're doing fine on your own."

He pointed to the chair. "Amalie, please sit and let me start over."

She sat on the cushion and crossed one leg over the other, swinging her booted ankle back and forth. She straightened her back and sat with the dignity of a queen. "I'm ready to hear your revised version now."

Declan clapped and let out a whoop. "Bravo on your performance, *Miss Fox*. You are a true thespian. Are you good enough to play a proud woman who wants to prove her worth to an intolerant pastor and his impartial congregation?"

"This really has nothing to do with you and Miss King?"

"You can't let her petty jealousy fuel yours. If you don't go tomorrow, she wins."

Amalie turned to Claire. "Have you emptied all my cases?"

"I have."

"Even the light gray one?"

"Yes." Mama Claire appeared stunned. "You're not--"

Amalie held up her hand. "Yes, I am, and the gown will be perfect." She turned back to Declan. "What time do I need to be ready in the morning?"

"Services start at ten o'clock."

"You'll accompany me, of course."

Why did he have this anxious flutter in the pit of his stomach? She'd given in too easily. "Yes, but what are you up to?"

"I'll give them a performance they'll never forget."

*****

Sunday morning Declan kept a nervous eye on the clock. The

Night Angel

minutes moved quickly toward the time they must leave or be late for the service.

Amalie sauntered into the lobby. His heart slammed against his chest at the sight of her. She stood before him a vision in white from her frilly lace bodice to the tips of her high-heeled boots. A white straw hat, tied with a white bow, primly covered her curls. He wasn't sure if it was the golden ribbon around the hat's crown that resembled a halo or the three inch gold cross hanging from a long coarse chain over her bosom that made him think of an angel. He moved around her appreciating what he saw, and let out a low whistle.

A slow grin spread across her face. "Do I pass?"

"You'll do. I checked to see if you'd attached a couple of wings to the back of your costume."

"I thought wings might be overkill."

He shook his head at her mettle. "I have something to make your performance more compelling."

He went into his room and returned with Judith's prized Bible. "Reverend King never had a chance, did he?"

"Let's go see." She took his arm and they strolled toward the church on the hill.

The bell tower pealed out the hour of ten as they passed.

"Fashionably late?"

"Better this way. More dramatic."

He pushed open the church's wide door. They stepped inside to the back of the room. When Amalie heard the cohesive gasp, she held Judith's Bible against her chest giving a pensive air.

Reverend King's face lit up at the arrival of his supposed new parishioner. He motioned for them to come to the front of the church.

Amalie rested her hand on his arm. "I can take it from here, Declan. Please wait for me."

"Not to worry, sweetheart. I wouldn't miss the next few minutes under any circumstance."

Pride filled him. She strolled down the aisle, stopping in front of the preacher, and placing her gloved hand into his outstretched palm.

"Thank you for the invitation to sing, Reverend King. I'm the Widow Renard. I'd like to perform Amazing Grace for you."

"I'm pleased you've decided to join us this morning," the usually stern man said, an appreciative smile crossing his face. He motioned for the choir to rise and turned toward the organist.

"Mrs. Braddock will you please start the music?"

"Of all the luck," Declan muttered under his breath. He'd not remembered Marinda Braddock played the church's music.

Marinda sat frozen on the organ bench staring at her sister. Amalie's face almost turned as white as her dress, but she quickly recovered. Ignoring Marinda, she started to sing without the music.

The clear enchantment of her voice filled the church. Like the first time, the hair on Declan's arms stood on end, sending chills through him as he listened to her voice. Amalie's talent far surpassed anything he'd encountered or anticipated.

Marinda brought the organ to life at the chorus and the choir accompanied her, keeping their voices in the background. He heard several intakes of breath when a beam of sunlight broke through the tall, clear windows. The bright glare illuminated the altar where Amalie stood. He observed around the pews. Nobody moved. Most of the parishioners barely breathed as Amalie shared her awe-inspiring talent with them.

At the end of her performance, Amalie moved off the raised platform with grace and confidence, pausing a moment in front of Phoebe. She nodded in recognition, giving the preacher's daughter a broad smile. He knew it to be a blatant act of victory. At least to everyone else, the gesture appeared a kind act of civility. He commended her audacity.

Amalie had accomplished what she'd come for and he was all the more proud of her for stepping up and taking the challenge. The preacher's nod of approval only proved his theory right. Amalie would achieve her dream. People would come far and wide to listen to her perform.

Amalie joined him at the back of the church. He noticed her stiff stance as they stood side by side until the service ended. She slipped her arm through his and they strolled down the steps onto the dirt pathway past buggies and tethered horses.

She paused after they'd separated from the crowd of mingling churchgoers. "Why didn't you tell me Marinda played the church's music?"

He shook his head. "I'm sorry. I forgot she was the organist. You know I would never have blindsided you on purpose, don't you?"

"I didn't think so, but--"

"Your sister looked more stunned than you did."

"I don't know who was more surprised, her or me."

"The congregation didn't seem to notice anything amiss."

Amalie grinned. "I thought my performance went quite well. What did you think? Did I win them over?"

He started to laugh. The jolly sound echoed around them. "Why do I have the feeling you already know the answer?" He brushed a stray curl away from her face. "You were wonderful, my dear. I've never heard Amazing Grace sung with such sincerity before."

"Thank you."

"You appeared very comfortable singing the popular hymn."

"My two sisters and I sang at church every Sunday." Her voice grew hard and resentful. "Singing was something I could do better than my sisters, and the only thing I earned praise for from my mother."

They continued downhill into town until reaching the bakery. He opened the door and motioned for her to enter. "We need to talk. Sit by the window while I grab a couple cups of coffee."

He set the mug in front of her along with a plate holding a sweet roll. "I am very sorry you had such a tough life as a child."

She gave a resigned shrug. "It's hard to let go of old resentments."

"Since I had such keen mothers, it's hard for me to fathom what your childhood was like. My own good mother loved me unconditionally, and Judith never could do enough for me. She and Angus took me into their lives and treated me as a son. I know now how lucky I was."

She picked at the roll while she sipped her coffee.

Declan wiped a spot of sugar from her lip, wishing he could lick the specks off instead. She had every right to feel resentment for her miserable childhood, but enough was enough.

"I promise to work on my attitude, but trust doesn't come easy for me." She stood and pushed the chair back under the table. "Ready?"

He paid their bill and escorted her back to the hotel.

Patrick waited for them in the lobby. "What's with your clothes, Amalie?"

"An audition." She handed the Bible to Declan. "Maybe Judith was with me today and that's why I was so well accepted."

"It wouldn't surprise me one bit. She would have approved of your hymn choice."

She pulled her gloves off. "I'm going to change clothes. See you in a few moments."

Patrick followed Declan into the dining room. "What was she talking about?"

"She's earned her first percentage point of profit." Declan grabbed a couple of cups and the coffee pot and set them on the table.

Patrick's face lit up as Declan explained the tale of the morning's activities. "Her actions never cease to amaze me."

Chapter Six

Marinda stood in the lobby when Amalie came downstairs after changing her dress. A beautiful little boy with a head full of dark curls held her sister's hand. She guessed him to be about three years old. With one finger stuck in his mouth, he gazed up at her with curious dark brown eyes.

Amalie reluctantly pulled her attention back to the poised woman next to him. "Hello, Marinda."

"I never thought I'd see you again."

Oh, this was going to be pleasant. The cold clip to her voice chilled Amalie. She wasn't quite sure how to approach Marinda face to face.

"Seeing you in church this morning was a shock." Her sister's scorn was quite evident by the tight set to her mouth.

"You know me, always turning up at the most unexpected times."

"Yes, and trouble always follows close behind you."

"Pull your claws back, little sister. I mean you no harm."

"Why are you in Paradise Pines?"

"I'm a resident now, at least for the time being." Amalie spoke with as calm a voice as she could manage under the strained circumstances. Marinda had certainly grown more guarded since they'd last met.

"I don't want you here."

"What's new?"

Marinda sighed. "My family and I are happy. I don't want trouble."

"I don't either. I've had enough to last a lifetime."

"That's not good enough. I want to know why you're here. Have you come to cause problems for me?"

Amalie laughed to hide her pain. Her family had always blamed her for their problems, real and imagined. "Do you hear yourself, Marinda? Do you think I have nothing better to do than cause you misery?" She balled her fists in frustration. "As far as I'm concerned, we don't even have to acknowledge each other after today. It's obvious you still hold a grudge against me, but, you know what, I don't care." She wouldn't be the one to break the emotional logjam between them.

"Fine, but I want you to understand when you ran off and left me to deal with Jonas Danforth's rage, you destroyed any sisterly feelings I had left."

"Maybe you did suffer because of my supposed carelessness with the banker, but it couldn't have been too bad by the looks of you."

Marinda stepped back a pace. "I'm done with you."

Her raised voice startled her son. He tugged at her hand. "Who's the lady, Mama?"

Amalie couldn't keep her eyes off the child even if he was the image of his father, Ethan. He moved closer to his mother and gave her a cautious smile.

If only-- She pushed the thought aside. Her baby boy was dead. Wishing for it to be otherwise was pointless.

"I'm your Aunt Amalie, your mama's sister." She bent toward him. To touch him would be heaven, but she hesitated. She didn't want to frighten the little boy. "What's your name?"

His dark brown curls bobbed when he lifted big brown eyes to his mother seeking her permission to speak.

"Benjamin." He held up three chubby fingers. "I'm three."

Amalie froze. She'd named her son Benjamin. "No!" Anguish ripped through her, tearing the scab off an unhealed heart. The pain hurt so deep she dropped to her knees and pressed trembling fingers against her chest. Tears she couldn't let go when her own little Benjamin died alone in his crib nearly four years prior, now flowed uncontrollably. Her baby had been the only good thing to happen in her life and certainly from her loveless marriage to Rupert. Strong arms wrapped around her shoulders. She leaned against his chest, absorbing the strength he so freely gave. Through the drench of tears, she focused on Declan's anxious frown.

"Let me help you." He coaxed her onto a chair by the hearth.

"Patrick," he bellowed, "grab the scotch from behind the counter."

Declan knelt in front of her. He took the bottle from Patrick and held the rim against her lips. "Take a swig, please. It'll calm you."

The potent whisky burned down her throat, scorching the pit of her stomach. He tried to give her another swallow, but she pushed his hand away. "That's more than enough."

He set the bottle on the hearth and rubbed his thumbs in a circular fashion over the backs of her hands. "Honey, can you tell us what's upset you?"

Amalie shook her head and leaned toward him. "Please hold me."

Pressed against his muscular chest, she drew from his strength. After a while, the shock of Benjamin's revelation eased. Her tears dried, but her heart overflowed with grief.

She peered over Declan's shoulder into her sister's eyes. Marinda's bewildered expression caught her by surprise. Drained of bitterness, Amalie slipped from Declan's embrace and gave him a quick kiss on the cheek. "Thank you, I'm much better now."

Her sister held out a white linen handkerchief. "My goodness, Amalie, I've never seen you cry before."

Not knowing what to think about Marinda's unexpected act of kindness, she accepted the lacy cloth and patted the dampness from her eyes.

Benjamin stood behind his mother. Tears glistened on his pale cheeks. She reached toward him. "I'm sorry I frightened you."

His warm hand rested against her cold palm. She gently tightened her fingers around his. "When you told me your name, I thought of my own little boy. His name was Benjamin just like yours."

Marinda's eyes widened. "You had a son?"

She reluctantly let go of her nephew's hand and blew her nose. "I can't face another confrontation with you today, Marinda."

"Don't be that way. Please, I want to know about my nephew and what happened to him."

Amalie took a deep, fortifying breath. "My baby only lived for two days. The loneliness since his death has been unbearable at times."

Declan moved closer. His fingers curved under her chin, turning her face toward him. "I am so sorry, Amalie. You're not alone anymore."

She stared into his eyes and wanted to trust what she saw. So far, he'd been straightforward with her, but past experiences held her back. The only way she'd survived the obstacles thrown in her way until now was by never relying on anyone but herself.

Marinda reached to give her a hug. "Declan's right. I wish I knew what to say. I can't imagine the loss of a child."

Amalie went ridged. "A couple of seconds ago you said plenty."

"Please, don't act this way. Maybe I was too quick to condemn you. Ethan says I always act before I think. It was such a shock to see you walk into church this morning. I had no idea you were in town and immediately became suspicious of your motives for being here."

"Marinda's right. It's time to start the healing," Declan said.

Weakness wouldn't drive her emotions again. It's something she buried a long while ago along with her precious son. She never wanted pity from anyone. "Benjamin's revelation caught me off guard. I thought I was over my grief."

"Won't you come home with me for a little while?" Marinda asked. "Ethan can give you something to calm you."

Amalie fought the memories of finding her son cold and motionless in his cradle. She didn't have the strength to deal with the visions right now, not with this beautiful, breathing little boy next to her. "Being with

Benjamin for a while would be nice."

"Go fetch Ethan, Patrick, while I take my sister home."

Patrick nodded and rushed out the hotel door.

"Would you mind fetching Darrah, Declan? It's time Amalie realizes she does have family. As unconnected from each other as we are, we're all she's got."

"I'll go if Amalie agrees." Declan searched her face for an answer.

She might as well get the confrontation with her other sister over, too. The day was ruined anyway. "I guess so."

"Good, I'll take you ladies home first."

"No need," Marinda said. "I have a buggy out front."

"Come, then." Declan helped Amalie to her feet and escorted the trio outside.

Marinda settled Benjamin on the seat between herself and Amalie. "Thank you. You're a good friend, Declan."

"Nothing you and Ethan haven't always been for me."

He gave Amalie a reassuring nod. "See you in a wee bit."

Marinda slapped the reins. The buggy bumped along Main Street.

Amalie wrapped her arm around her nephew, pulling him protectively close to her when they hit a deep hole at the edge of town.

Benjamin touched her hand. "Can I call you Aunt Ammy?"

She ran her fingers over the little boy's curls and brushed a few strays away from his eyes. "I'd be very pleased if you want to, Benjamin."

"Do you know my Auntie Darrah?" A smile brightened his dimpled cheeks.

Marinda took her eyes off the road a moment. "Darrah and Chase live a short way out of town on a horse ranch. They have a three year old son, Lance. She's pregnant again."

"Oh," Amalie said, her eyes tearing.

"You've met Chase, I believe?"

"You don't have to make small talk, Marinda."

Marinda pulled to a stop alongside the road. "I know, but we have so much to catch up on. I apologize for my shameful behavior earlier in the hotel. I was so blinded by my own anger I didn't give a thought to what might have happened in your life." She reached across her son's lap and placed her hand on top of Amalie's. "I'd like to put this unpleasantness behind us. Could we become friends as well as sisters?"

Years of distrust made her hesitant. Their parents had treated her as a stepchild for most of her life. Living in the shadow of her pampered sisters had left deep scars. "I don't know. My mind's too drained right now to think straight."

"We have time." Marinda turned her attention back to the road. She reined the horse up a slight rise and pulled to a stop under a huge, bare oak tree.

Amalie stood in front of a two-story, white house with its wide entry porch. She recognized their residence as one of those places she'd noticed from her hotel balcony. When she'd arrived in Paradise Pines, she never would have guessed she'd enter Marinda's home with her hand entwined with that of a little boy named Benjamin.

The aroma of apples and cinnamon greeted her. "Your place brings Grandma's kitchen to mind," she said, entering the cozy interior. Knickknacks which reminded her of their childhood home sat on various shelves. A small statuette of a girl who herded ducks caught her eye. She picked the figurine up and ran her finger across the delicate porcelain. "Wasn't this on that little mahogany table in Mama's dining room?"

Marinda nodded. "The housekeeper, Laura, packed several of Mother's favorite pieces plus some private papers and sent them to Darrah and me."

Amalie set the piece back on the mantel with care. "Laura was certainly the most unusual housekeeper Mother ever hired." She snickered. "Did you know she nearly threw me out of the house when I showed up unannounced on my last visit home?"

"Oh no," Marinda said with a shake of her head. "Laura acted very protective when it came to Darrah and me. She blamed you for a lot of our troubles."

She pushed away the memories, and dropped onto the settee. "I feel drained."

Marinda unlaced Amalie's ankle boots. "Put your feet up and rest. Ethan will be here soon."

Benjamin walked into the room with a carved wooden horse clutched in his hand. After Marinda draped a colorful afghan over her, he held out his toy. "I always take my horsie to nap with me. Maybe it will make you feel better."

Smiling at his endearing gesture, she took the treasure from his outstretched hand. "Thank you. I'm sure he'll make me feel a lot better."

"Come, sweetie, Mama will put you to nap while your auntie gets some rest." Marinda took her son's hand, pride radiated from her face. He gazed over his shoulder and waved as the two walked out of the parlor and up the staircase.

Amalie sat up, struggling to orientate herself. Raised voices from the back of the house drew her attention. She lifted the afghan and jumped to her feet.

A bout of dizziness set her back onto the settee. She waited for the room to stop spinning, then got back up and hurried toward the argument.

She poked her head around the corner of the dining room and caught Ethan's vent at Marinda.

"I don't want *that* woman in our house, Marinda. You're too kind hearted to forgive her. She's a fraud, and she'll bring havoc back into our lives again."

Amalie stepped through the doorway. Ethan's gesturing hands as well as his terse words told her all she needed to know. He still held a grudge against her for Patrick and Marinda's kidnapping. His anger was justifiably understood. She shook her head. Would her past mistakes continually get in the way of a better future?

"My God, you nearly died because of her selfishness. We've got our son to think of now."

Amalie rushed into the kitchen. "Ethan, stop" The room whirled, sending her into a vortex of darkness.

*****

Declan knocked at Ethan's front door. Nobody answered. He turned the knob and poked his head inside. Amalie's voice raised in distress kicked him in the gut. He slammed the door behind him and rushed toward the kitchen.

Astounded at seeing his lady crumbled on the kitchen floor, Declan shoved Ethan out of the way. "What the hell's going on? I thought you welcomed her here, Marinda?"

He slipped his arms under Amalie's limp body and lifted her against his chest.

"We can discuss whether she's welcome here or not later," Marinda said. "Put her in the room off the parlor." She led Declan through the house and pulled the deep blue coverlet back so he could ease her sister onto the cotton sheets.

He tucked Amalie under the coverlet and glared at Ethan as he entered with his medical bag. "Is she welcome or not?"

"Sorry, but this reunion caught me off guard." He set his bag at the foot of the bed.

"Doesn't your physician's code say you're supposed to bring comfort?"

"Calm yourself. After what's happened today, I'd bet her collapse is nothing more serious than nerves." He grabbed smelling salts from his bag and passed the mixture under Amalie's nose.

She sputtered awake. "Get away from me," she muttered, pushing away the vile-smelling concoction. Her gaze settled on Declan with relief.

"Declan, what's happened?"

With a light touch, he ran his fingers across her brow. "You fainted, honey."

She drew her attention from him and watched Ethan press his fingers against her wrist.

"I suspect you had a bad case of anxiety. My wife would hold me personally responsible if your recovery isn't complete. You might consider staying the night."

Ethan mixed a powder into a glass of water. "Drink this. The drug will help you relax."

The front door closed with a bang.

"Who's here?" Marinda called out.

"It's Chase and me." Their sister, Darrah, and her husband, Chase, walked into the room. Darrah proceeded to the bed and grasped Amalie's hand. "What's going on?"

Ethan motioned for the other two men to follow him out of the room. "I think these ladies have a lot of catching up to do."

He closed the door behind them and pointed toward the kitchen. "Let's grab a cold drink. We can go outside while the sun's still warm enough to enjoy."

Chase grabbed three glasses out of a cabinet while Ethan stepped into the cellar and returned with a pitcher of lemonade. They moved out back to the small, uncovered porch.

"What the hell are you thinking, Ethan?" Chase leaned against the rail with his arms crossed over his chest. "How could you let that conniving bitch into your home? Haven't we put up with enough of her tomfoolery?"

Declan's back shot ramrod straight.

Ethan grasped his arm. "Relax, having her in town is going to take us a while to adjust -- if we have to, that is. From past experience, she'll disappear again at the first sign of trouble."

"I had a hunch we might see the conniver when my partner read an article in a St. Louis newspaper a few weeks ago," Chase said.

He had Declan's full attention. "What article?"

"It was front page news. It seems she was seen wearing a piece of stolen jewelry. A ring. The man who designed it for his sister recognized it and reported her to the local authorities."

"Why would something as insignificant as a possible robbery be published on the front page?" Declan had an uneasy feeling he'd just learned the reason she refused Eric's interview.

"I'd say because the man hired a detective to find her."

Declan set his untouched glass of lemonade on the railing. "Do you accuse Amalie of the theft?"

"I don't think she stole the jewelry, but she knows her husband was a thief. What's worse she wears it along with several other pieces Rupert took the same way."

His heart dropped. He didn't want to believe the damning explanation, but knew Chase as an honorable man. He'd never sink so low as to blacken Amalie's reputation if he wasn't absolutely sure he spoke the truth. "Are you saying Amalie accepted contraband from her husband and wears it without conscious?"

"Sorry, Declan, but Darrah saw the stash when we ran into Amalie at Fort Laramie. She picked up her sister's bag and the handle broke. The carrier dropped to the floor, spilling the stolen jewelry at their feet."

"There has to be a good explanation." Chase's words hit him hard. How could he have been so wrong about her? "Amalie claimed she'd found the jewels and needed them to support herself until she found a rich husband to take care of her."

Ethan appeared as stunned as Declan. "Why didn't you turn her into the authorities?"

"Not enough time. Darrah and I had to catch up with Cappy before the wagon train got too far ahead of us, and the mail wagon I sent Amalie home on was leaving within minutes."

"Does anyone else know about the newspaper articles?" Declan asked.

"No. Cappy and I decided Darrah didn't need to have this new situation with her sister to worry about with the baby coming."

He'd heard enough. "Thanks. I've got to go."

Ethan blocked his way. "What are you going to do?"

"I don't know. I've got to think."

He walked around the corner of the house and strode along the gravel path to get his horse. There was good in Amalie, he could feel it. Troubled by what he'd heard, Declan settled onto the saddle and turned his mount toward the hotel.

He entered the lobby and proceeded behind the check-in counter. Grabbing the hotel's master key off the hook, he headed up the stairs two at a time. He stopped in front of Amalie's room, and turned the key over and over in his palm. *If I go inside and find the jewels, everything will* change. He stared at the key. Spying went against every moral fiber he valued. He couldn't do it. She'll have to tell him herself. He dropped the key into his pocket and walked back to the stairs.

By the time he reached the lobby, he knew he had to talk to Judith. She was the one person who could help him sort out this mess.

He found his violin on the top shelf of the storage room next to the stack of Judith's music books. He pulled the rectangle leather case down and blew the layer of dust off. He'd not touched it since the day Judith died.

Not far out of town, Daffodil Hill held the graves of the townsfolk. A mass of yellow blooms bid him welcome to the small cemetery. Colorful ribbons of deep orange, creamy white and golden yellow flowers grew in majestic, swirling patterns, flowing between the gravestones.

Declan hiked up the slight rise of the grassy slope until he reached his foster mother's grave. He dropped to his knees in front of the wooden marker he'd carved the day after her death.

"I'm struggling, Mama, and didn't know where else to turn." He brushed his fingertips across her name. "I wasn't sure if you'd hear my words, but know you'll feel my music."

He opened the case and removed the violin. Memories of the hours spent with Judith as she played her favorite songs ran through his head while he turned the pegs and adjusted the strings.

"I need your help. You always had great insight, and I am lacking. My heart tells me Amalie's the right woman for me, but I heard distressful news about her character today and don't know what to think.

"You'd love her spirit." Amalie's beautiful face appeared in his mind's eye. "She doesn't walk through life with indifference. She creates havoc, and pushes anything in her way to the side."

He slid the bow from the clasp inside the crimson lid. "How can my heart cherish someone my mind knows is wrong for me?"

Standing, he placed the rest against his chin and set the bow to the strings. A soulful melody rose off the violin, echoing around him and down through the canyon below. His consciousness became lost in the music sending his plea.

Sunlight faded into golden evening hues as he played. A soft breeze flowed around him. He pushed the bow faster, drawing from memory.

Exhausted, he lowered the violin and knelt next to Judith's grave marker. His chin rested on his chest. He opened his heart and waited.

A mist settled over him. Strangely enough it didn't bring a chill.

Warmth and contentment surged through his veins. He stood, laid the violin against his chin and played again. The knot in his chest eased. Hope strengthened his resolve with every beat of his heart.

Chapter Seven

Amalie actually thought she saw concern in Darrah's eyes. After years of ill feelings between them, she wasn't sure. With her nerves taut and the bedroom air as cool as her and Darrah's relationship had been for years, she thought she'd already been through enough today. What she wanted was for everyone to leave her alone, but knew her desire wouldn't happen anytime soon.

"You can imagine my disbelief when Declan showed up at the ranch and said you were in town, Amalie. He told us you'd had a shock at his hotel and I should come with him to see you."

Darrah accepted the offer of a chair from Marinda and moved it next to the bed. "Chase opted to use the buggy for my sake."

A warm sentiment filled Amalie's heart. Declan had been the one she turned to for strength. He'd given it without hesitation.

"What's this all about?" Darrah asked.

Amalie studied her oldest sister. Still wearing her hair in a long braid, she'd dressed comfortably in a light pink, high-waist dress. She appeared happy, radiant in her pregnancy. Four years had passed since they'd met at Fort Laramie and settled their differences -- at least she thought they had.

"I'm fine, only a little hysteria. There was no need for you to come rushing to my side." Amalie fidgeted with the dark blue coverlet, not sure she wanted to have a heart to heart. She sighed. Both women were stubborn enough to wait until she told them the whole hurtful truth. "I thought I was over the death of my son, but apparently not. Seeing Marinda this morning with her Benjamin caught me by surprise."

Darrah's jaw dropped. "You had a baby? When?"

"A few months after I returned to St. Louis, I gave birth to a son. I didn't know I was pregnant the last time we met at Fort Laramie." A knot tightened in her stomach. She pressed her hand against the dull pain and prayed she'd not embarrass herself by crying again.

"I'm so sorry." Darrah's eyes brimmed with tears. "I hope you weren't alone to deal with his death. It's hard to imagine how you coped with the loss of your child."

"It happens." Amalie fought to regain her composure. She shook off the melancholy, took a deep breath, and pasted a smile on her face. "I'd never been so alone, but managed. I moved on with my life."

Night Angel

Amalie looked away from Darrah's protruding stomach. She wanted to be happy for her sisters, but the old resentment was resurfacing. Even now Darrah and Marinda had beautiful children, while hers had been snatched away.

"The last time we spoke you were adamant about staying in the east. I'm curious, what made you pick a remote place like Paradise Pines to 'move on with your life,' as you put it?" Darrah asked.

"A chance at a job came up."

Wariness clouded Darrah's eyes. "I thought you liked all the excitement St. Louis provided. It doesn't make sense you'd come all the way across the country for the *chance* of a job. What's really going on?"

There was no doubt how Darrah would react if she knew the truth. Another tongue lashing similar to the first she'd received after her sister found the jewels is something she'd rather avoid. She brushed off Darrah's probe and changed the subject. "I ran into Patrick in Sacramento. His offer of a job at his saloon seemed a stroke of good luck. The offer didn't turn out to be quite as he stated, but we've come to terms. Now he's about to remodel an empty building into a music hall for me."

Darrah's mouth fell open. "Patrick's blamed you for everything wrong in his life since I met him. Why would he have anything to do with you?"

"Greed. My voice can line his pockets with gold, and he knows it."

"I can't say I approve, but it's your life. I hope you know what you're doing." She took Marinda's hand. "Did you know our sister was in town before this morning?"

Marinda shook her head. "Not until she walked into church. The shock of seeing her prance up the aisle with a Bible clutched to her bosom nearly made me forget to play. I wish you could have heard her sing." Marinda sat on the edge of the bed. "Amalie's voice is even prettier than I remembered. As soon as she started singing Amazing Grace, a hush fell over the congregation. I even forgot to accompany her until she reached the chorus."

"Church?" Darrah stammered. "You're singing in a saloon and at church?"

"The preacher made me an offer I couldn't pass up either."

Darrah leaned forward with a tight set to her mouth. "Why are you really in Paradise Pines?"

The familiar animosity between them resurfaced. "I feel the warmth, little sister."

Darrah's eyes narrowed. "I don't mean to interrogate you, Amalie, but having you show up on our doorstep from God knows where is suspicious. Don't you think we have the right to question your motives? After you ran off with my fiancé and then left Marinda to fend off Banker Danforth, even you must admit we have cause to act with caution. If you'd expected *warmth*, as you put it, you'd have let us know before now you were in town."

"Why, when this is exactly the kind of reception I expected from the two of you?" Amalie's voice rose to meet Darrah's steely tone. She punched at the two feather pillows behind her back and repositioned them. "It certainly wasn't for family since I obviously don't have one who gives a damn."

"I've never understood your way of thinking. All this drama over your baby's death seems staged to me, especially since it happened over three years ago."

Amalie jerked upright. The sharp edge of Darrah's barb cut deep. "I--" She started to speak, but couldn't find the words.

"Enough, Darrah. She wasn't faking when she collapsed on my kitchen floor, and I don't believe she was faking when she fell apart at the hotel."

"How can you tell? Everyone knows she's a good actress."

Suspicion brewed in Marinda's eyes. "Were you playing me the fool, Amalie?"

A bit surprised her baby sister's attitude had turned cynical, Amalie glared at her. "No. How can you think that of me? As mothers, you both must realize the emptiness I feel."

"Exactly what I thought, but I've misjudged you plenty of times before," Marinda said.

A chill settled over the room. "I've obviously made a mistake coming here." Amalie lifted the coverlet and spun her legs over the edge of the bed. She started to stand, but sank back onto the mattress and grabbed her throbbing head.

Marinda hastened to her side. "Are you alright?"

"The drug Ethan gave me must have taken affect because I feel lightheaded and nauseous."

Marinda helped her back beneath the coverlet. Tense as a bowstring, Amalie couldn't relax. She locked gazes with Darrah. "What's the use? I've fought your attitude all my life, and I'm tired of it. I thought we settled our problem concerning Rupert."

"I'm sorry. My comments were uncalled for. It's just--"

"Stop," Amalie said. "Please let the past die." She pondered her next words carefully before she spoke. Once said, life would never be the same again. "I know it's easy for you to hold me responsible for everything wrong with the family. Blame Amalie, she ran off with poor Darrah's fiancé. Blame Amalie, she ran off and Banker Danforth kidnapped poor Marinda. Look at what you have, loving husbands and healthy children. I have neither."

Patience had never been a part of her character. Her anger reached an emotional breaking point. "Surely you must see I'm not the one responsible for you and Patrick being kidnapped, Marinda. Jonas Danforth is. I had nothing to do with the hateful man's malevolence toward you."

Marinda frowned. She let out a deep sigh. "You're right. We all had a hand in riling the man. You weren't around. It was easier to blame you than accept any responsibility."

"Thank you for that much. Maybe I have a habit of not always using the best judgment, but neither of you are free of sins either."

"I doubt any of us are," Darrah said.

Amalie gathered her courage and spoke before she changed her mind. "While we're clearing the air, there's something I'd like to know. Why didn't either of you care enough to come to my defense when we were children and father treated me with indifference?"

Darrah leaned forward, her brows knit together. "Papa treated all three of us with kindness and love."

Frustration raged through Amalie. "No, he didn't. He gave his attention to you and Marinda, but not me, not ever. In the father stakes, I came in last."

Darrah frowned at Marinda before she turned back to her. "What are you talking about?"

Irrepressible bitterness dripped from Amalie's voice. "I was invisible. Didn't you think it strange Papa never included me when he took you places?"

"Amalie, I thought you hated going with us, not the other way around."

"Me neither," Marinda added. "We were all spirited children who irritated him on a regular basis. Why do you think he singled you out?"

"I wasn't his child."

A deathly silence settled over the room. Two identical pairs of light blue eyes stared at her in shock.

"Are you sure?" Darrah asked, clearly stunned.

"Of course I'm sure. I heard him say so." Pain cut through her heart, exposing raw emotions she'd never expressed before. "Mother was pregnant with me by another man at the time she married your father,"

Amalie blurted out, no longer able to hold back the tide of anguish she'd held inside for most of her life. "He took his disappointment in Mama out on me."

Marinda gaped at Amalie. "My God, no wonder you were always angry. I can understand why you carry such a deep resentment against him."

"What did mother say when you confronted her?" Darrah said.

"I didn't."

"For heaven's sake, Amalie, why didn't you?" Exasperation tinged Darrah's voice. "Mother's dead. You'll never know who your father is."

"I regret that I didn't ask, but at the time I was afraid I'd get in trouble for eavesdropping. Mama rarely stood against Papa when it came to me."

"How old were you?" Marinda asked.

"Mama insisted I have a party in celebration of my eighth birthday. Papa said no. I threw a temper tantrum. He ordered me to my room, but I didn't go. I hid on the stairs and heard the truth."

"This certainly explains a lot." Marinda shook her head, crestfallen. "If you feel this way about father, I can't understand why you helped get him out of jail?"

"Because I wanted to show him I was worthy of his love. Make him understand I have value."

"Did he?"

"I don't know. I haven't spoken to him since he left prison."

A knock drew their attention. Ethan opened the door and poked his head inside. "Marinda, you have a starving child and Chase is ready to take Darrah home before it gets dark."

Amalie checked outside the window. Tall oak trees cast long shadows across the yard. Where had the day gone?

Marinda turned to her. "Are you going to stay with us tonight?"

"Thank you, but no." She glanced over Marinda and glared at her husband. "Ethan made it quite clear he doesn't want me around his family."

"Yes, well, that's obviously not how my wife feels. You're welcome to stay if you wish. If not, I'll be happy to drive you home."

He didn't seem very enthusiastic about her staying. "Give me a while, and then I'll take that offered ride."

Darrah stood and brushed her cool cheek against Amalie's. The sweet scent of lavender touched her senses. "We can continue our discussion another time."

Alone at last, Amalie stared at the wooden beams stretching across the white ceiling. Marinda's nesting instinct brought a touch of homeliness to the room. Stifled, she pushed back the soft blue quilt. She needed fresh air.

She stood and waited a moment to see if the dizziness returned. Relieved the room didn't spin she walked into the parlor, picked up her boots, and slipped them on. She grabbed for the front doorknob.

"Are you sneaking out without so much as a good-bye?" A spark of anger radiated from Ethan's observant, dark brown eyes.

"I know you offered to take me back to the hotel, but I'd rather walk, clear my head." She moved onto the porch, but Ethan blocked her way before she could step off.

"As a doctor, I cannot let you leave this house alone after the medication I administered to you. As your brother-in-law, I insist on taking you home because you're family."

His stern expression indicated he was in no mood for an argument.

"Let me tell Marinda we're leaving. I'll get the buggy and bring it around front."

She sat in one of the brown wicker chairs on the porch and waited. Marinda and Benjamin joined her while Ethan hitched the horse to the buggy.

"Thank you for sharing with me," Amalie said, motioning toward the toy Benjamin clutched in his chubby hand.

He darted toward her chair. "Do you want to take my horse home? He can keep you company."

Amalie pulled her nephew onto her lap. "That's the nicest offer I've ever had, Benjamin, but I can't take him. He'd be lonely without you."

He shoved the wooden toy into her hand. "Please, I want you to have him."

Amalie gazed over his head at Marinda, silently questioning what she should do. He'd been so disappointed when she turned down the gift.

Marinda nodded.

"Thank you. I'll take very good care of him until it's time for him to come back home to you." She wrapped her arms around the sweet little boy and squeezed. When his small arms slipped around her neck, a jolt of warmth flowed through her. She closed her eyes and pushed away the threatening tears. *This must be what love feels like.*

Amalie didn't want to let go, but when Ethan pulled up front, Benjamin wiggled off her lap and ran to his father.

She took Ethan's offered hand and stepped into the buggy. Amalie nodded her thanks to Marinda. Words couldn't get past the lump in her throat.

Ethan maneuvered the buggy down the slope. "I hope you don't plan to work at Patrick's saloon tonight. It's going to take a while for the laudanum to wear off."

"I know I'm in no condition to perform." She stared at Ethan's profile as he guided the horse down the drive. "I don't know why you've changed your mind about letting me be around your family, but I'm grateful."

"Marinda says I owe you an apology. She's right, of course. I did blame you for Danforth's behavior. For my insensitivity, I am sorry."

"I never expected an apology, Ethan."

"When I couldn't find Marinda and Patrick, I was crazed with worry. You weren't around to question so I settled my rage on you before I dealt with Danforth."

"If I hadn't run, it would have been me who was kidnapped instead of Marinda. You'd been saved a lot of trouble."

A frown creased his brow. "You make me out to be an uncaring lout. Do you honestly think I would have let that bastard kidnap you and not done anything about it?"

"I'm sorry. I didn't mean to insult you." They bumped over a hole as they entered the outskirts of town. She grabbed the edge of the seat and held on tight. "I'm sure you'd have done the same for me or anyone else."

"Yes, I'm really a good person once you get past the meanness." An awkward smile brightened his face.

His good humor lessened the awkward moment.

He pulled to a halt in front of the Chaumers Hotel. The smile disappeared and his demeanor turned serious. "I don't know if having you back in our lives is a good thing or not, but I'm willing to take a chance on you."

"Thank you. I appreciate the opportunity to spend time with Marinda and Benjamin."

"My wife and son are my first concern always. Please don't do anything that'll make me regret putting my faith in you." He stepped from the carriage and walked around to her side.

She slipped her hand into his and planted her feet on the ground. "From my past mistakes I understand your apprehension, but you have nothing to worry about. I'm really a nice person, too."

He gave her fingers a light squeeze. "It's a truce then?"

"It's a truce." She waved as he turned the buggy homeward.

Disappointment flooded her upon entering the hotel. George worked the check-in counter instead of Declan.

"Evening, Mrs. Renard. I assume you're better?"

"Evening, George. Yes, thank you, I'm almost fully recovered. Is Declan around?"

"I don't know where he is. Reckon he'll turn up when he's ready."

She settled on one of the chairs by the hearth. Slumping against the soft cushion, she sighed. "I hoped he'd have a pot of coffee on the stove."

"He's not been around most of the day. If you're hungry, the small café in the plaza next door is open."

She perked up at the thought of food. "I'm actually quite hungry. Can you point me in the right direction?"

"I can do better than that. I'll escort you." He put up the 'be back in a moment' sign and moved from behind the counter.

Dusk had fallen by the time they stepped into the crisp night air. A short distance down the boardwalk, he pointed to a small entrance. It was dark and narrow. A single candle in a sconce lit the path. She gazed at him for assurance this was the right way. He motioned her forward.

Along the corridor several more of the delightful candles lit the walk into a small courtyard. The breath caught in her throat. A fountain flowed in the middle of the patio surrounded by several tables, each adorned with a flickering light in a clear glass holder. More sconces lit the walls around the perimeter.

"Are you pleased?"

"It's magical."

"My sister and her husband own the place," he said with pride. "Come and I'll introduce you."

An unexpected movement at the far end of the courtyard caught her attention. On a short set of steps a masked man dressed in black stood frozen. In a flicker of an eye, he was gone.

George held open the café door. "Mrs. Renard? Are you alright?"

She shook her head, clearing her mind. The drug Ethan gave her must be stronger than she thought.

Chapter Eight

Declan glanced at the lobby clock again. It's past three thirty and still no sign of Amalie. Enough. Did she plan on sleeping the entire day away? He reached under the counter for the newspapers he'd purchased earlier and went to find George. He located his clerk at a table in the otherwise empty dining room, his nose buried in one of those Wild West Magazines he always read. George looked up after he stuffed the last remnants of a sandwich into his mouth.

"If you're done with your food, I need you to work the counter," he said a bit brusquer than he'd intended.

George closed the book and grabbed his empty dish. "You do what you need to do, boss. I'll be right there."

Declan nodded his appreciation and headed upstairs. He tapped on Amalie's door, but she didn't answer right away. He banged with a heavy fist. Eventually the door swung open.

A bedraggled Amalie glared at him. "What do you want so early in the day, Declan?" She pulled her light blue wrap around her body and tied the sash, but not before he had a chance to appreciate her soft curves.

He moved into the room, stepping over the clothes she'd worn the day before. First, he picked up the skirt and blouse and tossed the wrinkled garments across the end of her bed, and then opened the balcony door and let in the invigorating warm air.

"Good afternoon to you, too, my dear. It's nearly four o'clock. Do you plan to face the world today or not?"

Amalie pressed the hall door shut and leaned against it. "Take pity on me. After yesterday I needed peace and quiet."

He tossed three newspapers across the bed in front of her. "I hope you enjoyed the peace while it lasted."

A gasp escaped her as she stared at the sketch of her face across the cover of all three of them. She sank onto the mattress, picked up a paper and started to read the bold ink printed on the front page of The St. Louis Herald. "Oh, no," she repeated several times as she read. "This is awful."

He studied her reaction while she scanned through the other two papers. Her fear turn into anger and then back to fear again. He hated putting her through this, but thought it better to be prepared than caught unaware.

Every one of the issues reported she was wanted for questioning in the murder of a young woman named Virginia Gibson and for the theft of an emerald and diamond ring belonging to the dead girl.

By the time Amalie finished, her face turned white as a sheet. "Where'd you get this trash?" She shoved the damning papers out of her way.

"The old gentleman down the road at the News and Novelty Store sold them to me."

He gathered the papers and tossed them onto the table by the window. "Chase mentioned his partner keeps up with the news from back east. The old man in the store says a few papers arrive every now and then, but not on a regular basis."

Declan sat on the bed next to her and wrapped his fingers around her hand. "If I'm going to help you, I need to know. Are the reports in the newspapers true?"

"No!" She pulled her hand from his and stood. "How can those bastards get away with publishing lies about me? Why I--" It took several deep breaths, but she finally calmed herself.

"My God, Declan, do you really think I could kill someone?" Her deep blue eyes, filled with pain, glistened with tears. "I'm deeply hurt you'd even ask."

He got off the bed and placed his hands over her shoulders. "I can't keep you safe unless I know the truth. Please, be honest with me."

"It's obvious I love jewelry. Denying it would be ridiculous." She moved to stare out the window. "The obnoxious man in St. Louis lost a lot of money at my poker table during the night in question. He'd downed several drinks during the card games. When I asked him to leave, he turned belligerent and threw around unsupported accusations."

"Like what?"

"He called me a murderer." Tears slid down her cheeks. "What those reporters say about other jewels obtained in a similar fashion is a lie. I'm being slandered. I didn't kill his sister, Declan. I got the ring from my husband. I swear it's the truth."

He sat on the table's edge and squeezed her hand. "I don't want to doubt you, honey, but Chase said you have a stash of stolen jewelry."

She snatched her hand away. "Chase told you that?"

He nodded. "While we were at Marinda's yesterday he explained about a lot of jewelry pieces spilling out of your bag onto the floor. Did Darrah see them when you were together in Fort Laramie, or was he lying?"

"It wasn't what it seemed, but my sister didn't want to believe my explanation. I didn't think she would tell Chase. Does anyone else know?"

"Ethan."

She turned away, clearly annoyed with his answer. "He's mistaken. I got all my jewelry from my husband."

"You have no stolen jewels in your possession?"

Her eyes grew wide. "There are none."

She was lying. It was as plain as the adorable upturned nose on her face. She purposely chose not to tell him the truth. He supposed that since she'd taken the jewels from Rupert's stash and not snatched them herself, she might not consider them as stolen. Frustration washed over him. How would he get through to her?

"You can't run from this. There's a bounty on your head."

"I surmised the spiteful man would do something, but didn't know about the reward before today." She pursed her lips. "It's scary to see he's taken his threat of revenge to this extent. A lot of miles separate Paradise Pines and St. Louis, though. Most likely nothing will come of it."

"When money's involved, vermin scurry out of the woodpile. I need to know what we're up against if we're going to be prepared to deal with what comes."

"Nothing's happened so far." She pointed at the date across the top of the papers. "Look, they're all several weeks old."

He raked his fingers through his hair. "What's it going to take for you to trust me?"

"I don't know, Declan. Trust doesn't come easily for me."

"Is it something I've done?"

"No."

"Then what is it that keeps you from letting anyone in?"

Her mouth twisted. "I'm afraid to trust my instincts after getting involved with Rupert. He hit me, often. His temper left scars in my soul, but lucky for me not on my face."

Declan wrapped his arms around her and held her tight, trying to banish the nightmares. "If he wasn't dead already, I'd kill him myself." He pulled back and slipped his finger under her chin, forcing her to look at him. "I'd never hurt you. Nothing on earth slithers lower than a man who batters a woman."

She nodded and brushed away the tear running down her cheek.

Her simple action stabbed through his heart. He pushed her disheveled curls off her face and touched her lips gently with his. "I'd kill any man who tries to hurt you, sweetheart. Count it as my sworn oath to you."

She wrapped her arms around his neck. "I wonder why you put up with me."

"You're a temptation too difficult to resist, my dear. Besides, I love a challenge."

"You consider me your challenge?"

"Uh hmm," he said, stroking her cheek with his thumb. "You are the one challenge I can never figure out."

She slipped her arm into his and guided him to the door. "You've given me a lot to think about. We can discuss what we're going to do later after I've mulled over my options." She pulled the door open. "Please, I need to get dressed."

Anger against Rupert Renard raged through his body. One way or another, the situation would be dealt with, with or without her cooperation.

*****

Amalie found the shortcut between the mercantile and barbershop where George told her to look for the News and Novelty Store. A bell tinkled and announced her presence as she stepped inside the small, musty establishment. Stacks of newspapers tied in bundles with cord stood in random piles around the floor.

A humped-over, gentleman who walked with a cane limped through a curtained doorway. "Help you, miss?"

She nodded at the old gent. "I hope so. A friend of mine picked up several Missouri newspapers this morning. Do you have any more copies?"

The man moved around the stacks checking the top paper. "Sorry, young lady. They was the last of 'um. Maybe we be gettin' more in another month or so, maybe not. Don't know for sure 'til they git here."

Hope stirred her heart. "Then you only had the one copy of each?"

"Can't tell ya for sure, but I'm thinkin' it be the case. Not too many folks around these parts want ta remember back home no more."

Her soul brightened as she left the shop. The coolness of the evening hurried her along. Being caught outdoors wouldn't be comfortable once the sun set. Declan would have a warm fire in the hotel lobby. Comfortable heat and a hot cup of coffee was what she needed right now.

A floppy straw hat displayed in the mercantile window drew her attention. A large-bosomed woman with salt and pepper braids, knocked on the window from the inside, motioning for her to come to the door.

"You're Widow Renard, aren't you?"

"Yes. Have we met?"

"No, but I heard you sing in church. A treat I won't soon forget."

"Oh, thank you."

"I look forward to hearing your beautiful voice again."

Amalie smiled, not knowing what to say. Singing in church again was not an option she'd considered.

"I have a bit of cleaning yet if you'd like to look around. Won't you come in?"

She moved past the clerk and tread inside the store for a quick moment. Every possible space had been utilized. Wooden ladders, wheel barrels, picks, and other mining tools were suspended from across the ceiling by giant hooks. Bins of nails, screws, and drill bits hung from chains alongside one of the walls. She strode across the uneven wooden floor, around barrels of grain, flour, sugar standing side by side. On the other side, she found household goods and ladies' finery displayed on tables.

The woman removed the straw hat she'd admired off the wooden stand. "This style would look lovely on you."

Amalie puckered her nose at her reflection in the mirror behind the counter. "Sorry, but this one won't do."

"I have several more styles in the rear of the store if you'd like to see them." The clerk pointed to a large, colorful display of hats and bonnets that hung across a mock clothesline.

Amalie checked out the window and noted the sun would set soon, but couldn't imagine a few more moments would matter. A new hat would most certainly brighten her spirits.

By the time she left with a promise to return the next day with payment, dusk blanketed the community. She picked up her pace to reach the hotel before total darkness hindered her way.

Entering the short walkway alongside Ethan's medical office, unease cautioned her. She glanced over her shoulder. No one was there. She hurried along. The closer she got to the boardwalk on the other side, the more heightened her senses grew. A few more feet and she'd be at the end of the alleyway.

Someone stepped from the shadows and blocked her way. A scream stuck in her throat. She stood still as stone. In the streetlamp's glow, she could see a tall man dressed in the same costume she'd seen on the stranger in the plaza last night. It hadn't been a hallucination after all.

He didn't make a threatening move. He didn't move at all.

Strange as it seemed, she no longer considered herself in jeopardy. How could she when his ridiculous, wide-brimmed hat had strange silver fluff balls dangling around the edge?

She wanted to laugh, but thought it might anger him. "Let me pass, sir."

He sauntered a couple of steps toward her with an exaggerated swagger. The man in black didn't break his silence until he stood a breath away. It was then she noticed the dark covering concealing his face.

The silk mask stirred a touch of fear in her. "What do you want?"

"Evening."

His voice sounded clear and crisp, not at all like she expected.

He stretched out a gloved hand. "I need you to part with your ring and the brooch on your collar, good lady."

She gasped. "How dare you."

He pulled the longest, most vicious knife she'd ever seen from alongside his neck. "I dare as I please."

She swallowed hard, trying to alleviate the sudden dryness of her mouth. Now would be the time to take the situation seriously.

"Please, I don't want to hurt you. Hand them over," he motioned with his fingers, "and you're free to leave."

She gawked at first, but decided the jewelry wasn't worth her life. Amalie undid the clasp to the cameo and slipped the pearl ring off her finger. She placed them in his palm as he directed, glimpsing his eyes through the small holes cut in his dark mask. Odd as it seemed, she'd swear remorse swam in their depths.

He took her hand and placed a kiss across the back of her knuckles. The warm touch of his lips through the silk melted her anxiety.

"Gentleman bandit?"

His chuckle rumbled from deep inside him. "As you wish, my lady."

A moment later, her heart raced from excitement instead of fear. She stood alone, curious about the man behind the mask.

*****

"I'm telling you he had a knife at least twenty-five feet long, Declan." Amalie paced the lobby floor. "I've never seen anything more lethal as the horrid pointy thing."

He closed the novel he was reading, and gave her his full attention. It wasn't easy to hold back his grin. Encountering Amalie on his way home from leaving groceries at Widow Jackson's gate had been an unexpected stroke of good luck.

"You must mean twenty-five inches long, sweetheart. Your description would make it a sword, wouldn't it?" She'd accepted the situation a lot better than he expected. "Besides, didn't you say he pulled the 'horrid pointy thing' out from alongside his neck?"

"You dare laugh at me? I could have been killed." In a huff, she dropped onto the chair next to the fireplace.

He sat on the hearth next to her. "I know you were scared, but now you're here safe with me."

"It's the strangest thing. The masked man didn't scare me except at first because he startled me. He was quite charming through the whole ordeal. Besides, I know how to take care of myself."

"Yes, that's obvious. You handled the situation very well."

"Next time I'll be ready for him," she said with great aplomb.

Bunny settled on the floor between them. Declan ran his hand along the dog's back.

"What does that mean?"

"Next time I'll have my bag with me."

"Are you goin' to hit him over the head with it?"

"No, I'll use my derringer. If I hadn't rushed out of here today without my bag, I'd have pointed it at him tonight instead of giving up my jewelry without so much as a fight."

His hand stopped. He could almost feel the cold piece of metal penetrate his chest. "You carry a gun?"

"Yes."

"Do you know how to use it?"

"Of course," she regarded her hands and fidgeted, "but I don't usually load the weapon."

He knelt in front of her. "Why not?"

She stared at him a long moment. At first he didn't think she would give him a straight answer.

"I have a flaw."

She was so sincere he didn't dare crack a grin. "I'm sure I must have one, too. Please, explain."

"It's the curse."

"The curse?" He gaped at her. "I'm afraid to ask, but what do you mean by a curse?"

"I faint when I see blood."

Leaning back on his heels, he crossed his arms over his chest. "Don't be ridiculous. I want you to tell me the real reason."

"I'm dead serious. My sisters do, too. I knew you'd laugh at me.

Most men snicker when they find out."

"Do I look amused? Don't try my patience, Amalie." He stood. "Of all the hair-brained ideas I have ever heard, this one is the limit. I can't believe you'd point an unloaded gun at someone unless you intended on using it."

A patron entered the lobby. "Evening, Declan."

"Evening. Have a good day?"

"Yes, a busy one." William Johnson paused before he headed up the staircase. "Would you have an extra pillow?"

"Yes, of course." Declan shot her a warning glare to stay put and fetched a pillow from the linen closet.

"Thank you. See you at breakfast."

The mood broken, Declan thought refreshments would ease the situation. "Can I get you a cup of coffee?"

"Thank you. I could use a hot drink."

He returned with a tray of cinnamon rolls, two cups, and pot of coffee. He set them on the hearth and pulled another chair next to hers.

"Do you have any idea how foolish you're being?" He placed his untouched coffee on the table and drummed his fingers on the armrest. "All you need to do is pull the trigger, close your eyes, turn, and walk away. Otherwise you could be killed while you lay passed out."

Leaning forward, Amalie set her cup down and chose the smallest of the rolls. "If you're so adamant about it, the next time the bandit stops me, I'll use a bullet and make sure I kill him."

"No, that's not what I meant." He searched for a plausible explanation. "Your bandit, as you call him, is highly regarded around these parts. People wouldn't take too kindly to anyone putting a bullet into him."

She gaped. "You know who he is?"

He sipped at his coffee. "He's called Night Angel."

"If he steals from people, why would they turn him into a hero?"

"As far as I know, you're the only person he's stolen from. I've only known him to help people in dire circumstance."

Amalie moaned as she dropped back into her chair. "Of all the rotten luck."

*****

"Mama Claire, what do you know about the Night Angel?" Amalie asked the next morning while buttoning the front of her white lace bodice and tucking it into the waistband of her brown skirt.

Claire glanced up from mending. "Why you wanna know, lass?"

Amalie dabbed rose-scented perfume on her wrists. "The rogue stopped me last night on my way home and stole my jewelry."

"Merciful heavens." The older woman leveled her gaze over the top of her glasses. "You let Declan know?"

"Yes." She picked her double strand of pearls off the vanity. "I still don't understand why this bandit is revered by Declan and the townsfolk. Is he right? Do the people around here think of him as an icon?"

"He's a folk hero. Been around Paradise Pines for years and, as far as I know, he's never taken from anyone before."

"Declan said the same thing."

Claire laid her sewing on the bed and stood. "Turn around." She fastened the pearl necklace Amalie struggled to clasp. "How strange, you being in town only a short while and all. Wonder what set him ta pick on you?"

"I wonder the same thing." Amalie slipped on her boots and headed for the door. "Guess I'll have to be more careful where I walk at night."

"Yes, you'd better." The older woman slipped the mended blue taffeta dress onto a wooden hanger.

"I'm off to buy a new hat at the mercantile. You've been mending a lot of my clothes. Are there any replacement supplies you need?"

"That's sweet of you to ask, honey." Claire pointed to her overflowing sewing basket. "Don't reckon I do." She gathered her scissors and thread and returned them to their place in the basket's lid. "You be careful that bandit doesn't catch you off guard again."

Amalie nodded as she grabbed her cape and bag. "I will. I'll see you later tonight."

Dazzled by the midday light, Amalie shaded her eyes and strolled down the boardwalk without paying attention to the town's busy activity. Sleepless hours, tortured by dreams of the Night Angel, had left her fatigued. Who was this mystery man who haunted her?

She stepped off the walkway toward the other side of the road, her mind focused on the man in black.

"Watch out!" Strong hands grasped around her arms. She lost her balance and thudded against a broad, rugged chest.

"Best be careful, miss," a deep, charismatic voice said.

She gawked at an ancient horse hobbling along the road in front of her. He struggled to pull a rickety green wagon protesting against its load with each turn of the wheel. The driver sat hunched over on a high seat, his expressionless face shaded by a huge straw hat.

Night Angel

When she turned, Amalie's breath caught. Dressed in dark trousers, a black shirt, and coat, the man could have stepped out of last night's dreams. His steel-grey eyes bore into hers, robbing her of speech.

"How can he possibly see?" she asked after she'd pulled her thoughts together.

"He's nearly blind."

"Oh, I thought the hat might hinder his vision."

The tall, clean-shaven cowboy chuckled. "I meant the horse. However, old Joe's just ornery enough he wouldn't care if he ran over a beautiful lady such as yourself or not."

"Thank you for keeping me from harm's way." She gave him one of her brightest smiles.

"The name's Maxwell Collins." He touched the brim of his dark, flattop hat. "Please, may I escort you?"

She took a second assessment of him before she slipped her hand through his offered arm. Once they reached the other side of the busy thoroughfare, he tipped his head. "Have a good day, ma'am."

She watched him as he sauntered back across the road and disappeared into Trick's. Later tonight she'd make sure to observe him more carefully, find out about him. Could be he's the devious bandit.

Amalie took her time peering into storefronts. She wanted to become acquainted with what the town offered. Several smaller shops stood tucked away on side streets, but for the most part people stayed along the main road.

She strode inside the mercantile. While the clerk finished taking care of two customers, she checked out the display tables.

"Aren't you Widow Renard?" one of the shoppers asked.

"Why, yes, I am."

"Mary and I were in church the other morning and heard you sing Amazing Grace. The whole town's abuzz about how lucky we are to have you singing with our choir."

Her friend nodded. "We all look forward to hearing your beautiful voice again next Sunday."

This was the second time she'd heard the same comment in as many days. In St. Louis her notoriety kept women like these ladies far from her door. Once they discovered she sang at Trick's, they'd change their tune and shun her.

"Thank you, but--" She looked around for an escape. The clerk motioned to her after she placed her purchase on the counter. "Excuse me ladies, it's been my pleasure meeting you."

She stopped in front of the mirror and tried on her new hat. Not the best in her wardrobe, but the brim would shade her face.

Amalie hustled down the boardwalk and around the corner of a partially-burned building. She noted a large lumber wagon in front of the music hall. Declan, along with two other men, unloaded lengths of wood. He'd pulled his shirt off. His muscles glistened with sweat. She took a deep breath, but even that didn't help slow her pulse.

A peddler meandering along the edge of the road beckoned her. Fruits, gleaming in blackened wicker baskets, were suspended from a pole bent from their weight across his back.

Declan heard the man's voice and waved at her as she walked across the road.

She waved back before returning her attention on the vendor. She didn't need Declan to see her blush while she gawked at his chest, naked except for the patch of dark hair.

One of the large, ripe oranges caught her eye. She plucked the piece of fruit from the basket and paid the man before heading toward the music hall -- and Declan.

Chapter Nine

"Afternoon, Amalie. It's a beautiful day to be out and about after the snow we had."

Declan leaned against the empty wagon watching her walk toward him. A wide grin intensified his dashing good looks, nearly buckling her knees. "Helpin' the local economy, I see."

She kept her attention focused on his face, hoping he'd put his shirt back on before she made a fool of herself. All that bare skin and rippling muscles were enough to make her weak.

His grin broadened.

Lord she prayed he couldn't read her thoughts. "Aren't you cold?"

"Naw, moving this lumber inside your music hall is a great stimulation."

That's not all that's stimulating. "Want to share?" she asked, pulling her attention back to the fruit.

He took the orange and reached for the knife secured in his boot.

Slicing the orange in half, he handed one portion to her while biting into the other.

She watched, mesmerized as the sweet citrus juice dribbled down his chin. He ran the back of his hand across his beard, but not before the juice trickled onto the mat of curls on his chest. He took another couple of bites, tossed the empty peel into the wagon, then stopped and stared at her. "Is there something wrong?"

"What do you mean?"

He nodded toward the untouched portion of fruit in her hand.

She shook her head. Now what did she do? Ask him to get dressed? *Pull yourself together. This fascination must stop before it becomes an obsession.*

"No, I think I'll save it until after I eat breakfast."

"Breakfast?" He let out a loud guffaw. "Breakfast ended a long while ago. How about letting me treat you to an early dinner at the Bell Tower Cafe?"

Not wanting to seem too eager, she pretended to consider the request before giving him an answer. "That sounds good. I need to discuss something with you."

"I'll be right back." He disappeared inside the building, returning a few moments later with a shirt on and running a comb through his damp hair.

"Not sticky anymore?" She smiled into his attentive eyes and delighted at the thought of spending some time with him.

"No," he shook his head and nodded toward the café across the road. "Shall we go?"

"Now I think about it, I am hungry."

He chuckled. "I'm certain we can find something to your liking."

The hens and chicken décor provided the restaurant a comfortable, cozy mood. Baking bread, mingled with frying chicken, wafted from the kitchen. Her stomach rumbled. She glanced at him out of the corner of her eye, but relaxed when he didn't seem to make an issue of it.

Declan nodded toward a table with a red and white checked cloth near the front window. He pulled a chair out for her and then sat on the other side of the table. "What would you like to eat?"

"Do they have a menu?"

He pointed to the wall behind a counter where a board listed the food for the day. "I'd suggest the meatloaf. Mrs. Clayton serves the best I've ever tasted."

"I can't keep my figure eating such a large portion."

"If none of those entries please you, the menu posts several other items you can choose from."

She ran her eyes up and down the bill and sighed in resignation. "I'll have the vegetable soup and toast instead."

The waitress placed two mugs on the table. She poured coffee into his before addressing Amalie. "You care for some, Ma'am?"

Inhaling the strong, rich aroma, Amalie nodded.

"Are you havin' the usual, Mr. Grainger?"

"Afternoon, Anna. Yes, we'll both have the meatloaf."

"Wait--"

Declan waved off Amalie's protestation.

"Is everything alright with you, Anna?"

The waitress shrugged. "I suppose you could say we've been having a bit of bad luck lately. I must work extra hours for a few weeks. My Johnny broke his arm jumping off the woodpile last week and now I've got doctor bills to pay."

"Sorry to hear it. Give the little rascal my best and tell him I'd better not hear he's giving his mother a bad time."

"Thanks. I'll be right back with your food."

"Why'd you order a meatloaf dinner for me after I said I didn't want it?"

"You're too thin. You need to put some meat on your bones."

She frowned at him. "I thought we agreed you'd stop being bossy."

"I did say that, didn't I? Sorry. I promise to work on my flaw."

She caught his inappropriate glance at her breasts and pursed her lips. His booming laughter warmed her checks.

"I know, I know," she said, interrupting him with exaggerated impatience. "You couldn't help yourself because my bosom is falling out of my bodice."

Anna arrived with two heaping plates of meatloaf and mashed potatoes. "You can't expect me to eat all of this?"

He had the first forkful of food in his mouth, nearly moaning from the taste. "Once you take a bite, you won't have a problem finishing it." He picked up his coffee cup and took a drink. "Now, what do you need to talk about?"

"People are being nice to me." She dipped her fork into the potatoes and gravy.

"That's a problem?"

"I don't know. Maybe. I guess I don't know how to fit in very well." She spooned the potatoes into her mouth. "The lady who runs the mercantile and two of her customers told me they loved the way I sang Amazing Grace. My two sisters hugged me yesterday."

"People being nice to each other is a pleasant way to live, Amalie. I suggest you relax and enjoy it." He shook his head. "Did you settle your differences with Darrah and Marinda?"

"They both seemed sincere with their acceptance of me, but now I wonder if they meant what they said."

"From my dealings with both of them, they've always been honest and forthright."

"After all the years of distrust and jealousy, I don't know what to think. The drug Ethan gave me might have muddled my judgment." She placed her cup on the table and rested her arm alongside it. "I don't know what their motives were for their kindness."

"You have to trust someone sometime. Why not let it be your sisters."

"I'll think about it. What about those church ladies? They enjoyed my voice so much they expect to hear me sing every Sunday from now on."

"Don't look so worried. The parishioners could end up being your biggest patrons. You can easily win them over with a little effort."

"Yes, but how will they react when they find out I'm a saloon-singing, poker player?"

"You're overreacting." He leaned his elbows on the table and rested his chin on his hands. "The odds are against them finding out."

"Why?"

"What husband would be crazy enough to let his wife know he's enjoying your talents at Trick's? That kind of admission would put an end to Saturday nights out with the boys."

"An interesting thought, but from my past experience the wives find out sooner than later." She pushed her empty plate away. "Life gets so complicated."

"Yesterday was very emotional. Give yourself time to heal." He stood and shoved his chair away from the table. "Come, I've got to get back to work. I'll walk to the hotel with you."

*****

Declan stopped at Ethan's office before he headed to the music hall. "How much does Anna owe for Johnny's medical bill?"

Ethan pulled out his payment ledger and stated the sum.

"Consider the balance paid." Declan dropped the fair amount of coinage onto the table. "As usual, you found this money when you arrived at your office this morning."

"Thank you. Your generosity never ceases to amaze me." Ethan placed the money into the cash box and stuck it back in his drawer.

Declan slipped into one of the chairs across from Ethan's desk. "What do you know about our ladies' situation yesterday?"

"It seems they are all sisters again." He shook his head. "Beats anything I've ever seen."

"I'm not sure how Amalie's handling the reconciliation yet, but time will tell." He leaned forward, taking a piece of maple candy from the dish on Ethan's desk and popping it into his mouth. "You've got connections in San Francisco, right?"

"I have quite a few. What do you need?"

"Colton still has crates of supplies Angus ordered years ago at the time he made plans for Judith's music hall. They're stored in a warehouse behind the Browns Hotel in San Francisco. I thought I'd go see what he's got. If I'm lucky, he'll still have those seats with the red velvet cushions and the curtains to match. I'm sure he'd love to get the boxes out of his way and, if we use what we have on hand, it would save me time and money."

"Are you still owner of Browns Hotel?"

"Angus left a nice investment for me."

When Ethan didn't comment, Declan added, "Amalie wants new

costumes. I promised to take her to the city to meet with Jenny Lind's San Francisco seamstress. While we're there I'd like to treat her to a night out. I heard Jenny Lind is supposed to perform at her namesake theatre sometime in the next couple of months. Do you have enough connections to make arrangements for Amalie to meet the Lady herself?"

"I'll tell you what," Ethan said, rising when a patient entered his examination room. "If Marinda and I can travel with you, I'll make all the necessary preparations."

Declan shook Ethan's hand. "Thanks, I appreciate your help. After the heated conversation we had the other day, I hesitated to ask."

"It's good for now. I told Amalie I'd give her another chance." Ethan stopped before he entered his examination room. "I assume you'd prefer to keep this San Francisco trip a surprise?"

"For now, yes. I hope to convince her I'm not only charming, but sensitive to her needs as well."

*****

Later in the evening Declan finished his bookwork and left George in charge of the check-in counter. Entering Trick's, he encountered a boisterous crowd of mill workers. Amalie sashayed across the bar with her usual strut.

"Evening, boys, I'm Lily Fox. I'm here to sing and dance for you tonight."

Hoots and hollers bounced off the rock walls. A low bow, giving them a healthy glimpse of her abundant breasts barely contained behind the lace of her deep blue dress, helped raise the room's temperature another notch.

He perused the crowd of intoxicated lumberjacks and leering miners. The men seemed even more excited than usual. A trickle of sweat ran down the side of his neck.

Is she intentionally provoking them tonight or is it becoming unbearably hot in here?

Amalie turned sideways, lifted the hem of her skirt and smiled as she exposed her leg to the knee. Pandemonium erupted. Drunken fools jostled their way to the bar.

A miner he recognized as Pickpan reached out and grabbed Amalie's foot. She screamed, proving to Declan she wasn't quite as in control of the situation as she usually was. She cuffed Pickpan alongside his head with the tip of her other booted foot. The shocked miner released her and wailed, grabbing his bloodied ear.

Patrick was quick to pull a large club from behind the bar. "Step back."

At the same time, the barkeep pulled Amalie to a safe place on the floor. He grabbed a rifle and leveled the gun on the raucous crowd.

Nobody moved, but Declan recognized her actions had fused dynamite and tempers were about to blow. If the patrons decided to push the situation to a fight, one club and a rifle would not hold them off for long.

He ducked into the music hall and grabbed the long-handled ax. He stepped back inside the saloon with the weapon raised over his left shoulder. Letting out a shrill whistle, he quieted the room. "Men, step back, all of you, or find your guts on the floor."

Dumbfounded faces stared back at him, but no one moved.

"You know what kind of damage this ax can cause. I'm not afraid to use it." His determination to maim the first fool who dared to test his threat must have radiated from his stance because they did as he demanded.

He lowered the splitter. "Find a seat or get out."

Loud grumbling rose above chairs being turned upright and scrapped across the wooden floor. Declan ignored the hostile glares and headed to where Amalie stood next to the barkeep. "Are you alright?"

"Yes."

"Are you sure? You're very pale."

"Thank you," she said, turning to include Patrick and Joe. "I wasn't prepared for their overzealous reaction."

"If you intend on staying, you might stay off the bar and keep to the box tonight. It's payday at the mill. Next time it could be gunplay," Declan said.

She moved from behind the bar. He noted she avoided the box, but did stand close to the piano and motioned for the pianist to start playing again.

Declan leaned against the wall near the entrance and rested the heavy ax head on the floor, keeping his hand on the handle, his attention on the crowd. Every now and then a patron would turn to see if he still stood guard over the lady, but none dared stir his ire again.

Camaraderie settled back over the gambling establishment. Some millworkers tied red handkerchiefs around their arms, thus becoming 'ladies' for their partners. Amalie sang. Men danced.

They looked ridiculous, but obviously enjoyed themselves. As long as the fools left the singer alone, he didn't care what they did for entertainment.

She paraded around the room, stopping in front of him. "You're casting gloom with such a scowl, Declan. Why don't you unbend a little and join the other men?"

Her face was flushed from the exhilaration of the evening, the fright of the near riot a half hour before obviously forgotten. Tension charged between them. He could barely compose his thoughts. "Saloons are not my first choice of entertainment."

"If you don't like being here, leave."

"As long as you continue performing for these horny drunks tonight, I'm staying put. I don't want to see you hurt, or any of these men. They work under incredibly dangerous conditions at the mill and deserve a chance to let loose."

Amalie's gaze riveted toward the door.

He turned to see what caught her attention. Maxwell Collins stood inside the room, checking out the place until he headed toward an empty table.

"You're right. I'm sorry. I'll play cards the rest of the night and let tempers settle."

Amalie stopped at Collins' table. Declan saw her eyes sparkled with interest as he opened a pack of cards and spread them in a semi-circle on the table.

"Mr. Collins, it's nice to see you again."

"Please, call me Max. Won't you join me?"

Amalie hesitated for a moment, a slim finger tracing pursed lips, then shrugged and eased into the seat.

His apprehension rose when Collins motioned the barkeep to bring two glasses and a bottle. A miner with slicked back hair and a new pair of britches stopped next to the table, tossing down a large deerskin pouch. "I've got gold dust. You got the grit to play with me, lady?"

Her success was never in doubt from the moment she skillfully fingered off the first card. The stubborn tilt to her chin confirmed her determination to show any man she was his match. Errant curls framed her oval face, but her expression hardened as she concentrated on the cards. Patrick spoke of her fame as a poker player in St. Louis, but failed to mention her impressive skill.

Hand after hand Amalie outplayed the others. She chaffed the losers while paying the few winners with grace. Collins had long since pulled away, watching her with hooded eyes. When she wasn't paying attention to him, the bastard puffed thick clouds of smoke from his cigar and rolled his eyes.

*****

Declan gazed at Amalie on the third floor balcony in the glow of a full moon. She'd not spoken but a couple words during the short walk from Trick's to the hotel. Now she appeared lost in thought, staring into the night.

Romeo, how would you act observing your Juliet? He was certain Shakespeare's character would have been undaunted at finding a way to scale the wall to reach his ladylove. That's when the ridiculous idea struck.

"Get your business done, Bunny. I've got something important to do." He hustled his dog toward the hotel entrance. While he had Amalie cornered on the balcony, he'd relieve her of the entire stash of tainted jewelry. Sounded simple enough, but with his lady nothing was ever easy.

He rushed Bunny inside, pulled his extra costume from the hidden drawer in the armoire in his bedroom, and bounded up the stairs. On the third floor he unlocked the door leading to the attic. Once dressed in his Night Angel garb, he grabbed the longest length of rope stored in the supply box and edged his way through the opened window. He prayed his cockamamie plan wouldn't send him to his death.

He quickly ascended the rungs of the fire escape ladder. The brick chimney stood halfway across the flat roof. He secured the rope around its base and, peering over the ledge, dropped the length down alongside Amalie's balcony. Noting the distance to the ground, a knot tightened in his gut. After a sharp intake of air, he grabbed hold of the cord and stepped off the roof's edge. The strand slipped easily through his gloved hands during the downward slide until his boots thudded on the plank deck behind Amalie.

She whirled around and shrieked.

"Please, don't be afraid." He raised his hands, showing he held no weapon. "I mean you no harm."

Once she recognized him, she relaxed. "No? Then why are you here?" She held up her palm. "No, don't tell me. Let me guess -- to steal from me again?"

"You wound me." He placed his hand over his heart. "I heard you sing again tonight. I came to bow at your feet, kiss your hand, and thank you."

"You were at Trick's?" Her brow puckered. "Did we speak?"

"I am everywhere, my dear. Have you not heard I'm an angel?" He chuckled. "A heart used to beat in here." He tapped his fingers against his chest. "You've stolen it. I came to reclaim it, but, alas, now standing in front of you I find the task impossible. It's too late to recover something which by rights belongs to you."

Amalie leaned against the wrought iron rail, her hands clenched tight. "I'll swap your heart for the jewelry you relieved me of the other night."

Another hearty chuckle burst from him. "*Touché.* The lady has a sense of humor."

"Your arrogance intrigues me." She sauntered toward him. "Have I seen you without your mask?"

"On occasion, but you don't recognize me as the man who has a place in your future yet."

She stopped a mere foot in front of him, the glow from the table lamp shined through the window and across her face. He lowered his head, making it impossible for her to see his eyes and waited, curious as to what she'd do next.

"Give it back."

"What?"

"I want what you've stolen from me." She held out her palm. "I want my jewelry."

"Too late, the jewelry's gone." He took her hand and kissed the back of her knuckles. "I'm afraid you're right at why I'm here tonight." He slid the bracelet off her wrist and nodded at the necklace she wore. "I need the pearls as well."

Amalie ripped her hand from his grasp. "No!"

He exhaled an exaggerated breath and shook his head. "Does that mean I must pull my nasty knife out to retrieve the necklace?"

She stiffened and narrowed her gaze on him.

He shrugged. "The choice is yours, but I don't intend to leave without them."

Pools of tears welled in her eyes. If he didn't think them a ploy, he'd feel more a heel than he already did for stealing from her. Only the thought of her going to jail if she got caught with the ring kept him from backing down. "I would steal a kiss instead, but am bound by this mask."

"Why do you take from me when you give to others?"

"Quit stalling." He opened his palm. "Give me the pearls."

She clutched at the necklace. If looks could kill, he'd be dead.

"Don't try my patience." He spun her around, catching her off guard. Once the necklace rested securely in his pocket, he whispered in her ear. "That wasn't so difficult was it?"

She tensed and broke from his grasp. "Why don't you make both our lives easier and take the rest of my jewels right now?"

"Precisely my thought, too, my dear." He pointed toward the open door. "After you."

"You cannot possibly think I'm serious?"

"Maybe you are, maybe not." He pulled a black velvet bag from his pocket and held it toward her. "I am, so go inside and fill this."

She moved away. "No, get the bag away from me. I'll scream if you don't leave."

"If you were going to cry out, you'd have done so before now."

The determined expression on her face alerted him he'd made a strategic mistake. As she screamed a high pitched screech, he seized the rope and jumped to the rail. "Search your soul. You already know why I take from you."

Her cry echoed around him during his quick descent. Before anyone became overly curious, he'd slipped behind the hotel and sprinted for the back window to his bedroom. He only had a few minutes until she'd be at his door.

Chapter Ten

"This has to stop," Amalie raged at his parting back.

She held her breath while the Night Angel slid down the rope. For a moment she contemplated following him, but changed her mind after she noted the great distance.

What did his puzzling answer mean? How could she possibly know why he took her jewelry?

Amalie rushed into her room and locked the balcony door with a firm click. She opened her hatbox and ran her fingers over the cache of jewels still hidden under the secret lid. Did he know how Rupert got these pieces? It's the only probable explanation for his comment, but how? Until yesterday she didn't think anybody knew about the jewels except Darrah. Now she wasn't sure.

The emerald and diamond ring sparkled in the light. Her favorite piece slid onto her finger as if it belonged there. The man in St. Louis said he'd had it designed as a special gift for his sister. Under the lamp's glow, red, blue, and gold prisms glittered off the diamonds around the green stone. What had Virginia looked like and how old had she been when she died? Now she understood the damage Rupert had inflicted on the immigrants. Nausea churned her stomach.

Amalie tugged the ring off her finger, dropped it back into the folds of velvet and locked the lid. She'd not given thought to the people who owned the jewels or how Rupert's killing spree had ended their lives. She tossed a suitcase on the coverlet, determined to escape the guilt. She swung the armoire door open and stared at her neatly hung costumes until the bright colors blurred before her eyes. A vision of Declan filled her mind. Her heart pounded. With a cry of despair she slammed the door closed and sank onto the feather mattress. Sooner or later she had to stop running. The time was now.

Declan's bossiness annoyed her, but his continual protectiveness might prove a good thing. She wanted to tell him the truth, but held back. Instinct warred with reason when it came to trust. Always suspicious by nature, she hated to ask for help -- even now, but in this instance, she had no choice. She needed his assistance. The irritating bandit would not intimidate her again. She'd had enough of his larceny.

Amalie shoved the hatbox behind the decorative front of the tall armoire. The more she thought about the Night Angel demanding all of the jewels, the angrier she got. By the time she reached the lobby, she was mad as hell.

"Declan." She stepped behind the counter and knocked on his bedroom door. "Wake up."

He didn't answer her plea. She banged with both fists. "Declan!"

The door swung wide. He stood bare chested, pushing disheveled hair out of his eyes. "What the hell's going on? Are you trying to wake the dead, or is the place on fire?"

Words stuck in her throat.

"Amalie," he uttered in a near whisper. "Don't look at me like that, not when my bed's but a few yards away."

She pulled her gaze from his and straightened herself.

He grabbed a shirt off a nearby hook and snapped the door shut behind him.

Declan ushered her toward the chairs in the lobby. "I hope you have a good explanation for rousing me and probably half the hotel guests."

"He robbed me -- on my balcony -- where you said I'd be safe."

"What are you talking about? Who robbed you?"

"Just now your gentleman bandit assaulted me on my balcony."

"You had a bad dream. Go back up to bed. We'll discuss this in the morning after we've both had some sleep."

"Declan, please listen to me."

"You're being overly dramatic again. Your room's on the third floor for God's sake."

She tapped her foot. "I was attacked. Don't you care?"

"Come on, I'll fix some coffee. It's obvious you're not going to let me get any sleep until this is settled."

He set the pot on the stove and stirred the embers back to flames. "It's been a long day, so let's get this over with."

"I don't understand your attitude." Amalie sat on the bench across the table from him. "Tonight you stood guard over me at the saloon and now when I need help you don't care."

He yawned. "I'm listening."

"The Night Angel dropped onto my balcony from the roof."

"Did he hurt you?"

She shook her head. "He came down by rope and slid a bracelet off my wrist and pearls from around my neck. Of all the nerve. He also ordered me to fill his bag with the rest of my jewelry, but I wouldn't do it."

"I'm sorry, honey. If I'd had any idea the room would open you to possible danger, I'd have chosen one without a balcony. I'll relocate you first thing in the morning."

He started to get up, but she grabbed his arm and pulled him back down on the bench.

"I won't move anywhere. The thieving swine will not get away with inconveniencing me more than he has already."

"I'm afraid I must insist. There's a small sitting room in the attic I can fix up nice for you. It's most unfortunate I boarded up the little window after the squirrels got inside last summer. Still, considering what happened tonight, I'd rest easier knowing you're safe even if it means you won't be as comfortable."

"I won't change rooms. I like the one with a window and balcony. Think of something else."

Declan went to the kitchen and returned with two cups and the coffee pot. "I suppose Bunny could sleep next to the door. Would you feel better with him as your protector?"

She gazed at the sleeping dog. "I don't think so."

"Bunny would probably rise to the occasion if he sensed you were in danger."

A low snore emanated from the mutt.

"Maybe not," he said with a chuckle.

*****

His attempt at humor did not lighten her mood.

"I'll notify the sheriff in the morning." Declan filled their cups and sipped his coffee.

"Can't we deal with the robberies on our own?"

"Why? This is the second time you've been reluctant to involve Matt."

"Please, find the Night Angel. Make him tell you why he steals from me and make him stop."

"You had the chance earlier tonight. Why didn't you ask him yourself?"

"I did."

"What's the problem then?"

"He said I already know why."

"Do you?"

She shook her head.

"How on earth do you expect me to find him when nobody knows his identity?"

"We can start by making a list of possible candidates."

Declan couldn't believe he was doing this. The entire situation raged out of control, but Amalie didn't leave him any other choice but to go along with her outlandish scheme. To do otherwise, might raise her curiosity. "The Night Angel started his night visits about three years or so ago."

"Good. Do you have a piece of paper? We might as well get started."

"Now?" He let out another big yawn, hoping she'd get the hint. "It's after midnight, and I have to get up at six."

She cast him an expectant look from behind her long, sooty lashes. "I'd feel better if we have something positive to work on in the morning."

"There's no way I can talk you out of this?"

Amalie shrugged. "It's up to you, but I'm going to start with or without your help."

Her answer didn't surprise him. He wouldn't have expected anything less. Grabbing paper, pen, and ink from behind the counter, he set the supplies on the table. "Write down what you remember about him."

"He's tall."

"Tall as me?"

"No, I'd say much taller, maybe a couple of inches. His shoulders are broader, too." She wrote the details. "Oh, and I saw his eyes for a moment that first time. I think they're gray."

"Hmmm, I can't think of any six foot, six inch, gray-eyed, smooth-talking men in Paradise Pines able enough to slide down a rope to assault you."

She rolled her eyes. "You don't have to be sarcastic. I can name at least one."

"Who?"

"Maxwell Collins."

Declan jumped to his feet. "Have you lost your senses, woman? Collins would no more put himself in danger for anyone or any reason except his own self-preservation."

Amalie glared at him as she chewed on the end of the pen. "Perhaps, but maybe it's what he wants everyone to believe so they'd never suspect the truth."

"Nonsense." He sat again. "Don't say I didn't warn you. Might I dare ask how you came to this reasoning?"

"Both times I saw him he wore black and he was in the saloon this evening."

"That's to be your criteria?" He pointed to his trousers, which were the ones he'd had on earlier when he'd supposedly assaulted her. "I'm wearing black. I was in the saloon tonight."

She stacked the paper in a neat pile and set the inkwell on top. "If you're not going to take me seriously, I will find the thief by myself."

"Don't be foolish. You can't go searching for a man alone. We don't know anything about this bandit for God's sake. Your life could be in danger if you investigate his identity. What if you anger the man? Next time you encounter him, he might use the long knife you say he wears over his shoulder to harm you. Did you stop long enough to think about all the possibilities?"

"Don't raise your voice to me." She glared daggers at him. "I'm determined on this, Declan. I won't be his victim again."

"Alright, put my name on top of the list. I'm six foot, four inches."

"Oh, please, there's no way anyone would believe you're the Night Angel. I don't want to hurt your feelings, but you do have the Scottish accent. As charming as it is, the Night Angel doesn't speak with your burr. Besides, you were asleep while he was up on my balcony stealing from me -- again, I might add."

"You blame me?" He jabbed his forefinger into his chest.

"It *is* your hotel."

"Yes, it is." He stood and motioned her to move in front of him. "It's time for both of us to be in bed."

"What are you going to do?"

"Secure your room for the night and deal with you and your situation tomorrow when I'm not so likely to lose my temper." He followed her out the door and upstairs.

She opened her unlocked door.

"I'm glad you take your security so seriously."

"I've had enough for one night. Stop scolding."

Once inside the room, he unlocked the balcony door and made a show of checking the area before securing the door behind him. "Give me a hand, will you?"

He passed her the lamp, then picked up the small table from in front of the window and set it upside down on the bed.

"What are you doing?"

"You cannot stay here unless I secure your room." With his back and shoulders against the side of the heavy oak armoire, he slid it past the window toward the balcony door. The cabinet caught on the baseboard and wouldn't budge. Amalie grabbed the other end and directed him. With one huge shove, the hatbox fell off the top almost colliding with his head.

"What the hell?" He snatched the box from the floor.

Her eyes grew wide with what, fear? "What do you have in here, a hoard of rocks?"

She held her hands out. "Personal items I'd rather keep private. Please, give it to me."

He held the container toward her. It bothered him she still didn't feel confident enough with him to explain the jewelry. At least now he knew where she stored the stash.

She slipped the hatbox under the bed. "Sorry, Mama Claire told me to put the ridiculous thing where she wouldn't keep tripping over it."

One last shove positioned the cabinet where he wanted it in front of the window while still blocking the door. "Do you feel safer now?"

"It'll do until I put an end to the gentleman bandit's night raids."

"I'll bid you goodnight one more time then." He snapped the door shut behind him on his way out.

He took the stairs two at a time to the lobby. In his room, he kicked the door shut and dropped onto the bed. His mind raced over the events of the last hour. He never anticipated she'd take hunting the Night Angel with such zeal, but guessed he should have expected the unexpected from a woman like Amalie. This quest of hers merely pointed out what he already suspected. She was a very clever, determined woman with no intention of backing down from her search, and it bothered him -- a lot.

Frustrated, he rested his hands under his head and stared at the flickering lamp on his bedside table. How would this foolishness end? The idea of her *interviewing*, as she called it, all the prospective Night Angel candidates worried the hell out of him.

The drunken miners and mill workers who gawked at the ripeness of her bosom tonight had infuriated him. He'd itched to use the ax on someone, anyone who dared push him too far. Now she expected him to stand back while she made her list?

The lobby clock struck three times. Six o'clock would get here far too soon.

He stripped out of his clothes and started to toss the trousers across the chair, but stopped remembering her pearls and gold bracelet.

The pieces dropped out of his pocket into his palm. Thoroughly disgusted with himself, he placed the jewelry alongside the others in the hidden drawer of his mother's spice box. He returned his keepsake to the top of the bookshelf, then snuffed the lamp and slid into bed.

If only she'd wear the damnable emerald and diamond ring so he could be done as a thief.

*****

Declan set his hammer on the floor and stood, wiping sweat off his face. The six men who'd showed up this morning already accomplished an incredible piece of work assembling the stage's underpinning.

He grabbed his tool chest and headed toward the loft.

"Afternoon, boys." Amalie entered the building and strolled around stacks of scattered lumber toward the men who stood gaping at her. "May I join you for a few moments?"

Harold Eriksen pulled his cap off as she approached. "Ma'am, Mr. Grainger's in charge."

"Yes, but it's you men I'd like to speak with. May I ask a couple of questions?"

"Amalie, why are you here?"

She pulled a pad of lined paper and pencil from her bag. "I need to add these men to my list if you don't mind, Declan."

"Let me see who you've got so far." She'd already written several names and information with regard to each candidate in neat columns.

"Where's my name?"

"We discussed this last night. You're not a contender."

Was he going crazy? He must be. Only a lunatic would be jealous of his own self and her damnable compilation of Night Angel suspects.

"Do as you wish, but don't take all day." He motioned to the men. "Miss Fox needs help with a survey she's doing. I'd appreciate your cooperation so we can get back to work. Please, stand in a line in front of her so she can see you."

With a wide grin on each of their dirty faces, the men did as he asked.

"Ma'am," a tall man with a Swedish accent said, "what do you look for?"

"It's a quirk of mine to know who's working on my behalf."

Amalie studied each carpenter, asked his name, and wrote the information on her paper. "I thought there'd be more men here."

"Sorry, Ma'am," the Swede answered. "That preacher fella's bad mouthing you and this place. Lots of men who need the pay won't go against his demands."

Amalie's face turned scarlet. A muscle twitched in her cheek.

Declan turned to his crew. "Take your noon break."

He waited until they'd all left the building. "Unclench your jaw, Amalie."

"That man's going to regret he messed with the construction of my music hall. I won't stand for his meddling. I kept my part of the agreement. I sang in his church and he gave me his approval. What's his problem?"

"Don't worry about Preacher King. I'll find him and straighten out the situation."

She rested her hand on his arm, stopping him before he could leave. "No. I can't resist the challenge, I'll do it."

The mutinous twist to her mouth worried him. He had no intention of letting her leave until she'd calmed down. "First, let me show you the work we've gotten done today. The men almost have the stage built. Wait 'til you see what Harold intends to carve in the panel across the edge. We discussed the plans this morning. He's far more talented at woodworking than I expected."

She ran her hand along the boards. "The performance area is so much larger than I expected." A bright smile lit up her face.

A breath caught in his throat. "You're glad you decided to stay in town?"

"Very glad! Can I stand up there for a moment?"

He grabbed a couple of boards and laid them across the floor joists. "I'll give you a boost."

"Wait." She unhooked her boots and slipped them off, then placed one foot into his cupped hands. With ease, he balanced her by taking one of her hands and raising her level to the unfinished stage. She held his hand until both her feet stood firm on the boards.

"Won't you christen your music hall and sing something for me?"

"It would be my pleasure, sir." She tossed her curls and held her chin high. Her clear voice flowed over him with ease. "I don't have time to be proper--"

The words surrounded him, echoing from the high ceiling and off rock walls. The farther back he moved, the more her remarkable talent mesmerized him.

Amalie stopped singing.

A commotion behind him drew his attention. He turned and noticed Phoebe King and two other women inside the doorway.

"Phoebe, what are you doing here?"

The preacher's daughter gave him one of her brightest smiles. "My father asked us to fetch Widow Renard."

Amalie frowned, her lips pinched. "Why?"

"You're late for choir practice." Phoebe's voice oozed contempt.

Amalie lifted her chin and moved to the edge of the stage. "Will you help me down, Declan?"

He grabbed her hand and balanced her until she sat on the edge.

"Wait a minute and I'll help you with your boots." He dusted the sole of her foot before slipping her boot on. "I didn't think you intended to sing at church again."

"I don't. It's apparent Reverend King has a lesson to learn."

He gave her a quick glance as he grabbed her other foot. "What's that supposed to mean?"

"Nobody takes me for granted."

"What are you going to do?"

She patted his arm. "Don't worry I can handle a presumptuous ass." Amalie shoved the paper and pencil inside her bag and headed for the door.

Chapter Eleven

Amalie shoved Phoebe out of the way and marched up to Reverend King. "How dare you send your daughter after me? I am not an errant school girl."

The reverend pulled off his glasses and tossed them onto the opened account book. He stood, pushed away from his cluttered desk, and glanced at his daughter. "What's she talking about?"

Phoebe rested her hand on his sleeve. "I'm sorry, Father, but I couldn't think of any other way I could get her here."

Caught off guard by the change of circumstances, Amalie glared at Phoebe. "Wait. Just. One. Minute! You mean your father didn't demand I be here to rehearse with the choir?"

Phoebe's cheeks turned crimson, but she said nothing in her defense.

Amalie wanted to smack the look of satisfaction off the spiteful girl's smug face. How dare the impudent twit involve her father in such a selfish scheme?

The reverend glowered at his daughter. "What excuse do you have for this ridiculous confrontation?"

Phoebe's gaze narrowed on Amalie. "She came to Paradise Pines and ruined everything." Venom dripped off her tongue. "Tell her we don't want her here, Father."

"We?" Amalie pulled herself up to her full five foot four and one half inches. "Don't you mean *you* don't want me here because you're a jealous bitch?"

"Widow Renard." Reverend King turned his sharp gaze on her. "You are in God's house. Watch your language."

"I am *not* jealous." Phoebe stamped her foot. "You're a vulgar cow. No wonder everyone says you're a constant embarrassment to Declan."

"Enough!" The reverend slammed his fist against the desktop. "Phoebe, you know better than to use such language in a house of worship. I insist you follow proper decorum while you're here."

He pointed to the open door. "Get the choir practice started while I finish my discussion with Widow Renard."

Phoebe's bottom lip jutted, and she looked as though she might commit a mutiny.

"Go," he motioned, "and close the door."

With a huff, Phoebe lifted her chin and left in a surge of indignation, slamming the door behind her.

Reverend King returned to his chair and motioned for Amalie to sit across from him. He leaned back observing her. His face might have been carved from stone for all she could tell. It infuriated her the way he stared impervious to her discomfort.

"My daughter's right, Widow Renard, I don't see any future for you in this community. Be gone by morning." He picked up his spectacles, dismissing her as he started back on his books.

His impertinence stunned her speechless. She thought the top of her head might blow off at his arrogance. Who the hell did he think he was, God?

The cleric gazed down his nose at her. "Is there something else?"

The stale air in the room stifled her. Instead of answering him, she got up and moved to the large window overlooking a grassy knoll. If she didn't find a way to tamp down her temper, she might as well leave town without a fight.

A young goatherd caught and held her attention for a moment. How simple his life appeared. She lifted the window and sucked in deep breaths of fresh mountain air. A soft clinking resounded from small brass bells tied around the goats' necks. The gentle tone drifted into the room and soothed her distressed nerves.

"Widow Renard, what are you doing?"

"Your pompous attitude has sucked all the pure air from the room," she said, glancing over her shoulder. "I've replaced it."

"You have a quick tongue, don't you?"

She closed the window and turned, but stopped midstride noticing his malicious leer. He turned his face away, but not before she'd seen his lustful gaze rake over her. In that unguarded moment, the power shifted.

Her confidence restored, she sashayed across the room and rested a hip on the edge of his desk. "What do you know? The good reverend's harboring impure thoughts."

His eyes narrowed. His face turned deep red. She thought he might have a heart attack.

"Get out. Don't stop until you're on tomorrow's stagecoach to Sacramento."

She didn't move. "You want to run me out of town because--hmmm," she rolled her eyes and ran the tip of her finger over her lips, "you lust after my body?"

"How dare you."

When he rose out of the chair, she gasped and pressed her hand across her mouth. Oh, this is too good to be true. "Seems you've proven my point, sir," she motioned to the bulge in the front of his britches. "You use your daughter's jealousy to hide your sin. How sad."

She straightened her skirt with calm determination.

"You go too far, woman. I'll ruin you in this town if you don't leave." He towered over her, using his size and authoritative manner to try and intimidate her. The glare in his eyes, so cold and calculating, rooted her to the floor but she didn't flinch. Instead, she flaunted her confidence with a haughty smile and a few well-chosen words.

"By the time I'm through with you, Reverend King, the people of this town will say a poor widow was unjustly ordered out of Paradise Pines by a devious, power-driven zealot."

The room went still except for the tick-tock of the wall clock. Pure malice radiated off the man. "What would you expect, you harlot? You strut around in provocative clothes tempting any man beyond his limits. You," he wagged his finger at her, "deservedly have earned my contempt and censure."

His vicious comments swamped her with rage. "Contempt? Didn't look like contempt to me. A few moments ago you were ogling my breasts. You afraid someone will figure out you're a fraud?" She headed for the door. "Let's get one thing straight," she said before turning the handle, "I'm one woman you can't control. I'm not leaving town and if you try to turn people against me, you'll find out just how good of an actress I am."

She strode into the hallway and let out a shuddering breath. *What have I done?* She massaged her brow in an attempt to push away a headache. Declan's voice niggled her mind. *The reverend could make it very difficult for Patrick to open the music hall if he gets his hackles up.*

How could she turn what happened around to her own advantage? She had to act soon before the arrogant fool had a chance to recover his composure.

Worried her dream might slip away, she decided it didn't matter what she had to do to secure the success of her music hall. After all, acting is her profession. She could do this to keep what she'd wanted most of her life. Straightening her posture, she dug deep and pulled out every strand of humility she could find.

She knocked first, then opened the office door, and stuck her head inside. "Reverend," honey dripped off her tongue, "I apologize for my outburst earlier." She closed the door behind her. "After second thought, I've seen the error of my ways. What will it take for you to change your mind about me leaving town?"

Night Angel

The smirk on his face turned her stomach. No doubt the cost would be great. He'd make this as humiliating as he could.

"There's no reason we can't be civil. All I ask is for you to stand in front of my congregation and denounce your immoral ways." King's stern voice made his demand more than clear.

Could she humble herself as far as he demanded? She had to try. "If I do as you ask, what will you do for me in return?"

"Regardless of what you think, I'm a gracious man." He pointed to the chair across from his desk.

She took the seat and sat poker faced, clasping her hands in her lap.

"Accept the wisdom I preach as gospel and, if you keep your mouth shut about our deal, I'll promote your music hall for a percentage of the revenue. I'll also expect you to attend church and sing with the choir to show your good faith."

Bile churned her stomach. She thought she might be sick, but bowed her head and allowed him his temporary victory. "I'll do as you wish."

*****

"You didn't sound tone deaf last Sunday." Amalie stood in front of the choir and wanted to scream. How would she ever pull these voices together and make them sound even remotely passable? She hoped concentrating on the task in front of her would help alleviate her frustration with the reverend. Patrick would be furious with her if she ruined their chance to open the music hall.

"It's because we weren't singing. You were," Asia Murdock said.

Amalie pulled her attention back to the chubby young woman's cherubic face.

"We know we sound terrible, but don't know what to do about it."

"Obviously Miss King doesn't either," Amalie said with a quick nod toward the preacher's daughter.

Phoebe turned her back on Amalie. "I'm sure the Lord is happy with our voices the way they are, Asia."

"Yes," Amalie pushed Phoebe aside, "but I'm certain even the Lord would have a difficult time accepting this caterwauling in his church, Miss King."

"We're a small choir who strives to give a proper presentation at services, but if you think you can do better go ahead and try." Outrage sparked from the depths of Phoebe's brown eyes, daring her to take up the challenge.

"Sit down, Phoebe. I've had more than enough of your temper for one day."

The entry door swung open at the back of the room. Marinda, with Benjamin running a few steps behind her, hurried up the aisle. "I apologize for my tardiness," she said, pulling sheet music from her bag along the way.

Amalie's heart warmed. Benjamin noticed her and his eyes lit up. He ran toward her with his arms open, a grin spread across his dimpled cheeks. "Aunt Ammy."

She caught him against her. He smelled like the out-of-doors, fresh and alive.

"You're sisters?" Phoebe stammered, staring dumbstruck between Marinda and her.

"Yes, that's right." Amalie smiled at Benjamin and squeezed his hand. "You see, I do have ties to this community, Phoebe, and I don't intend to let your jealous tantrums deny me my right to live close to them."

Phoebe dropped onto the front pew and cast Amalie a hateful stare.

Marinda motioned for her son to return to the back of the church to play with his toys. "What's going on?" she said soft enough so only Amalie could hear.

"The good reverend has ordered me to leave on the next stage out of town. Can you believe his audacity?"

Marinda frowned. "Why?"

"Jealousy." She nodded at the preacher's daughter, who continued to glare at her. "It's apparent Miss King's not happy with my relationship with Declan Grainger. Had her sights set on him, and I've spoiled her plans."

An odd expression crossed her sister's face.

"What, Marinda? You look like you've just discovered the entrance to the mother lode."

"Is there a relationship growing between you and Declan Grainger?"

Amalie couldn't hold back the smile or keep the telltale sign of a blush from heating her cheeks. "I'm not sure what's going on yet, but I can't deny the gorgeous Scot knocks me off kilter."

Marinda squeezed her hands. "I'm delighted for you. He's a wonderful man. You could certainly do a lot worse for a husband."

"It hasn't gone far enough to think of marriage, little sister, but thanks for the approval."

"Widow Renard?" Asia called from the choir pews. "Are you staying?"

Amalie nodded at the young woman. "Yes. I want everyone who sings bass to move to the back, tenors over to the left, altos to the right, and sopranos in the front."

Nobody moved.

"You don't understand, do you?"

They all shook their heads.

"I'm sorry, but I don't know your names. Mine is Amalie, by the way."

She pointed to the three women she knew had the deepest voices. "Please move to the back." Then motioned to the others one by one, placing them where she thought their voices would work best.

"Remember, your attitude while you sing makes the difference. Don't be afraid to raise your voices. Let them carry to the very edges of this room." She pointed around the perimeter. "Listen to each other, blend together. Make the parishioners experience your joy at singing for the Lord."

"This isn't a theatre," Phoebe said. "I know what you're up to and it's not going to work."

"Please, we need her help, Miss King." A young woman turned from Phoebe to Amalie. "You will stay and help us, won't you?"

"Father won't be happy after he hears you're changing our routine order of songs."

Amalie ignored Phoebe's outburst. "If you follow my instructions, I'm certain we can delight the congregation come Sunday."

"We'll do it," Asia chimed in. "We're tired of singing the same songs every week."

Amalie nodded at Marinda and motioned for the choir to sing Amazing Grace.

"Stop." She waved her hands back and forth at the screeching. "Something's not right."

She motioned for Asia to step forward. "I'm sorry, but your voice isn't working well with the others."

Asia's eyes overflowed with tears. "Please, don't make me quit."

Amalie didn't want to see the girl disappointed, but it wasn't fair to the other choir members. She moved to a window and stared outside pondering her options. The goatherd was still on the hillside. Hearing the bells again sparked an idea.

"Stay put, I'll be right back."

Amalie approached the young man. "Hello there. Do you have a moment?"

The disheveled youth got to his feet and sauntered over to her.

"I noticed your goats wear bells. Do you suppose you might sell a couple of them to me?"

"You want my bells?" he asked, taken aback. "My grandfather brought them from Germany. He might be mad if you take them."

Amalie pulled coins from her pocket. "Is this enough to cover their value?"

A huge grin spread across his smudged face. He gasped at how many coins rested in her palm. "Maybe he won't care that much."

"If it's a problem, you can let me know and I'll return them."

He knelt next to one of the goats and unbuckled the lash. "Sure you don't want more than two?"

"Thank you, but two will be fine." She took the first one while he caught the second nanny goat and removed her bell.

She nodded her thanks and returned to the church with a much better outlook about the choir's performance on Sunday next.

"Asia, take these. The bells are your new voice. Watch for my signal and let them do their magic."

The girl shook them with a lot of vigor every time Amalie nodded. Amalie silenced the choir. "Remember, Asia, the bells are not to outshine the voices. Let me hear you ring them with easy swings, echoing the voices around you.

She turned to her sister. "Marinda, start again."

This time Asia's bells blended in with the choir. The radiant smile on the girl's face assured Amalie she'd done the right thing.

She nodded at Marinda. "Pick up the pace."

*****

"Declan, duck tail!"

A stack of lumber thundered over him a moment after he dove under the portable workbench. Sweat beaded across his forehead. To fight off the suffocating closeness of being shut in a tight place, he drew slow, calming breaths until Ethan removed the last board.

"Are you alright?" Ethan extended his hand and helped him to his feet.

He nodded. "Thanks. That was a bit too close for comfort."

Swede sat across from him with a red-splotched white cotton cloth held over his temple.

"Is your injury serious?"

"I'm fine," the giant of a man assured him. "God gave me a thick skull."

"Good. It's a mighty fine one at that, Gunnar."

Ethan pointed to an overturned box. "Sit so I can check you out as soon as I get Gunnar's forehead bandaged."

"I'm fine, too."

"Let me be the doctor, will you. After I tell you what Amalie's up to, I think you'll no longer be fine."

Dread washed over him. "What the hell does that mean?"

"Relax, man, or you're going to have a heart attack."

Declan scowled. "Don't try my patience, Ethan. What the hell has Amalie gotten into now that's going to rile me?"

"About an hour ago she dropped Benjamin and Marinda at home and took the buggy up to the mill."

"She drove alone?" Declan balled his hands into fists and fought the urge to swing at something. What the hell was she thinking? "That damnable list of hers is going to get her hurt or, even worse, killed." He was furious at her lack of sensibility.

He grabbed his gun belt and picked up the rifle he now kept inside the front door. "Will you come with me, Ethan?"

"You don't think you're overreacting? Amalie's used to handling men. She does it every night at my brother's saloon."

"Not last night."

*****

"Grainger," Ace yelled, waving his arms to catch their attention as they galloped into the logging camp almost a half hour later. "About time you got up here to git that saloon singer outta here."

Declan nodded at the mill foreman and bounded out of the saddle. "Where is she?"

"The men have her between those two buildings." He motioned toward the edge of the yard, away from the main milling shed.

Ethan grabbed the rifle. Declan pulled his pistol from the holster. They rushed toward the sound of voices raised with hilarity and raucous laughter.

They rounded the corner and came to a quick halt. Ethan almost collided with his back. Stupefied, Declan stared at Amalie poised like a queen on the stump of a giant sugar pine. Her court stood around her absorbed in the naughty ditty she sang. After she'd finished, she gave them a quick curtsy and a bright smile.

He shoved his way through the group of mill workers and into the small clearing.

Amalie's eyes opened wide at the pistol he held in his hand and then at Ethan's rifle. "What are you two doing here, preparing for war?"

He returned his gun to its holster and reached for her. "Don't be glib. You know why I'm here. Get down. You're leaving with me right now."

Once her feet hit the ground, she poked the tip of her finger against his chest. "You're the second man to tell me what to do today and, quite frankly, I'm tired of it. I'm staying here until my list is complete. Either help me or stay out of my way."

His fists settled against his waist. He wanted to strangle that delectable neck of hers. "You expect me to help with this tomfoolery?"

Tension sparked the air between them.

"I don't expect anything from you, Declan."

"Excuse me." Ethan stepped between the two of them. "Are you going to stand here all afternoon arguing, or are you going to let her finish so we can get off this mountain? In case you haven't notice, it's growing darker by the moment."

"Do what you have to do, Amalie." Agitation sharpened his tone. Declan waved her off. "Just finish, and be quick about it. We'll wait over there." He motioned for Ethan to follow him to the edge of the clearing.

The two leaned against a shed, watching mill workers line up and give her the information she sought.

"What's going on, Declan? You mentioned a list earlier at the music hall."

"Amalie's accumulating the names of men who could fit the persona of the Night Angel."

A puzzled frown crossed Ethan's face. "Why?"

Declan checked to make sure no one could hear him. "The Night Angel's been stealing that ill-gotten jewelry from her and she doesn't like it."

Ethan stared at him with dark amusement. "Considering who you're dealing with, you'd best be careful."

Declan ran his hand back and forth across his neck. "I feel a bit singed already."

"I suspect she's as stubborn as Marinda. Don't take too long to tell her who you are and your reasons why."

"I can't. Amalie's starting to trust me. I need more time to win her confidence."

Ethan was relaxed, grinning now. "Can I say, I told you so, or would you hit me in the mood you're in?"

"I heard you loud and clear the day we had our conversation in the coffee shop."

"Sorry, but you caught me off guard with your confession. The last thing I expected to hear you say was you were in love with my devious sister-in-law."

"It didn't matter by then anyway. I knew the moment my hand touched hers I couldn't be happy without her. She stepped off Lucas's coach straight into my heart." Turning his gaze back to Amalie, he snickered. "I only hope I survive what's sure to come."

"I'll pray for your quick recovery."

Declan raised his brows. "I'll probably need all the help I can get."

"You still want to take the lady to San Francisco?"

"Did you get the tickets to see Jenny Lind?"

"It's the reason I stopped by the music hall earlier, to tell you this Saturday is the only time we can go. I have four seats reserved in Senator Bidwell's box."

A smile teased the corners of his mouth. His mood lightened. "Perfect."

"What are you thinking, Declan?"

"I plan to make sure this trip works to my advantage. By the time we return home, the lady will be convinced I am the man she wants to spend the rest of her life with."

Ethan shook his head. "If you're sure it's what you want, I hope it works out, buddy. I'm not sure it's your wisest decision, but good luck."

Amalie strutted at a brisk pace toward them. "I'm ready to go now."

Declan ushered her to the buggy and tied his horse to the rear. The narrow dirt road widened, but Declan still couldn't see very far in front of them. Darkness settled everywhere except places where the moon cast shadows, especially along the side of the road with a steep drop off. Ethan led the way on horseback with a torch. The other two gleams of light came from the lanterns secured to the front of the buggy he drove.

Relief washed over him at seeing the street lanterns of town flickering ahead. Amalie hadn't said one word on their way down. He'd not either, wanting to use all of his concentration on getting them off the mountain in one piece.

Declan pulled the buggy to a stop at the hotel entrance. He jumped down and walked around to help Amalie before untying his mount. He offered his hand. She barely glanced at him, but did stop to thank Ethan.

Ethan tipped his hat and tied his horse to the back of the buggy. "Talk to you in the morning, Declan," he said before directing the horse to move the buggy along.

"Why the attitude, Amalie?"

"Your scowl worked as well today as your ax did last night. You turned what was a friendly get-together into a wake. How dare you follow me around like I'm an incompetent fool?" She turned in a huff and marched inside the hotel.

Stunned at her mindset, he headed to the stable and retired his horse. By the time he got upstairs, he'd developed an attitude of his own. He knocked on Amalie's door, but she didn't answer.

"I guess you're not interested in the tickets I have for Jenny Lind's performance in San Francisco this Saturday night." He headed toward the stairs.

"Declan?"

Trying not to grin, he turned at the sound of his name.

Chapter Twelve

Amalie's taught nipples strained against the sheer lace of her white cotton nightgown. She might as well not have anything on considering the amount of covering it provided. For the life of him, Declan couldn't stop staring.

"Oh," she shrieked, noticing where his gaze rested. "I'll be right back." She crossed her arms over her chest and ran back into the bedroom. She returned in a blue and gold striped dressing gown.

"I believe you mentioned San Francisco."

"I'm not in the mood to talk about your surprise anymore." No way would he let her manipulate him so easily. It might set a precedent he'd regret later.

She grabbed his arm before he got to the staircase. "Why are you acting so pigheaded?"

He studied her face, his gaze resting on her pouty lips. It took every ounce of strength not to smother their softness with kisses. "A moment ago you didn't want anything to do with me. Now that I dangle irresistible tickets in front of your nose you're happy to see me again? Don't play me as a fool. Good night, Amalie."

"Fine, take the shrew Phoebe King with you then." She sank to the carpet and dropped her face into her hands. Her heart-wrenching sobs cut straight through him.

Although she could be very dramatic when she wanted her way, this time the tears appeared genuine. He scooped her from the floor and kicked her bedroom door shut behind them. For once, the bed wasn't covered with clothes. He sank into the deep feather mattress. She settled on his lap and slipped her hands around his chest. Her close proximity roused his senses.

"I'm a mean, heartless swine. Forgive me?"

She gazed at him with her huge sapphire eyes still brimming with tears. Denying her anything at that point was next to impossible.

"Uh huh." Amalie brushed the dampness off her cheek. She rested against his chest, wiggling her derriere as she moved. Declan fought in vain to control his arousal. He loosened the top button of his shirt, ran a finger around the inside of his collar drenched with sweat. "Please sit still, Amalie, or I swear I won't be responsible for my actions tonight."

"Stay with me, please?"

All of a sudden, the room turned hot. It was all he could do not to strip the gown off her shoulders. "Amalie, control yourself. It's not proper." He shoved her onto the mattress and put enough space between them so he could slow down his raging emotions. He wanted more than sex with her. When they came together, it would be an act of love. He'd not settle for anything less.

"I'm sorry. I had little, if any, sleep last night because of the Night Angel, and I can't think straight."

"Did anyone hurt you at the mill?"

She shook her head. "Everyone treated me like a lady."

Relieved, he gave her a quick smile. "You are a lady, a very intelligent and clever one."

"If that's how you feel, why'd you follow me to the mill? Everyone, including me, could see you were mad enough to commit murder. You embarrassed me breaking through the crowd with your guns drawn."

A twinge of guilt nipped at his conscious. "I may have made a big deal out of you going to the mill alone, but after what happened last night at Trick's can you blame me?"

Her eyes opened wide and she shrugged, but her growling stomach broke the tense moment.

"When's the last time you ate?"

"Sometime yesterday."

"I'm hungry, too. Change into a more decent garment and meet me downstairs. I'll put something on the stove so we can both eat."

He stopped at the door. "Five minutes, or I'll be back and carry you downstairs."

"Yes, master," he heard as he shut the door. He chuckled all the way downstairs. Her spirit was something he appreciated about her, except when she dug in and drove him to distraction.

Soon strips of ham sizzled while he opened a container of beans and brewed coffee. Amalie strolled into the dining room looking good enough to eat in a simple lace bodice and blue skirt. He transferred their food to the table.

She sat and placed one of the napkins in her lap. "I'm ravenous smelling this spicy food." She pointed at the platter he'd set next to the ham. "What's this stuff?"

"You have so much to learn about how Californians eat." He picked a tortilla off the plate. "A lot of locals use these in place of bread." He showed her how to fold it over and stuff beans, ham, and cheese inside.

He watched highly amused as she tried to eat without making a mess. "Here, let me assist you." He wiped the drips off her chin with his napkin and grabbed another flour tortilla. With practiced motions, he loaded it with beans, cheese and pieces of ham and then tucked the sides as he folded it. "Now, lean over your plate and do the best you can."

Amalie managed a second tortilla like an expert. "Thank you, kind sir. What a delicious treat." She rested her elbows on the table and leaned her chin on her hands, staring at him.

"Do you have something you want to say, Amalie?"

"I'd like to ask a big favor."

"Certainly."

"Your girlfriend lured me to the church on a pretext this afternoon. It wasn't her father who wanted me there, it was Phoebe herself."

"What?" He never expected *that* to be what bothered her. He'd hoped she had decided to trust him and mention the stolen jewelry. "Phoebe's not my girlfriend."

"This is very embarrassing, so let me make the explanation without more interruptions, please."

A pinkish tinge crept up her cheeks. He moved around the table to sit next to her. "I'm man enough to hear whatever disparaging remarks she said about me."

"Your arrogance astonishes me." She ran her fingers over his scruffy beard and gave a gentle tug. "It's me, not you, she turned her venom toward."

He leaned back, a bit embarrassed at his blunder. "I'm sorry. I had no idea she'd go so far."

"It gets worse. She demanded her father order me out of town on the first stagecoach."

He slammed his fist against the table. "Sonuvabitch!"

She grabbed his arm. "You can't blame her for the dramatics. If you didn't have so much sex appeal, she wouldn't be chasing after your affections."

He quirked his brow. "Do I dare ask what you did about it?"

A grin spread across her face. "I challenged her to a dual at sunrise, of course."

"Bravo!" He stood applauding. "I shall polish the old dueling pistols and be your second. We'll dazzle her with our fancy footwork." He shuffled his feet around in a circle.

She rolled her eyes and burst into a fit of mirth, but her relaxed mood didn't last. Pain soon replaced the spark of humor in her eyes.

"Sweetheart, please what's bothering you? I understand Phoebe is a thorn in your side, but you're hiding something from me. What is it?"

"Reverend King insinuated I'm a whore along with a few other offensive slurs."

It took every ounce of strength he could muster to control the rage boiling inside him. "Did the bastard touch you?"

"No, but the bulge in the front of his trousers confirmed he's an indecent man. Before I remembered he could ruin our chances to open the music hall, I commented on his erection."

"Amalie! Your bluntness shocks me sometimes."

"I'm afraid it gets worse." She entwined her fingers with his. "When I returned to his office, I cowered in front of him and let him think I'd go along with his demands."

He wanted to throttle her. "You never should have given him that much power."

"I didn't mean it. I wanted to buy some time until I could figure a way to fix the mess."

"What'd he threaten?"

"To withdraw his support for the music hall if I don't tell his parish I believe his gospel at church this Sunday, and pay him a percentage of the revenue from the show tickets."

"My God, will that man stop at nothing to satisfy his lust for power? You'll never know how sorry I am for placing you in a position for the preacher and his daughter to attack you like this."

"Declan, this isn't your fault."

"It's true. If I'd seen Phoebe for who she was earlier, she would never have had cause to stir up such a hornets' nest." He let loose of her fingers and paced. "If you haven't figured it out already, the 'good' reverend's playing a dangerous game and you're the pawn. He thinks he can control me and hurt you at the same time."

He paused in front of her and crooked his finger. "Come here."

She stepped into his open arms. "Sweetheart, I most definitely will never let you go anywhere without me." He closed his eyes, losing himself in the sweet hollow of her throat.

His lips moved to her mouth, savoring the softness driving him to distraction all evening.

She eased the top buttons of his shirt open. Her fingertips roamed across his chest and stirred a bright flame to a full raging firestorm. "You tempt me beyond limits," he moaned, then dipped his head to catch her lips again. His kisses deepened as he wrapped her in the cocoon of his arms, pulling her into his embrace where he could keep her safe.

The stagecoach rumbled to a noisy stop in front of the hotel. Frustrated, Declan dropped his arms and rested his forehead against hers. "Dammit, Lucas is here," he rasped out. "Sorry, sweetheart, I've got guests coming in tonight."

His hands shook as he tried to button his shirt. Finally he got the job done and tucked the tails back inside his britches. He stole one more kiss. "Wait in the lobby. I want to tell you all about the plans I've made for tomorrow."

Declan led a young couple inside. After he set their luggage in front of the counter, he winked at Amalie. The smile she returned warmed his heart a touch more.

Once the new arrivals signed in and headed upstairs, he grabbed two cups of hot coffee. "Here's the plan." He handed one drink to her and sat, taking a sip from his. "Tomorrow about noon we leave for the dock at Sacramento on the stagecoach. We'll travel all night aboard ship and pull into San Francisco Harbor early enough Friday for you and Marinda to visit the dressmaker and get fitted for costumes."

"Marinda's going, too?"

"Yes, Ethan as well -- chaperones."

"We need chaperones?"

"No, sweetheart, I'm teasing you. It'll give you and your sister a chance to have fun together."

Excitement danced in her eyes, a radiant glow lit her face. "I can't wait."

"Have you ever been to San Francisco?"

"No, I was headed there, but Patrick found me. I chose to come here where I had the sure thing of a good job, or at least I thought it was a good job on a stage." An impish grin tugged at her lips. "Guess it all worked out for the best anyway."

She got up and waltzed around the sleeping dog, dropping to her knees in front of Declan. "I'm such a fan of Jenny Lind and have dreamed of meeting her for so long. Do you think we'll get the chance?"

"I hope the trip turns out to be all you hope for, honey. As for what's going to happen, you'll have to wait and see."

Her face contorted into a deep frown. "You're not telling me more?"

"No, except I'm going to be busy during the day."

Her chin dropped.

"You won't even miss me. Marinda has many great friends who will be delighted to show you all the best places in the city. From what I've heard from her and Ethan, you'll fit in well with them."

"Why don't you want to show me around San Francisco? Isn't it one of the reasons you wanted to take me there?"

He set his cup on the table and leaned toward her. "Years ago Angus ordered a lot of equipment for Judith's music hall. We might be able to put it to use now. All the crates are stored in a warehouse behind the hotel where we have reservations. With Ethan's help I should be able to check through them in record time."

He reached for her hand and pulled her to her feet. "I'll stop at Claire's and ask her to help you choose an appropriate wardrobe. Then I'll deal with Patrick about you missing some performances before I seek out Reverend King."

He walked behind the check-in counter and grabbed his gun belt off the hook.

Amalie grasped his arm and pushed the barrel of the gun toward the floor. "Why do you need a gun?"

"Don't interfere." He buckled the belt around his waist. "Trust me to do what needs to be done."

"You won't do something stupid, will you? I couldn't bare it if you got hurt." She slipped her hands around his neck. "I learned a long time ago if you lose your temper, your temper wins and you lose."

"If what you say is true, then why didn't you follow your own advice earlier today?"

Her eyes darkened. "I admit I didn't do a good job hiding my displeasure, but I tried."

His finger tipped her chin. "Like you did upstairs earlier with the tears?"

"Whatever do you mean?" She blatantly batted her eyelashes. "I have no idea what you refer to."

"Hmmm, a likely story." He gave her a quick kiss and headed for the door. "I promise to try to do as you ask, but no assurances. I'll let Patrick know not to expect you until Tuesday at the earliest."

*****

Declan knocked on the door of the King house and waited. His fingers drummed along his pant leg. By the time he'd made the arrangements with Claire and dealt with Patrick's bad humor, he was ready to put this altercation with the reverend behind him. At best he'd try to hold back his temper, but doubted he'd keep his promise to Amalie.

Phoebe pulled the door open. "Declan, what a pleasant surprise." She reached for his hands, but he snatched them back.

"I'm not here to see you. Where's your father?"

"She got to you, didn't she?" Phoebe's voice rose to a high, hysterical pitch. "Don't believe a word the harlot said. She's a liar."

"Watch your tongue. You've said enough for one day."

"I haven't even begun." Phoebe stomped across the porch and punched him in the chest. "You gave me the impression we'd be married. Why'd you do it when you knew all along what you really wanted was some fast woman to bed?" She threw a couple more jabs and kicked him in the shin. "You despicable liar."

Declan grabbed both her wrists. "Shut your filthy mouth, Phoebe. Not one more word."

She struggled to get away from him. "You swine, I hate you!"

A motion at the window behind her caught his attention. Mrs. King shook her fist at him before she dropped the curtain.

He finally released Phoebe and stepped back, throwing his hands up in defense. "Just tell me where your father is -- now."

"He's at the church. He always spends evenings there while he writes the sermon for Sunday."

The front door swung open. Mrs. King stepped outside with a broom in her hand. She raised her weapon and wacked him across his backside. "You get yourself off my porch, *Mister* Grainger. We don't want your kind of trash around our daughter."

"Fine." Declan turned to go and received another smack. He cursed his stupidity for not sensing the true nature of the King family before now.

Declan hurried up the hill to the church. The door handle turned easily in his hand. He paused and then entered the church with caution. The reverend had been adamant about keeping his church locked at night. He stepped inside and glanced around. A tall, white candle stood aglow at the pulpit and another at the hallway door that lead to his office. Who could King expect at this time of night?

Sickened by what happened earlier, Declan sat on the back pew and stared at the ceiling. Those last few moments at the King house weighed on his mind. "Jesus," he said, running his hand through his hair, "how the hell did my life get to this point?" Judith would frown on him for using profanity in church. He needed another graveside visit again, and soon.

He stood and headed to face one more confrontation. After his sharp rap on the parish office door, Reverend King bid him enter.

"Evening." Declan strode to the preacher's desk.

The reverend snapped shut a ledger and slid the book into his bottom desk drawer. The man acted guilty of something. Declan was sure of it, but shrugged the idea off to the mood he was in.

King pulled a key from his vest pocket and locked the drawer before he motioned to the chair across from him. "I'll be with you as soon as I finish my thoughts on Sunday's sermon."

Declan sat and waited. His anger deepened along with his impatience. Time limped along to the tick of the wall clock. He pulled the knife sheathed in his boot and cleaned imaginary dirt from under his fingernails. Still, the reverend ignored him. Out of patience, he jumped up and drove the knife into the top of the man's desk. "We can be civil or pain can be involved. It's your choice."

Startled, the reverend gawked at him as if he'd gone mad, but said nothing.

"I want to know why you gave my lady a problem over the music hall. I thought we had a deal."

King set his pen down. "You jilted my daughter."

"What are you talkin' about?"

"All I've heard since you've accepted my wife's supper invitations is 'Declan said this' and 'Declan's so wonderful.' Quite frankly, I'm sick of your name mentioned in every conversation in my home. Phoebe thought you were about to propose marriage. Now this saloon singer comes to town and you've no time for my daughter anymore."

"Enough." He'd had his fill of the man's vindictiveness. "I admit I might be guilty of being insensitive, but nothing more. I've *never* given Phoebe a reason to believe I was interested in marriage."

"What matters right now is my daughter, not your pride."

"No, what matters now is you've insulted my lady and I want to know why." His fingers itched for his gun. "Let go of this vendetta you have against me and apologize for the insults you hurled at Amalie today. The music hall's going to happen whether you back the venture or not."

The reverend's eye twitched, but he remained mute.

"I couldn't believe my ears when I heard you promised to support the music hall, Amalie's dream -- for a price." Sensing he finally had King's full attention, Declan leaned toward the older man. "It's hardly what I'd expect from a man of God."

Declan moved to the library shelf. He picked a book at random and dropped the volume on the edge of the desk. The sound reverberated around the room. "I won't stand by and let you hurt Amalie's career."

Declan reached for a second book. A light knock on the door aroused an earlier suspicion. Abby Russell poked her head around the door. He caught surprise on the woman's face and knew for certain his hunch was correct. Something was not right.

"Go on home to your children, Mrs. Russell. The reverend won't meet with you tonight."

She mouthed, 'thank you' and closed the door.

His gaze locked with King's. "You bloody bastard." If his suspicions proved true, he'd see the hypocrite hang. "I want an answer, Reverend. Why'd Mrs. Russell come here tonight?"

"Get out!"

"What about the vows you made?" Declan picked up the Bible and shoved the book at the reverend's balled fists.

King snatched the sacred book. "Get out of my church, or I'll throw you out."

"Amalie was right, wasn't she? You use your power to manipulate people."

"You go to hell and take her with you."

Declan pulled his pistol and cocked it.

Chapter Thirteen

Rage drove Declan. He shoved the preacher backward across his desk and jammed the pistol barrel against the man's temple. "I've had enough. You start talking or I swear I'll blow your bloody head off."

Sweat dampened King's flushed face. He clamped his jaw shut and glared back. Pure, venomous hate poured out of his steely gray eyes.

Declan itched to pull the trigger, end the preacher's devious dealings with his townsfolk, but his conscience wouldn't let him. Instead, he fired the shot into the ceiling.

King jumped. He swallowed hard and nodded. "I'll do what you say, just put the gun down."

Declan eased off, but kept his pistol readied. "Now I know what it takes to get your attention."

"It's not what you think." The reverend straightened his clothes with a quick tug.

"For your sake, I pray not."

King pulled a handkerchief from his pocket. "Mrs. Russell comes by here every Wednesday night to drop off a payment on the debt she owes me." He removed his eyeglasses and wiped the sweat off his brow. "I'm telling you nothing inappropriate happens."

"Do I have fool written across my forehead?"

"I swear on the Bible. She's only here long enough to give me her pay and then goes home to her son and daughter."

"I must be missing the obvious. A widow with young children sneaks into your church to pay you money? Do you run a money lending business from your parish cloaked under the veil of darkness?"

Outrage crossed the man's face. "I am a man of God first and foremost and demand respect from you, Grainger."

Declan's jaw dropped at the man's audacity. "Respect?" He took a deep, steadying breath. "Don't push me, you ass. If any demands are made, they will be mine. Now give me a straight answer or I swear I'll shoot you, with the utmost respect, of course." He leaned close.

The reverend threw up his hands. "If you will listen to me--" He shifted in his seat. "The widow hasn't paid me in full for her husband's funeral service yet."

"What?"

"I've tried to be patient, but she's not met her financial obligation."

Night Angel

King shoved his thinning gray hair out of his face and leaned back in the chair. "Being a generous man, I found her a night job cleaning at the mercantile while her children sleep. She comes by once a week and gives me her pay."

It took every ounce of willpower Declan had not to pull the trigger after all. "You mean to sit there and tell me you don't have a problem with Abby Russell leaving her young children alone every night to pay for a job already covered by the salary this town's council pays you?"

"It's none of your business how I run my church, Grainger."

Declan banged his fist against the desk. "In the name of God, what kind of man are you?"

"I've told you what you wanted to know, now get out."

"I'm not going anywhere until you give me all the money you've taken from Abby Russell and anyone else who's paid you these outlandish fees to date."

King stood and pointed at the door. "Get the hell out of my church."

Phoebe rushed into the office with a rifle in her hands. She glanced at Declan and then her father. "Papa, are you alright? I could hear your bellow all the way outside."

"What are you doing here, daughter?" He reached over and grabbed the gun from her hands.

"Jack Jameson stopped by the house to report he heard gunshots coming from here. While he looks for the sheriff, I decided to come and see for myself. Mother and I were worried after our unpleasant encounter with Declan earlier. It looks like we were right to be concerned."

A few moments later Sheriff Stanton strode into the parish office. His brow puckered at seeing the guns in the men's hands. "Put the weapons on the desk."

Declan set his pistol near the edge close enough to grab if the situation erupted out of control. King ignored the order.

The sheriff pulled his firearm. "Put the gun down, King."

The preacher left Phoebe's side and leaned the rifle against the side of his desk.

"Will someone tell me what the hell is going on here?"

"I demand you arrest this man, sheriff. He's broken into my office and threatened both my daughter and me. Look at her. He's near scared Phoebe to death."

Declan had to give King his due for audacity.

"Do you have something to say in this matter, Declan?"

"I'm not sure what we have going on here, Matt. I'm trying to figure out if the preacher is a common thief or if his criminal acts go deeper."

"You speak sacrilege, Grainger. You dare insult my character without proof? I demand your immediate apology."

Declan's temper snapped. Through a red haze, he grabbed the preacher by his lapel. "Shut up, King. You're done making demands tonight." He shoved the man into his desk chair. "Get out of that seat at your own risk," he said with his index finger pointed in the preacher's face.

He turned back to Matt. "I don't know how far the larceny goes yet."

"Are you certain, Declan? Those are strong accusations."

"I'm not sure of anything, but by God I'm going to find out."

"Get him out of my office." King pumped his fists, but didn't stand.

"Enough for tonight. We'll discuss this after tempers cool. Let's go, Grainger. We can stop at Trick's for a drink on the way down the hill."

Declan picked up his pistol and tucked it back into his holster. He turned to go, but halted before he reached the door. "I'm not done dealing with your reprehensible behavior with my lady earlier today. You give her anything to be upset about again and I won't hesitate a moment to follow up with another visit. Next time I won't be so pleasant."

He stomped into the hall and let out a deep moan. "It's taking every ounce of strength I have not to kill the bastard, Matt. I've spent a lot of time with King and never guessed his true nature."

"Don't be so hard on yourself. It's not gone so far you can't fix it."

On the way back to the hotel his mind ran in a thousand different directions. If Amalie hadn't told him about King's behavior, he might never have discovered the double dealings to his townsfolk.

"Thanks for the offer of a drink at Trick's, Matt, but I'm escorting Amalie to San Francisco tomorrow for a few days and have chores to finish up before we leave."

"The time away will be good for you. I've never seen you lose your temper like you did tonight. Is there something else going on involving Mrs. Renard?"

"The *good* reverend leveled some nasty comments against her character earlier today, ordered her out of town along with a few threats I still intend to deal with at a later date."

"I trust you'll not take the law into your own hands."

He slapped Matt on the back. "You can count on me for being a law-abiding member of this community, sheriff."

*****

Declan situated Bunny outside his bedroom door before he shut and locked it. He pushed his bed away from the tunnel entrance and entered the dark void.

Dressed in Night Angel garb, he treaded along the narrow tunnel until he reached the exit behind the church. He doused the lantern and stuck his head outside, sucking in deep breaths of fresh air until his heartbeat slowed.

Assured no one lurked around the area, he ran his hand along the church's back wall until his fingers brushed against the hidden latch. When Angus built the fire escape door, he'd teased him about being able to sneak into church and hide from the devil. Now the devil waited inside. Declan looked to the heavens. "Put in a good word for me tonight, Angus. This man's treachery must be stopped."

The hinges creaked as the small door pulled away, gaining him entrance to the storage room. Loud voices emerged from the parish office. He cracked the storage room door open and listened.

"Please, Papa, you've got to calm down or you'll have a heart attack."

"Enough, child. You brought that scoundrel into our lives, and now look at the mess I have to deal with."

"I'm sorry. It isn't my fault Declan's a liar."

"Nothing is ever your fault, Phoebe. Now stop the tears. I've heard enough of your bawling for one night."

Declan eased the door open enough to have a visual of the two. He needed a diversion to get inside that room. His gaze rested on two bells on a shelf. Perfect.

He waited until both King and Phoebe had their backs to the door. With his knife in his right hand and a bell in his left, he entered the office and shook the bell. "I'm ringing for the truth, Reverend King."

King spun around, wrapping a protective arm around his daughter. Phoebe's eyes grew wide before she shrieked. "Father, do something."

"What are you doing here, Night Angel?"

"Move." He motioned toward the bookshelf.

Not as controlled as Declan would have expected King to be, the reverend checked out the rifle still leaning against the side of the desk.

"Don't be a fool, sir. I can drop you with my knife before you blink your eye."

Phoebe pulled her father along by his arm until their backs rested against the bookcase.

Declan picked up the rifle, checking to see if it was loaded. He shook his head. Just like Phoebe to carry an unloaded gun into a ruckus. He tossed the firearm on top of the desk and leaned his backside against the edge. "Now, what's this I've heard tonight about you cheating my people out of their hard earned money, Reverend King?"

The man tensed and pulled away from his daughter. "I'm a decent, God loving man. Did you hear the scandalous lie from Grainger?"

He stood silent in hopes King might inadvertently let something important slip.

"Humph. Well, don't believe a word of it. Grainger has plenty of reasons to lie. He's a scoundrel and I can prove it." He glared at his daughter. "Tell him. Tell the Night Angel what kind of man Grainger is. He needs to know how Grainger made you all kinds of promises and then dumped you when a piece of trash rode into town with her flashy clothes and filthy mouth."

Declan's fingers held a death grip on his knife. It took every ounce of strength he had not to anchor it between the bastard's eyes, but his secret persona kept him from doing anything to give his identity away. Amalie's words echoed inside his mind. *If you lose your temper, your temper wins, or in this case, King wins.*

Phoebe for once didn't utter a word. He'd have thought she'd have plenty to say about his supposed unsavory moral fiber.

"Speak, child. Don't keep the man in suspense."

"I've not come here to debate the character of the hotelkeeper. I want the money you've stolen from my townsfolk. Hand it over."

The reverend glimpsed the knife and scoffed. "You parade in here under the guise of an angel dressed in black. You threaten us with your ridiculous blade. Your reputation is highly exaggerated. From what I've heard, people love you while still fearing you. It's probably not fear of you hurting them, but fear of your incompetence that scares them."

Declan ran the tip of his boot knife into the desk. He reached along his neck and extracted the longer knife from the shoulder sheath. "My mission is to undo the wrongs and protect the innocents." He twisted the blade back and forth. "My sharp friend here has been of great assistance in my endeavors. Would you like to find out firsthand how sharp the point is? How easy it would stop the beat of your heart?"

"You boast empty threats."

"Maybe I do exaggerate. I withdraw part of my comment, sir. I am in doubt my blade would encounter a heart at all. Prove me wrong. Return the money you've illegally taken from your parishioners, and I will no longer detain you."

"Papa, please do as he asks."

The reverend's eyes narrowed.

"You're testing my patience, Reverend King. Your daughter is a lot smarter than you are. Don't be a fool. Heed her good advice."

With the room dim enough and the two of them standing in the shadow of the single light, he decided to take a chance. Putting an end to this encounter without bloodshed was worth the risk. Declan stepped close enough to the reverend so his breath brushed across the man's face. "Oh, I understand your reasoning. If you give me the money, you'd be admitting you're a thief." He pressed his hand against the reverend's chest and ran the edge of the knife along the large man's bristled cheek. "Too late, the secret's out. I know you're a thief, and so does the law. Make it easy on yourself and your lovely daughter, and hand over the money."

King's eyes grew huge, nearly bulging from his crimson face. "How dare you come into my church and make such vile accusations."

Declan grabbed the man's arm and spun him around. He held the blade to the edge of his neck. "You dumb, stupid, ass, tell your daughter where your stash is."

"Not necessary. I know where he keeps it." Phoebe reached into her father's vest pocket and pulled out a small key.

"What are you doing, Phoebe?" Reverend King spit out.

Declan could feel the rage soar through the large man's quivering body while they watched her move to the desk.

She unlocked the middle drawer and pulled out a ledger and wooden box. "Here, take them." She tossed both items on top of the desk.

King went rigid. Phoebe had handed him the proof he needed to put the reverend's larceny to an end.

He shoved the man toward his daughter and pointed in the direction of the door. "Take your father and get out."

He followed them through the church and bolted the door behind them. Back in the office, he sat at the desk and opened the cash box. His jaw dropped at the amount of paper money it contained, in neat piles, plus stacks of gold eagles.

What he read in the ledger turned his stomach. "Damn, does that bastard stop at nothing?" Page after page listed charges for christenings, sick patient visits, weddings, and counseling. He scratched his head. Why hasn't anyone come to him or the sheriff about what the reverend had forced them to do?

All these people, most of them his friends, would be compensated. He'd see to it. Nobody deserved treatment like this, especially by a man whose character should have been trustworthy.

A thought occurred to him. If the reverend wanted his parishioners to pay their supposed debts to him, why'd he block the able bodied men from the work he offered at the music hall? It didn't make sense unless power and arrogance drove the man more than the money. He supposed King couldn't give them an opportunity of earning a proper salary. A good paying job would give them a chance to break free from his hold.

After he and Amalie returned from their San Francisco trip, he'd investigate further. He tucked the ledger inside his shirt and started for the storage room.

Rage pumped through his body. It pushed him through the tunnel into the cavern in record time. He pulled off his hat and veil, tossing them along with the wooden box on the counter. He sank onto the overturned ore cart and pulled the ledger from inside his shirt. He glanced through the pages again. Disgust nearly suffocated him. What in the hell have I stumbled onto? He'd encouraged the town to hire the bastard. King had represented himself as a compassionate man of God. Where'd it all go wrong?

He snapped the book closed and dropped it on top of the box. He couldn't get out of his clothes fast enough. Naked, he ran to the underground creek flowing along a prehistoric riverbed and ventured into the knee high water. The melted snow chilled him to the bone, but the cold revived his hot, sweaty flesh. He sat and then lay back, letting the rush of water flow over him until his skin prickled.

Refreshed, he used brisk rubs to rid his body of the chills. Dried and dressed in his street clothes, he headed back through the tunnel to his bedroom.

Amalie waited for him in the lobby. She turned at his entry and rushed toward him. "Declan, you're back. I didn't see you come in. Where've you been for such a long time?"

He dropped his hands over her shoulders. "Slow down, I'm fine. Coffee?"

"Yes, I'll join you in the kitchen and you can tell me what happened."

She sat on a three-legged stool and watched as he pulled a bucket filled with water out of the hole in the floor. "You have a well inside the kitchen?"

"You forget I only have the most modern equipment in my hotel. It's a standard Angus and Judith drilled into me."

"They were wonderful parents, weren't they?"

"As I grow older I realize it more and more. Someday I hope my own children will pass on their teachings."

Her eyes widened. Sadness reflected from the brown depths. She rushed out of the kitchen into the dining room. He found her sitting at the table, her head resting against her hands.

"I'm sorry for my insensitivity. Forgive me for not remembering you've lost your child?"

She gazed up at him, tears glistening in her eyes. His heart restricted. He sat and pulled her into his arms and held her while she wept.

"What's happened to me, Declan? I think I've probably cried more in the past few days than I have in my entire life. It's not like me."

He held her away from him and tipped her chin so she'd look directly into his eyes. "I am not an expert at women's emotions, but my guess is that for the first time in your life you feel alive and loved. You're experiencing all kinds of new emotions -- your confrontation with your sisters, thinking about the death of your son, and possibly caring for me?"

"Maybe." She pushed away and composed herself. "I'd like the cup of coffee you offered, Mr. Grainger."

"I am your humble servant." He stood and bent slightly at the waist. He turned before he stepped out of the room and studied her. How would he ever get through to Amalie, get her to trust him enough to give him her heart? He had to find a way to convince her she wanted to be his wife. With her temperament, he couldn't push her too quickly or she'd bolt. With her trust problem, she'd run from him anyway once she discovered he hadn't been forthcoming with his social standing. One of the surprises he had for her in San Francisco could possibly turn into his folly.

Chapter Fourteen

Amalie pressed her palms against the butterflies fluttering inside her tummy. Tomorrow morning she'd be in San Francisco. She'd heard someone say once the city is a magical place. Exactly what Declan had planned for her was a mystery she anxiously awaited for him to unfold.

She and her sister stood side by side on the top deck of the steamship. She barely took her eyes off the water's edge as they traveled down the Sacramento River. "Those white birds with spindly legs are beautiful."

Marinda caught her enthusiasm. "Look over there. I love watching the large herons as they take off and fly." She pointed out several more species of birds. "Traveling by steamboat is certainly better than the dusty ride to Sacramento in Lucas's stagecoach. The man's incorrigible."

Amalie nodded. "For certain, he's a most rude man."

"Ladies?"

They both turned. Declan and Ethan approached. Amalie caught her breath at how dashing Declan appeared as he strolled toward her in his dark brown trousers and leather jacket.

"Are you ladies ready to go in for supper?" Declan asked. "I've reserved a table for the four of us by the window so you won't miss any of the view."

Amalie entered the dining area and gasped at the elegance of red, white, and gold. The room, divided into two levels, held an assortment of passengers. Declan pointed at a table on the lower floor with a reserved sign set on the red tablecloth. Amalie gripped the brass handrail and stepped down the wide staircase of the Delta Rose.

A waiter approached as soon as the four of them were seated. He poured everyone a cup of coffee and left with their order. Rolls of crusty brown bread, creamy clam chowder and coffee started off their meal, soon followed by baked halibut, boiled potatoes in a cheese sauce, and large red strawberries with cream. After the main course, she glanced over the cart with several different desserts and moaned. Every delectable treat tempted her.

Declan leaned close to her ear. "You see something you'd like?"

"All of it, actually, but I couldn't eat another bite."

"You mean you've finally filled your stomach? No growling tonight?"

Night Angel

"I don't think I've ever eaten so much food at one sitting. Do you think we could take a dessert for later?"

Declan's wink summersaulted her very full stomach. He lifted a piece of cake off the cart and placed it on the table in front of her. "Does this meet your fancy?"

"Yes, thank you." She leaned over the small plate and inhaled the cinnamon and nutmeg essence. A long time had passed since she'd indulged in her favorite food -- apple cake smothered in cream. She glanced across the table at her sister. "Do you remember the apple cakes our housekeeper used to serve us at Sunday suppers?"

"Oh, don't tempt me to take a piece. The apples were from the tree out back by the garden shed, if I remember correctly."

"Yes. I used to pick them for Laura and set them on the counter where she would be sure to see them." Amalie snickered at one of the few happy times from her childhood. She loved climbing that tree.

After the waiter cleared their plates, Declan placed his hand over hers and squeezed. "Having fun?"

In high spirits, she glanced around the busy room filled with passengers. "Yes. How could I not?"

The steamship's captain rose from the head table and stepped up a short rise onto a stage not far from where they sat. "Ladies and gentlemen, I proudly announce San Francisco's own Tucker Morrison and his musicians are here this evening to entertain you. We always encourage our guests to come on stage where they can sing with the band or share a talent, so don't be shy. Who's first?"

Immediately, a hand shot up. The captain pointed to an elderly gentleman who picked up three plates on his way to the stage. He juggled the white dessert dishes along to the beat of a spirited tune Amalie didn't recognize. His act crashed to pieces on the floor along with his confidence. The gent threw up his hands and returned to his seat with a very flushed face.

"Anyone else?" The captain scanned the room. When his gaze settled on their table, his jaw dropped. "Is that you, Grainger?"

Declan raised his hand and waved.

"Come on up here. I'm sure the crowd would enjoy one of your ballads."

He shook his head and waved the captain off. "Not tonight, Joey."

Amalie's jaw dropped. "What's he talking about, Declan? You sing?"

Declan shrugged. "Very badly, I assure you. I'd compare my voice with a randy old tomcat on the prowl."

"Let's hear some encouragement, people. I grew up with this man. His voice is a treat you shouldn't miss."

The room abounded with applause.

Declan rolled his eyes at her. "I haven't sung since Judith died. If I tried, I'd embarrass myself."

She squeezed his hand. "Then it's time you started. Go on, do it for her."

"I know you're not shy, Declan. Get up here."

Declan sauntered to the front of the room and grabbed his friend's outstretched hand. "Good to see you," he said with a wide grin. "How are you?"

"I'm good. You're not going to disappoint us are you?"

Amalie's heart warmed at the fleeting look Declan shot her. Pride raced through her as she settled back waiting for Declan's performance. She took a quick glance at Marinda and Ethan.

Declan pulled a tall stool to the middle of the stage. "As you can tell from my accent, I was born and raised in Scotland. At the age of nine, after my mother died, my father and I sailed to America. The memories I have of my homeland still live inside me. I'd like to share with you tonight the ballad I wrote years ago from the memories of a young Scottish lad."

Sitting, he strummed a banjo. His voice deepened with the added touch of his Scottish burr.

"In lands rising so close to heaven,
Scots hear the flutter of angels' wings,
Flying over mountains chiseled from stone.

Bagpipes echoing from glen to glen,
Gather men to band as fighting forces,
To save their mountains chiseled from stone.

Highland mists settling across rich forests,
Blessing countrysides filled with lochs and glens,
Gracing the mountains chiseled from stone.

My heart still feels the call of this land,
Where my mother taught me to love and grow,
To stand tall in the mountains chiseled from stone."

Amalie stood along with Marinda and Ethan, appreciating the

audience's emotional response. He'd delivered his song with the passion of a child who'd left part of his heart in his homeland.

The next time he caught her attention, he held his hand toward her seeking permission to bring her on stage with him. She smiled and nodded her approval.

"I'd like to introduce my lady, Lily Fox. She should be up here instead of me. I guarantee her voice is the best you'll ever hear."

A man in the audience yelled back. "I wanna hear a real singer, not some lady friend of yours."

Declan pulled a coin from his pocket. "I'll put up this twenty dollar gold eagle against an apology from you for insulting my lady if she doesn't live up to my praise."

The heckler skimmed the room until his gaze settled on her. Amalie stood. "When you apologize, good sir, I'll take the gold eagle."

The audience enthusiastically egged the man into accepting Declan's bet. He waved his hand and sealed the deal.

Amalie stepped onto the stage. "Evening everyone, my name's Lily Fox and I'm here to entertain you." She slipped off her white lace wrap and handed it to Declan before motioning him out of her way.

"*Alas, my love, you do me wrong--*" The crowd sat motionless listening to Green Sleeves sung like they'd never heard it before. The age-old song reverberated throughout the steamship, drawing crowds from other areas. Amalie finished and took her bow. Everyone stood clapping, most with tears dampening their cheeks.

"Thank you," she said as the applause continued for several minutes.

The grin on Declan's face as he stepped next to her and held up the gold eagle gave her great pleasure. His action brought another round of applause.

He faced the audience. "All right, ladies and gentlemen. What's your choice? Who should take this coin home?"

"Lily!" reverberated around the room.

He placed the coin into the palm of her hand and wrapped her fingers around it. "It's just the first of many, my dear."

"You were amazing, Miss Lily. Take your coin with my good will," the loudmouth hollered.

The captain joined them on stage. "I don't suppose you'd treat us with another song, Miss Fox?"

"Thank you, Captain. Maybe a short one would do?"

"I'm sure whatever you choose will be fine. By the way, the name is Joe."

Amalie belted out one of the ballads the gents in St. Louis requested frequently. Again, the appreciation of the audience sent a bolt of pride through her. She was born to sing.

Declan slipped her shawl over her shoulders and escorted her back to their table.

"You're both full of surprises," Ethan stood and pulled a chair out for her. "By the sounds of things this evening, I don't think you'll have any trouble filling the music hall."

"Thank you, Ethan. I consider that high praise."

Marinda squeezed her hand. "Honey, you sounded wonderful. I'm so proud of you."

Her sister's praise struck a happy cord. With their history, she never expected they'd become friends. "How very nice of you to say, little sister. I appreciate the compliment."

A waiter stopped by the table with a bottle of white wine and four glasses. "Delivered with compliments from the captain."

Declan accepted the bottle and thanked the waiter. He pulled the cork and started pouring. "Everyone want a glass?"

Amalie grabbed his wrist. "What are you doing? I didn't think you drank alcohol?"

"This seems an occasion for changing the rules." He filled all four glasses. "*Slainte*, I salute the beautiful Benjamin sisters who've captivated the hearts of the men who've fallen in love with them."

"I guess we've fooled them, Marinda. He thinks we're both lovable."

Declan kissed the back of her knuckles. "Very lovable."

"If you don't mind my asking," Ethan said, "why is it you've become a teetotaler? It seems odd considering the amount of time you spend at Trick's."

Declan caught Ethan's grin. "The reason I spend time in Trick's now is *Lily Fox*. As a young lad, I had the job of cleanup in the bar area of our hotels. The stale smell of spilled whiskey and vomit turned my stomach. I've never participated in the drinking ritual."

"Maybe it was your foster father's intention all along," Ethan said.

"There's no doubt Angus was a very clever man. It was a lesson well learned and not forgotten."

The band started. Tables were pushed out of the way to form a small dance area. Amalie watched couples sway to the music. "Do you dance, Declan?"

"Do I dance?" He brought his mouth close to her ear. His voice dropped low. "If you're willing to risk your toes being trampled on, I'll give it a try."

His fingers wrapped around hers and he led her onto the dance floor. A spark of mischief gleamed in his eyes. She caught a faint smile before he slipped his arm around her back and held her right hand over his heart. The tempo of the music slowed. His light steps carried them around the dance floor with grace. The devil, he'd been less than truthful about his dancing ability. She pressed against the hard, muscular warmth of him. He whirled her around other couples with grace and expertise.

She was disappointed when the music stopped and he escorted her to their table. Placing his arm along the back of her chair, he dared to stare at her with a self-satisfied smirk. It wasn't in her to let him off easy. She pulled off one of her shoes and rubbed her toes.

"Uh oh," Marinda commented. "Declan step on your feet too many times?"

"You have no idea." She sent him a smug grin. "I hope Ethan brought his medical bag. I'm certain all my toes must be broken."

Declan grabbed his heart. "You wound me."

"What I don't understand is why you thought you had to misrepresent your dancing skills."

"It's been so long, I figured my feet must have rusted since the last time I guided a lady around the dance floor."

"He's actually the best partner I've ever had," Amalie finally conceded.

"Thank you, my lady. The honor was mine, I assure you."

"We have a long day tomorrow. I'm ready to turn in now. Marinda?"

"You go ahead. I'll join you after a stroll around deck with my handsome husband."

"Make that two times around the deck," Ethan said, winking. They joined hands and left the room.

"I guess their departure leaves us alone, sweetheart. Shall we go?" With Declan's arm wrapped around her shoulders, they strolled along the long, narrow hallway to her and Marinda's cabin. They stopped in front of the white cabin door with a bronze No. 8 nailed on it. A soft light from the lantern bolted onto the wall between the two beds lit their entry.

Declan took both her hands and pulled her toward him, but didn't hold her. "I'm certain by now you realize I've fallen in love with you." He searched her face and gently cupped her chin. "You stole my heart the moment I saw your glare from inside Lucas's stagecoach the night you arrived on my doorstep."

"I glared at you?"

"Uh hmmm, you did."

"I'd forgotten, but don't doubt it. You must have thought I was some kind of uppity bitch the way you laughed every time Lucas made those brash comments."

"Not even for a moment. In fact, when you stepped onto the walk, held up your chin, and strutted past me into the hotel like a queen, I admired your strength of character." He brushed his fingers along her cheek. "When you asked about sleeping in my bed, I almost choked. You displayed both guts and pride. Qualities I admire in a woman."

"You certainly know how to flatter a girl, Mr. Grainger."

"That's because I find you absolutely irresistible. When I said you *are* loveable, I was quite serious."

The warmth of his gaze turned her knees fluid. She grabbed hold of his shoulders to keep from toppling to the floor. "I don't know what to say."

"You don't have to say anything." He leaned toward her until his lips covered hers, and wrapping both arms around her back, he squeezed her against him to a point where she could barely breathe.

He released her. She lost her balance and stumbled against him.

"Whoa." He caught her by the shoulders. "Are you alright?"

She nodded, but Amalie wanted more. She wrapped her arms around his neck and pulled his mouth back against hers, thrusting her tongue against his.

"Sweetheart," he whispered with a raspy voice after he unlocked her fingers. He placed her hands over his erratic heart. "See what you do to me. I want to make love with you, but not now, not tonight."

"Declan, please, I don't understand. Why won't you stay with me?"

He touched the tip of his nose against hers, peering deep into her eyes. "Don't misunderstand, Amalie. My body aches for you. I want nothing more than making love with you right this moment, but I won't be able to walk away once we've shared a bed." He cupped his hand along her cheek and smiled at her with tenderness. "You are the only love for me, but if you don't feel the same way--" He ran kisses along the sensitive part of her neck up to her ear.

"I don't know how I feel, Declan, except scared."

"I know." He rested his forehead against hers. "I'm scared, too. I've lost everyone in my life I've ever cared for. I'm tired of living with memories. I want a special love of my own. Someone who loves me back. A family."

"I wish I could be so sure of what I want." She placed her hand against the flat of his palm, entwining her fingers with his. "I know I can act frivolous and self-centered, but a lot of the time it's bluff. I can thank Rupert for that." She fought the tears, but they streamed down her cheeks anyway. "He killed part of me, too. Hell is too good for him."

"Sweetheart, you don't have to make a decision tonight, this moment. I know it's a big step for you, for both of us." He brushed the wetness away. "When you're ready, you won't have to wonder if loving me is right or wrong. Trust your instincts. Your heart will guide your decision."

"One more kiss might help." She gazed at him from below her thick lashes.

He chuckled, breaking the seriousness of the moment. The sound warmed her heart. Why couldn't she take the first step toward happiness and grab the kind of love he offered?

"Come here," he said, crooking his finger.

Tenderness wrapped around her heart, easing her fear. His strong hands ran up and down her back as he pulled her against his chest.

"You don't have to ask a second time."

She closed her eyes, losing herself to his passion. Sensitive to his touch, his kiss just about devoured her, drove her to deeper depths. God help her, she wanted what he offered. She wanted him.

He released her. Without his warmth pressed against her, a chill seeped through her gown. "Please, won't you stay?"

"I can't. Not until you're sure my love is enough to last you a lifetime."

His eyes reflected what it cost him to refuse her. She hated his stubbornness. Patience definitely was not one of her virtues.

"Sleep well, my love." He placed a light kiss on her forehead and went to the door. Giving her one last glance, he walked out, firmly shutting it behind him.

Disappointed he hadn't stayed longer she undressed and slipped between the cool, cotton sheets. She settled onto her back and stared at the light. Would she ever trust again? She didn't want to go through life always suspicious and doubting the people she cared for.

When Marinda came into the room, she closed her eyes. Not ready to discuss her future with her sister yet, she feigned sleep.

*****

The Delta Rose sailed into San Francisco Bay the next morning under a thick blanket of fog. "It's a beautiful sight, isn't it?" Declan asked once the mist thinned and they could see the city built on hills.

"Yes, very beautiful," she returned, but her gaze was focused on him, not the scenery. In the morning light she recognized how easily she could love him if she gave the relationship a chance. Declan was a good man. After he'd left her last night, she could think of nothing else but his affectionate words and promises.

Commitment still scared her. Maybe by the end of the weekend she'd have her heart sorted out. She slipped her hand into his and watched as the ship sailed through the entrance of San Francisco Harbor. Sailing ships from around the world docked at the vast quay. Declan pointed out several large vessels taller than some buildings she'd seen. A string of fishing boats rang bells as they passed on their way out to sea.

Marinda joined them at the rail. "Isn't this harbor huge? When Ethan and I came through here in 1850, this entire area was a graveyard of abandoned ships."

Seagulls shrieked overhead, seamen tossed giant ropes to dock workers, and soon the Delta Rose's long bow rested secure against the pier. The heavy gangplank dropped onto the wharf. They walked past nets full of fish swinging from boats lined up along the dock. The colorful language of the sailors caused Amalie to smile. Memories of the hours she'd spent along St. Louis's busy wharf came to mind.

Declan hailed an open air buggy. The four of them rode through Portsmouth Square. Struck speechless by the activity around them, Amalie's head whipped back and forth trying to see everything at once. She was in San Francisco at last. The city was everything she'd imagined and more.

Four and five-story buildings stood regally side by side at the edge of the square. The sign on the front of the hotel where they stopped boasted it housed the finest gambling hall in the city.

"Why are we stopping here?"

"This is our hotel, sweetheart."

"Are you sure? The sign says this is a saloon."

"Trust me. You'll not be disappointed in our rooms." He disembarked from the buggy and held his hand up to help her. A porter greeted Declan and placed their bags inside the entrance, stating he'd see their luggage safely delivered to their rooms.

The four of them strolled past the reception desk without checking in and walked up three flights of stairs. Declan pulled a key from his pocket and opened a pair of double oak doors. He moved back, motioning for them to enter.

She gaped at the opulence. "Are you sure this is where we're supposed to stay?" Finely carved furniture, delicate lamps, and as fine a collection of porcelain figurines and rich oil paintings as she'd ever seen dominated the room. Someone with great taste had given the space warmth as well as grace.

Declan frowned. "Aren't you happy with the suite?"

She moved farther into the room and spun around. "Oh, no, I'm very impressed you've found these rooms. How could I not like it here? Are you a friend of the owner?"

She caught Ethan grinning at Declan. "Are you two tricking Marinda and me? Are we trespassers?"

"Don't keep her in suspense, Declan."

"The suite belongs to me as well as the entire building except for the gambling saloon. I have a partnership with Colton Brown who runs the bar and gaming tables while I'm not here, which, as you know, is most of the time. I choose to live in Paradise Pines and run Chaumers."

Her mouth fell open. "All--of this--is yours?"

"Yes, my inheritance from Angus and Judith."

She surveyed the beautiful pieces of art around the room. "Did Judith do all of this?"

"Yes. She was quite talented, don't you think? Angus let her have free rein to decorate all the hotel rooms, but her essence is in these rooms where we lived until we moved to Paradise Pines."

A couple of young men placed their luggage inside the suite. Declan handed out a few coins and closed the door behind them. He picked up the Braddocks' suitcases and nodded toward a door. Amalie placed her handbag on a small table and followed close behind.

"Will it do?" he said to the other couple, laying the suitcases on a stand against the wall. "It's the grandest of our bedrooms. I thought you'd enjoy the view from in here."

Marinda danced around the spacy area. "It's so regal."

Amalie surveyed the corner bedroom, decorated in soft apricot with green accents. It was quite large with a window overlooking the back garden. An oil painting of a strikingly beautiful, dark haired woman hung on the wall across from the bed. "Is this Judith?"

"Yes, lovely wasn't she?"

"Very lovely." A stab of envy shot through her. How could she compete with a woman so perfect?

"My foster mother had the same interest in music as you."

"How nice," she answered with as much enthusiasm as she could muster.

He turned to Ethan and Marinda. "Get settled and then we'll go down and have something to eat." He grasped Amalie's hand and led her into the parlor, closing the door behind them.

He ushered her into another room at the other end of the suite. "This one's mine. While we're here, you may use it as your own. I'll sleep on the small bed in the office."

The beige and shades of blue décor suited him. Mementos sat on two bedside tables and the tall oak armoire. A daguerreotype of a youth and two adults caught her eye. She picked the frame up and stared at the people. "Is this you with your foster parents?"

"Yes. It was taken when I was nine, right after we arrived in New York. Judith wanted a keepsake of the day we became a family."

She replaced the photo on the table. "Is their last name Grainger?"

"No. My father's name was Roderick Grainger."

"What was theirs?"

"Carnegie."

She thought she knew Declan. Obviously he wasn't the hardworking hotelkeeper she'd been led to believe. "You're very wealthy, aren't you?"

He gave her a guarded look. "Does it matter how much money I have?"

"It might." Something didn't add up here. She was almost afraid to ask the question nagging at her since she'd stepped inside the suite. "It's you, not Patrick, who's building the music hall for me, isn't it?"

Declan's eyes grew wide, but he said nothing. A tight knot formed in the pit of her stomach.

"Am I right?"

"Yes."

Disillusionment overwhelmed her. Until now, she'd thought of him as honorable and above deception. "Why?"

He grabbed her hands.

She jerked them away. "Don't touch me."

"Calm down. If you don't lower your voice, your sister and Ethan will be in here."

"I don't care."

"I do. This is between you and me."

"Patrick, too, of course," she threw back at him.

"For God's sake, Amalie." He took her by the arm and escorted her to a settee in the parlor. He settled next to her. "There's no reason you should be so angry. Let me explain."

She tilted her chin and shot him a mutinous stare. "You're wasting your breath."

"It's mine to waste."

"Well, I won't listen. You and Patrick have been in cahoots behind my back. You've made a fool of me. Patrick doesn't have my interests at heart and you know it. I thought you were different. Every man who's deceived me always has a good reason."

"I understand you're hurt. Believe me I felt a heel for misleading you. When I made the decision to have Patrick front the music hall, I feared it might come to this."

She let out a long, dramatic sigh. "Then why'd you do it?"

He cupped her chin and forced her to look at him.

She didn't want to listen, but after seeing the devastation in his eyes, she paid more attention to his explanation.

"When I heard you sing at Trick's, your voice drew me to you. I *had* to build the music hall. I suspected you wouldn't accept the offer from someone you didn't know so I hedged my bet and asked Patrick to make the offer for me." He leaned back and let go of her hand. "I ask you to please accept my apology for not dealing with my dilemma in a more appropriate way."

She rose and walked to one of the large bay windows without saying a word. She stared through the sheer white lace for a long time. Words eluded her. Declan had an excellent point. Maybe she overreacted, but the fact remained he'd manipulated her.

What am I supposed to do? She leaned her forehead against the cool glass and stared into space, rethinking his explanation. Did it really matter why or how he built the music hall? He was doing it because he loved her. She was stupid not to have appreciated his motivation from the beginning. *He loves me.*

Oh, dear God, and I'm in love him. The thought overwhelmed her, sucked the breath from her. She turned to tell him of her discovery and found the room empty.

Chapter Fifteen

He'd had enough. If Amalie wouldn't give him the benefit of the doubt, what else could he say?

Declan grabbed work clothes from the armoire and pulled on his britches. A light knock rapped against the bedroom door. He quickly buttoned the crotch and picked up the light blue shirt. "What is it?"

Amalie poked her head inside. "Declan?"

"Not now."

"I only need a moment. It's important."

He fastened the last button on his shirt and tucked it inside his pants. "For God's sake, Amalie, I built you a music hall. My actions were never intended to hurt you."

"So you just explained. It's not what I wanted to discuss with you." A blush tinted her cheeks.

Her obvious embarrassment surprised him. Another one of her stabs at manipulation no doubt. He battled between throttling her or kissing those pouty lips. "Can you give me one logical reason why you carried on like I've committed murder or some other crime as heinous?"

"No, but--"

"I thought not." He had no intention of saying something he'd regret later. He pulled a handful of bank notes out of a safe and handed them to her. "Pay Madame LaCroix after you've chosen your new wardrobe today."

"What should I order?"

"I don't care. Whatever you need for your performances," he snapped. "I'll see you this evening." He strode to the door cursing himself as a fool. Would he ever figure out the woman?

Colton Brown caught up with him along the path to the warehouse. "What's the hurry, Declan? Those crates have been here all these years. Can't you take the time and greet your partner?"

"Colton." He clutched the outstretched hand. "I've got a lot on my mind."

"I have no doubt. I've heard the gossip about your arrival with a beautiful woman on your arm."

"The woman in question is mine." He shrugged and grinned. "Or at least she will be as soon as I convince her."

Colton clasped his shoulder. "Well, good luck. I look forward to meeting the lady."

"Thanks. How's everything going?"

"Profits are up. I hired a new bartender last month and he seems to be working out satisfactorily."

"Good. Did you have any luck hiring transport wagons?"

"The Mitchell brothers arrived about half an hour ago."

"All right, I'll catch you later." Declan continued on his way.

John and Jess Mitchell leaned against the side of their large wagons waiting for him.

"As soon as you open up, we'll pull the rigs inside," Jess said. "You can lower the crates directly into the back if you'd like."

"Let's do it." Declan unlocked the doublewide doors and pushed them open. The dirt floor held tables, spare bed frames and boxes labeled with various linen supplies. He yanked on a pair of heavy leather work gloves. It didn't take long for the three of them to move most of the boxes out of the way to make room for the wagons.

Jess eased the first transport into the space. At the top of the ladder Declan pushed away cobwebs and stepped onto the loft. The first box noted the contents stamped across the top. Four seats per container totaled a lot of chairs to tote back to Paradise Pines. He hooked the pulley onto the crate and motioned for John to lower it. Once the box rested on the wagon bed, he returned to the floor.

"Dammit!" A two-inch hole chewed along the base didn't bode well. He grabbed a metal lever off the top of a nearby barrel and pried the lid off. With the first two red velvet seat cushions out of the crate his worst fear was corroborated. He'd found rat devastation. He rummaged through the packing and found two other cushions plus wooden backs, armrests and legs. Further inspection showed minimal damage easily repaired. He whooshed out a sigh of relief.

"Ready to get the rest of them boxes, boss?"

With a nod, he scampered back up the ladder.

Ethan entered the work area two hours later. The first wagon stood loaded and John was in the process of backing the other one inside the warehouse.

Declan waved to his friend once John placed the transport under the loft.

"Can you take a break and come eat?"

Declan wiped the sweat off his face and tucked the handkerchief into his back pocket. "Now you mention it, I am hungry." He jumped off the ladder. Before he left with Ethan he sent the brothers off to take their meal break.

"Let's eat in the garden." Ethan pointed along the walk to a shaded area. He set the basket on the table and pulled out lunch containers.

Declan stretched his legs out on the bench. He took a long drink of hot coffee and bit into a chicken sandwich. "What are you grinning at? Amalie spin you a good tale after I left?"

"You can't tell me you didn't expect that kind of reaction."

"Yes, but I didn't think she'd still be mad once I explained why I asked for Patrick's help. She calm down yet?"

"Marinda's friend, Genevieve Vellechamp, was waiting in the lobby when we went downstairs for a meal. I couldn't get a word in edgewise throughout breakfast. My guess is the only thing on her mind right now is clothes, shoes, and whatever else they think she needs at Madame LaCroix's establishment."

"Good." He stuffed the remainder of the sandwich into his mouth, then downed his coffee and put the cup back into the basket. "You know what's really got me worried?"

"My guess would be the Night Angel?"

He nodded. "If she got this angry because I didn't tell her of my wealth and about the music hall, what will she do if she finds out I'm the one who's been stealing her jewelry?"

*****

Genevieve's driver pulled the buggy into an alley close to the wharf. Amalie noted a small shop with a sign tacked over the door -- Madame LaCroix, Dressmaker. Colorful pink and yellow flowers peeked out of boxes from under two display windows.

Genevieve led Marinda and Amalie inside the cozy establishment. A small bell attached at the top of the door announced their arrival.

"One moment, if you please," a voice called from a back room.

While they waited, Amalie and Marinda rummaged through boxes of buttons and laces displayed on a table in the corner. Genevieve sat alongside the windows searching for costume ideas in one of the large books with pattern sketches.

A petite, older woman stepped from behind a deep blue curtain. "Ah, it is you, Genevieve, and look who you've brought to Madame LaCroix. Marinda Braddock, it's been much too long since you have come for more of my beautiful creations, *non*?"

Marinda gripped the shop owner's hands and smiled back. "Much too long, Madame." She motioned toward Amalie. "Please, let me introduce my sister, Amalie Renard."

Night Angel

"Ah, the woman who wishes to have many costumes made. Turn around, *s'il vous plait*."

Amalie did a quick pirouette.

Madame pinched her lower lip while scrutinizing. "You must stand up straight, lift your chin. Yes, yes, you'll do nicely. Follow me ladies."

The world behind the curtain bustled with activity. Four seamstresses sat at long tables covered in fabrics, cutting tools, and threads in a rainbow of colors.

"Continue down that hallway and wait in the room on the end until I can join you." Madame LaCroix pointed toward a beaded entrance.

They found a well-lit area filled with more fabrics and accessories. "Oh," Amalie gasped noticing a woman on a platform with her back to them. "Sorry, we didn't mean to bother you."

"Please, do not distress yourselves. You do not disturb me." The lady turned. "I wait for Madame LaCroix."

Jenny Lind, the much adored Swedish singer smiled at her. Amalie gasped. Her mouth went dry. She tried to speak, but what did someone say when she came face to face with her idol?

"I understand one of you is a singer?"

Still unable to speak, Amalie nodded. Finally she squeaked, "Me."

Miss Lind moved toward her. "Madame LaCroix has shared with me you will attend my performance tomorrow night."

"Yes."

"What's the matter with you, Amalie?" Marinda asked.

Warmth rushed to her cheeks. "Don't embarrass me, little sister. This is Jenny Lind."

The singer let out a light chuckle. "I understand. It happens a lot. I'm honored you're impressed with my fame. Come sit. We can talk until I must endure more pins."

"Miss Lind, I'm honored to meet you. For years my dream's been to hear you sing. Now, sitting here with you, I don't know what I should say."

"Thank you for your kind praise. Please, call me Jenny."

Amalie rolled her eyes at Marinda and Genevieve. Her heartbeat finally slowed to normal. All the questions she wanted to ask her idol started to form in her mind. "Won't you tell us about your professional life? I dream of a career such as yours."

"Yes, I've had success on the stage and I don't regret a moment of it, but this is my last tour."

Deep disappointment surged through Amalie. "Why? So many people will be unhappy if you no longer perform."

"I'm going back to Sweden to marry. My dream is having a family of my own." She laid her hand on Amalie's arm. "I hope you have your career and that the fame is everything you want it to be. Remember though, you can't take the applause to bed with you. Nights can be long and lonely when you sleep alone, my dear."

"You've been lonely?" She couldn't believe anyone as adored as Jenny Lind could suffer loneliness.

"Yes, but now that I have my own true love, my heart sings from joy not ambition. I'm truly happy."

"How could anything be more important than standing on a stage and singing for an audience?"

Before Jenny could answer, Madame LaCroix strolled into the room with several books and a tape measure draped around her neck. A frazzled young woman followed close behind.

"You," she said, pointing at Amalie, "get out of your street clothes so Minette can measure you." The coil of dark hair pinned atop the petite lady's head bobbed as she issued her directives. "You," she said, pointing at Jenny, "back on the platform so we can have your dress finished for tomorrow night's performance."

Genevieve and Marinda helped Amalie undress down to her undergarments. Measurements were taken. Afterwards they paged through books choosing the costumes which would add zest to *Lily Fox's* wardrobe.

"Do you have a gown for the performance tomorrow night, Mrs. Renard?" Madame LaCroix asked while she sat on the floor pinning Jenny's dress.

"Only those I brought from my current wardrobe."

"*Non*, that will not do." Madame turned toward Minette. "Girl, run upstairs to the closet in the green workroom and get the unclaimed engagement dress."

"Yes, Mama." The girl nodded and rushed from the room.

"I have an unusual silk you might consider wearing. I made it for a lovely young woman, but the family's fortunes changed and the girl didn't take it."

Amalie hesitated.

"You have a problem?"

"Wearing someone else's gown doesn't seem right."

"Of course, it's your choice," Madame LaCroix said. "We shall see."

Once Minette returned with the garment, Madame unpinned the drape protecting the gown. Amalie's breath caught in her throat. The silvery silk fabric sparkled with diamond-like brilliance. She ran her fingers across the soft material, barely able to control her enthusiasm at attending Jenny's performance in the spectacular gown. She would definitely accept the dress.

"The gown suits you, yes?" Madame LaCroix asked.

"Yes, very much."

"Let's see if alterations are needed." Madame helped Amalie slip the soft silk over her head and buttoned down the back. She motioned for her to turn.

"We need a few tucks at the waist and, as far as the bust, hmmm," she stood back and motioned to a mirror. "What do you think? Too tight or do you like showing off your glory?"

Amalie gasped at her reflection. She glanced at the other women. "What do you think?"

Marinda beamed. "You'll be a sensation."

"You must wear the dress, Amalie," Jenny said, nodding.

She spun around, observing her reflection in the mirror. True the bust fit a bit snug, but she liked what she saw. Tomorrow evening she'd definitely catch Declan's attention. She missed him and wondered if his temper had cooled yet.

"You like what you see?"

"Oh, yes, thank you. I'd be foolish not to wear this dress tomorrow night."

"Good. I'll have alterations done immediately and deliver the garment to Browns Hotel later today."

The rest of the afternoon went by in a blur. Fabrics, patterns, laces, trims, and accessories were chosen. Amalie's head spun from the enormity of it all.

Genevieve suggested they stop at a harbor front café for tea before they headed back to the hotel.

Amalie turned her nose up at several fishermen stacking boxes of bait along the dock. "This place has a pungent fish odor. Are you certain it's alright to eat here?"

"Trust me, you've never tasted anything as good as the cookies Mrs. Martin bakes." Genevieve smacked her lips. "They're definitely worth the inconvenience of the wharf's unique fragrance."

Inside, Marinda pointed toward a small table situated along a row of side windows overlooking the harbor. Once they settled, Amalie turned to Genevieve. "Do I have you to thank for meeting Jenny this afternoon?"

She nodded. "You were pleased?"

"Yes, very much. How'd you manage it?"

"I mentioned your wish to meet Jenny to Madame LaCroix. She did the favor for me."

"Thank you."

Genevieve squeezed her hand. "Madame sounds strict, but she has a big heart. My mother and I have purchased dresses from her for years, and so did Declan's foster mother."

The pot of tea and Scottish shortbread Genevieve ordered arrived. She slid the plate of cookies across the table toward Amalie. "Try one."

The cookie actually melted in her mouth. "You're right, Genevieve. Who cares about the fish smell? These delectable cookies are heavenly."

"Would you both consider coming to the tea my Mother's hosting at the house tomorrow morning?"

Marinda nearly choked. She set the cup on its saucer and stared at Genevieve. "What are you thinking? Your mother would have another attack if my sister and I called at her mansion."

"You misplace your perky spirit somewhere in Paradise Pines, Marinda?" A twinkle sparked in Genevieve's deep brown eyes.

"What are you two talking about?" Amalie asked.

"Mrs. Vellechamp invited Ethan and me to her home to discuss having our wedding in their garden. I might have mentioned Chase could possibly arrive wearing a bear fur with sequins sewn on it. Genevieve's mother couldn't take a joke and faked a heart attack."

"What?"

Marinda started to giggle. "Sorry, but just thinking about my behavior makes me laugh. Mrs. High-Society-Matron Vellechamp announced it wasn't appropriate for our wedding to be held at her home because of my low position in society. Her degrading statement made me angry enough to forget Mama's upbringing. I'm afraid I didn't show her my best side."

"I think the funniest part was Marinda telling Mother he would probably wear sequins on his bear fur while walking her down the aisle."

"So, did you have your wedding in her house?"

Marinda grasped her hand. "Yes, and it was beautiful. I wish we'd been friends then and you could have attended as well."

A shot of envy tore through Amalie, but she quickly tamped down her jealousy. "Well, don't keep me in suspense. What color sequins did Darrah sew on Chase's fur?"

All three burst into laughter. "Chase showed up in an evening coat and red cravat. He had my mother panting at his good looks." Genevieve winked. "That man's a handsome one."

"Hmmm, guess I'd better give him a second glance. Maybe I missed

Night Angel

something the first couple of times."

"You don't think he's a looker, Amalie?" Genevieve asked.

"When I saw him at Fort Laramie, he was angry at me most of the time and the other day at your house, Marinda, I only saw him for a moment."

"Now you're part of the family again, I'm sure you'll see him in his best humor."

Genevieve looked between the two of them. "So, will you accept the invitation or not?"

"It's not a good idea for Amalie and me to show up without your mother's personal invitation. Ethan won't be with us in case she goes into vapors or something else as dramatic."

"Oh, but we must go. You can't deny Genevieve's mother the pleasure of meeting the 'bad' sister."

"I agree," Genevieve said. "Mother can't disapprove of your status now, Marinda. If you say yes, I'll send the carriage at eleven tomorrow."

Marinda peered at Amalie. "You sure this is how you want to spend your time tomorrow morning?"

"I'm sure. I bet I can think of something to liven up the party."

Marinda giggled. "It might take the pressure off me if you do."

Amalie actually looked forward to meeting San Francisco's best. "It'll be a great distraction for a few hours before we need to get ready for the theatre. Besides it might be interesting meeting someone more dramatic than me."

Marinda grinned at her. "Who said Mrs. Vellechamp is more of a drama queen than you, *Lily Fox*?"

*****

Declan strolled into the room about half an hour after the Braddocks left for their supper with John Bidwell. His beguiling smile stole her breath away and dispelled her apprehension. Amalie's spirit soared at his good humor.

His clothes were covered with dust, his rolled up sleeves accentuating his muscular arms. She couldn't pull her gaze away. His ruggedness appealed to her sense of adventure, just like his gentleness calmed her panic.

"Did you have a good day, Amalie?"

She pulled her attention back to what he was saying and nodded. "I have so much to tell you."

"Give me a moment, will you? Let me get out of these filthy work clothes and wash up."

As soon as Declan returned, he closed the heavy drapes and tossed a couple of oak logs onto the fire. "The evenings can get a bit chilly here when the fog comes in. This should keep the place warm now that the sun's going down."

He turned toward her and held out his hand. "Come, sit with me and tell me about your day." He slipped his arm around her shoulder, pulling her against him.

"I have something I must say before I tell you about my day."

"What's wrong?"

She inhaled a deep breath and spoke the words she'd tried telling him this morning before he left in a huff. "I haven't apologized very many times in my life so I'm not very good at it."

"Apologize for what?"

"My behavior this morning was appalling."

"It's over."

"No, it's not. You built a theatre for me. How could I not consider it an honor? Well, maybe honor isn't the right word. Hmmm--"

"Loved, cherished, adored?"

Amalie chuckled, relieving a bit of her pent up anxiety. "Yes, all of those words." She rubbed her fingers over the top of his hand. "My only excuse is not recognizing kindness when I received it. I'm sorry."

"Apology accepted." His warm lips grazed hers, slowly pulling her into a deep, penetrating kiss. His love wrapped around her like a soft cocoon. Contentment stole over her.

Declan relaxed his hold. "Did you enjoy meeting Jenny Lind today?"

"You knew?"

"Yes. I hope the surprise pleased you."

"Can you believe I was speechless when she turned around and I recognized her?"

He shook his head, chuckling. "That's hard for me to believe, you-of-so-many-words. Did you have a chance to discuss your career plans?"

"Yes, and I liked her a lot. I can't believe her performance tomorrow night will be her last. How very sad it is for her fans."

"Yes, very sad. I'm glad we've the chance to attend one of her performances before it's too late. Did you order all the costumes you're going to need? Better yet, do I still have money left, or was it all spent on your new wardrobe?"

"Ooh." She pulled away from him and grabbed her bag. "Here's what's left of the money you gave me for costumes this morning. I think you might have enough left so we can enjoy a supper out of the hotel this evening."

*****

They stepped into a light mist. Amalie pulled her cape tight around her shoulders as they moved along the busy boardwalk, working their way around street vendors who hawked everything from newspapers to jewelry and bouquets of flowers.

Declan stopped at a display table of jewelry made from jade, pearls, and ivory in gold and silver casings. He picked out a good size, lustrous pearl from the Chinese vendor and had it put on a delicate gold chain.

"You said the Night Angel stole your pearls so maybe this necklace will help replace them. Turn around so I can hook the clasp."

"Declan, it's beautiful." She beamed admiring the pearl as it lay above the crown of her breasts. Rising on her toes, she placed a kiss on his cheek.

"It looks lovely on you." His warm gaze focused where the pearl rested between her breasts.

"You're an impossible rogue, Declan Grainger."

"No, I'm a man who appreciates beauty." He took her hand and led her up a couple of steps. "The restaurant's owners tolerated me when I was a lad. They will adore you."

He pushed open the door and motioned her into a world fragrant with the aroma of garlic and various spices she didn't recognize. Declan waved to an elderly man and pointed at a table near the front window.

She took the offered chair. "Did you find what you expected at the warehouse today?"

"I must say I'm very pleased with what we found. You'll have a theatre full of red velvet seats with gold armrests and backs. Once we get the stage finished, I'll hire local seamstresses to resize the red velvet curtains. There are only two chandeliers, but they are large and I think they'll work nicely once they're cleaned properly. Your patrons will assume they're made of diamonds, not glass prisms."

"It all sounds perfect. I can't believe I'll have my own music hall soon."

"The wagons' travel time could take a week or two, so we should be able to open the doors in less than a month like we'd planned."

"It's a good thing I like the color red," Amalie said. "I don't suppose you'd change the color if I didn't?"

"Nah, I'd change singers first."

She playfully slapped his hand. "I missed you today. I hated you were angry with me."

"Me, too. Let's try and avoid the situation again."

The older gent approached their table. "I thought it was you, Declan. Greta will be happy to see you in here. It's been a long while."

The waiter nodded at Amalie. "Evening."

"Otto, meet Amalie Renard."

"I'm pleased to meet you, Fraulein." He turned to Declan. "Will you have your usual order or would you like a menu?"

"Are you adventurous enough to try something different, Amalie? Greta serves the best German sausage and sauerkraut in the city."

"It sounds interesting. I'm game for a new eating experience."

After Otto headed back to the kitchen, Declan rested his elbows on the table and his chin on his hands. "There are certain to be times we're angry at each other, but hopefully they'll be few and far between. I meant what I said last night. You are a very loveable woman, Amalie. I would like to spend the rest of my life showing you how much."

She surveyed the restaurant decorated with a German flair. Several couples had come in after them. "I wish there was some place where we could be alone a few moments."

He stood and held out his hand. "Grab your cape and come with me. I have the perfect spot." On the way down the hall, he poked his head into the kitchen. "Greta, I'm showing my lady the view."

"Ack, you come give Greta a hug first, you rascal." After he wrapped his arms around her and squeezed, the heavyset woman let out a rumbling laugh. "Who is that you have with you?"

"Hello, I'm Amalie Renard."

Greta gave her a welcoming nod and pointed toward the door. "Be quick about it. I won't be having my boy eatin' cold food."

Declan led her along the narrow hallway and up an extremely steep, rickety set of stairs. On the roof, San Francisco lay at their feet under the glow of a full moon. Above the fog, the lights flickered in a light mist. A foghorn sent out its warning message in a low pitch.

"It's very romantic up here. How'd you find this place?"

Declan leaned against the roof's waist-high ledge by one of the three lamps highlighting the restaurant's sign. "While I was growing up, Otto would let me tag along and help him with his birds."

She frowned. "What kind of birds would someone keep on their roof?"

"Doves. He built coots all along the side of the building. If Otto was busy, I came up here and fed them. I loved the sound of their cooing." He pointed at a tall building located a short distance from the restaurant.

"See those windows on the top floor? The one on the left is my room -- the one you're using while we're staying here. I could see the cages."

He wrapped her in his warm embrace. "There were times I'd dream on the stars from here."

"I can imagine you doing it. They look close enough to touch."

He tipped her chin. "Will you make those dreams come true and take a chance on me?"

She touched the side of his cheek. "Yes. I'll take that chance."

The expression on his face went from surprise to incredulity to a broad smile. "Yes?" He grabbed her by the waist and spun her around the rooftop.

His animated response warmed her heart.

"You're sure? I mean, really sure about this, Amalie?"

"This morning I tried telling you I'm in love with you, Declan Grainger, but you refused to listen."

"I'm glad you've told me now." His hands cupped her face. His lips caressed her mouth. She wrapped her arms around the back of his neck and lost herself in their kiss. When he pulled away, she gazed into his eyes and knew without a doubt he loved her.

"You have no idea how difficult it was to walk out on you. I'm sorry my bullheadedness kept us from this fun earlier."

"It's behind us now." She nibbled on his lower lip. "I don't suppose you have another perfect kiss tucked away somewhere?"

He rolled his eyes. "Possibly."

"Can you give me a hint?"

He touched his mouth. "Try right here. Every time we kiss is perfect, my love."

She ran her fingers over his warm lips. "Kissing is one thing we'll never disagree on, Declan." She rose on her toes and continued the pleasure he'd started.

He squeezed her arms gently and put a little distance between them. "Sweetheart, we'd better return or Greta will send Otto after us."

She nodded. "Alright, but I want to say one more thing first." She studied his beloved face for a long moment. "Our disagreement earlier was as serious as life gets for me. If I thought I couldn't trust you, I would run as far and fast as I could. Promise me from now on you won't give me any reason not to have complete faith in you."

"I am well aware of the importance of trust."

His voice sounded tight as he spoke the words. He stood stiff and looked toward the hotel when she glanced at him. "Declan?"

"I swear... I swear from this moment forward I will never give you reason to... doubt me, but you must realize trust goes both ways. You have parts of your life you've not shared with me yet. When you think you can tell me, I swear I won't be judgmental."

"Thank you."

The mist thickened, cloaking them in a blanket of thick fog. "Come, you're shivering. We need to get you out of this dampness."

"There you are." Greta greeted them at the kitchen door. "Stand by the stove and warm yourself, Fraulein."

She tossed another log into the stove. "Declan, have Otto bring your table settings in here where it's warm."

Greta pulled a small table closer to the oven.

After Declan dragged a couple of chairs in from the dining room, Otto reset their places.

"I can't believe it's permitted to eat in their kitchen," Amalie whispered in Declan's ear.

"It's expected. I've eaten in here since I was a teenager and talked them into adding my name on their ever growing list of special people."

Greta set two plates on the table and motioned for her to sit. "My Otto and me don't have children, so we bring them off the streets and feed them. This one here," she patted Declan on the shoulder, "he was always hungry for my wursts."

Amalie frowned at Greta. "Wursts?"

Declan chuckled. "German sausages."

"Oh."

Greta's light blue eyes twinkled. She motioned toward the food. "*Echt gut?*"

Otto placed his arm around his wife. "See, Mama, I told you the boy is happy."

Amalie watched the interaction between the older couple and Declan. It was déjà vu, reminding her of the night she was introduced to Mama Claire. He had an engaging way of connecting with everyone, no matter their age or background. She admired him for this knack and envied him, too. He had everything she'd always wanted -- family ties with these dear people, Claire, Judith, and Angus. Envy raged through her. All she'd ever wanted as a child was David Benjamin to act a father to her, accept her as part of his family. Something she never got.

She took a bite of sausage. It was spicy, but had a delightful taste. She smiled at the older woman and tried to repeat the German words. "*Echt gut.*"

"I am happy you enjoy." Greta smiled her approval.

"I like your friends," Amalie said on their way back to the hotel.

"They adore you."

Declan slowed his steps to match hers. "You sound surprised. You don't think I'm adorable?"

His cocky smile almost buckled her knees. "It's not that I'm surprised, silly, but jealous. I wish I'd had your life growing up, loved and adored wherever I went."

"Surely you cannot be serious. I find it hard to believe your amazing talent and beauty hasn't brought you many admirers over the last few years. If you're throwing out a challenge to make you feel adored and loved, I accept with pleasure."

"I suppose it makes a difference who's giving and why, don't you think?"

"Sweetheart, with the mood I'm in tonight, you might not want to know what I'm thinking."

Chapter Sixteen

The suite had cooled while they'd been out for supper. Declan grabbed for the screen in front of the fireplace, but her statement stopped him cold.

"You're having tea with Elizabeth Vellechamp?" A nerve in his right temple throbbed at the thought of Amalie anywhere near the quarrelsome matriarch.

"Genevieve invited us while we were out with her today. I've heard the woman's quite an interesting lady."

"Lady?" he scoffed. "Mrs. Vellechamp may think she's a lady, but she's far from it."

"You know her?"

His confrontation with Elizabeth Vellechamp had altered his life. Being a foster child never bothered him until she referred to him as the upstart son of a fisherman. Her barbs attacked his pride. She'd accused him of taking advantage of the Carnegies' money and position after they'd so generously taken him into their home.

He stoked the embers and tossed a couple more oak logs on top. "Come sit with me." Once they'd both settled onto the settee, he spoke cautiously. "The entire Vellechamp family is -- ah -- unusual."

Amalie frowned. "Genevieve was kind to me today."

"I'm well aware of Genevieve's charms."

"She didn't mention knowing you."

"I doubt our association seven years ago meant as much to her as it did to me."

"How well acquainted are you?"

He searched her face, surprised at seeing a trace of uncertainty. "It was a long time ago, another life, no longer important."

She unhooked the buttons on her boots. After slipping them off, she wiggled her toes. "I'd have thought she would've mentioned knowing the man who paid for the clothes today."

"What happened between the Vellechamps and me has nothing to do with you. Mrs. Vellechamp insulted my father and told me I wasn't good enough for Genevieve."

"She said that to your face?"

"I've been called worse." He patted the top of his thighs. "Put your feet up here."

Soft moans escaped her lips as he massaged her arches and toes. Lying against a fluffy pillow, she eyed him with contentment.

"I think I've finally found how to tame you, my little kitten."

Amalie peered at him from under long, sooty lashes. "Are you certain that's what you want?"

The smoldering heat in the depth of her blue eyes aroused his body to a slow, consuming burn. He nudged her feet to the floor and reached for her. "Give me a kiss, you little minx."

His lips covered hers, while her fingers wove through his hair, pulling him closer. A fierce longing pushed him to reach something inside her, to strip away any hesitation she might still have in becoming a permanent part of his life.

"Is that the best you can do?" she purred at him.

He chuckled. "I'm just warming up."

She pushed him away and sat up. "What's that noise?"

He rushed to the window and saw people running from the building. A fire wagon rounded the corner as he watched.

Ethan burst through the outer door. "There's a fire in the kitchen."

Declan jumped to his feet, pulling Amalie with him. "Grab your shoes."

"Where's Marinda?" Amalie shrieked as they ran to the door.

"She's helping people out of the hotel."

"How bad is it?" Declan hurried Amalie down the stairs in front of him.

"There's a lot of black smoke."

"The gaming room?"

"Colton's clearing patrons by the back staircase."

They reached the restaurant's entrance and encountered a rush of people in and out of the building. "Where the hell is the racket coming from?" He pushed Amalie toward the outer door. "Go with Ethan."

"No, Declan, don't go in there," Amalie screamed.

He ignored her plea and rushed into the smoky restaurant. The sound drew him toward the kitchen. "Victor? What the hell are you doin'?" He reached for the bulky cook floundering around the room, slamming lids on the stove.

Victor Bernardino pushed him away. "Get your hands off me. I gotta save my stove."

The man was a fantastic cook when he was sober. Unfortunately he was drinking more and more. Declan could smell the powerful spirits even through the thick smoke from the burning stove. He grabbed the man's arm with a firmer grip and propelled the intoxicated man out of the building. His eyes stung like sin. Racking coughs broke from his dry throat.

He met Ethan on the boardwalk. "You'd better see to Victor's burns."

Amalie rushed to Declan's side and helped him across the street. "Are you alright?"

He drew in another deep breath and nodded. "I'm not hurt, just covered with soot."

Ethan joined them.

"How is Victor?"

"The burns will hurt like hell for a while, but he'll survive. I'll see he gets to the hospital unless you shoot him for what he did to the restaurant."

Declan sank to the ground, slumped over to rest his head on his filthy hands. "Don't think the thought hasn't crossed my mind."

The fire captain caught his attention. He got up and sauntered back across the street with Amalie and Ethan close behind him.

"Fire's out. You were lucky. The worst damage is contained to the kitchen."

"Thank you. It's safe for everyone to return to their rooms?"

"All clear."

He turned to Amalie close at his side. "It's cold out here. I want you to go back upstairs. I'll stay for the cleanup."

"Let me help."

He brushed his lips across hers. "Sweetheart, I need to know you're upstairs and tucked in my bed where you're safe. I'm the owner. It's my responsibility to supervise the work."

He grabbed another quick kiss and returned to speak with the firemen.

*****

The following morning Amalie traipsed into the other bedroom. "What are you wearing to Mrs. Vellechamp's tea?"

Marinda held up a silk beige skirt and pointed to the delicate, white lace bodice on the bed.

"I'm not sure what I have on is appropriate. What do you think of this?"

Marinda's gaze ran over her dress. "I never expected to see you in something as subdued as that dark blue gown."

"It's my fault. I should have paid more attention to what Claire packed."

"We have to leave for the Vellechamp mansion soon or we'll be late. If you plan to change, do it now. What else did she pack?"

Amalie rustled through her bag. "Nothing appropriate for high tea."

Marinda opened her own carpetbag. "Take your pick."

Amalie frowned at her sister. "I can't wear your clothes."

"You have no other choice." Marinda held up a scooped neck lavender dress of fine linen.

"It's nice, but the skirt's too long. All your skirts are going to be too long and the bodices too tight."

Marinda inspected the hem. "I have an idea. Get out of those clothes and let me see what I can do." She rummaged through Ethan's medical bag.

"Are you going to shorten the skirt with sutures?"

"Don't be silly." Marinda pulled two packets from the medical bag. "I'm glad Ethan's obsessed about having an ample supply of tape. Hold the bottom so I can make the new hem smooth."

A few moments later Amalie slipped into the gown. "Your idea worked perfectly except for buttoning the bodice. It's unfortunate you don't have my 'glory' to contend with."

Marinda pushed her hands away. "Let me do the buttons."

Amalie sucked in her breath. The bottom two slipped into the holes with a bit of effort, but the other three weren't even close.

"This isn't going to do. Take the dress off." Marinda ruffled through her case and pulled out a corset. "We'll cinch until you fit into mine."

Amalie wrapped the stiff garment around her torso. "Will it work?"

"Hold your breath and we'll see."

Marinda tugged the lacings until Amalie thought her ribs would crack. "Stop! You're squeezing the life out of me."

"Quit fussing. One more pull should be enough." Marinda tugged the last breath out of Amalie's lungs and tied the laces.

"If I'm supposed to be breathing, this thing's too tight."

Marinda slipped the dress back over Amalie and shoved the remaining buttons into their holes. "There we are. We're late, let's go."

Amalie grabbed a pair of white lace gloves and small bag from her room. Genevieve's driver waited for them outside the hotel's entrance. With his help they stepped inside the carriage and were on their way.

"I don't know about this, Marinda."

"You'll do fine." Marinda pulled a pair of surgical scissors from her bag. "If you start to turn blue, I'll cut you out of the corset with these. Pray it doesn't come to that."

"Yes, but I'd prefer living through my performance."

"Performance?" Marinda's face paled. "You're not going to do something embarrassing, are you?"

"When you accepted the invitation, did you think I'd waltz into the spider's web and dance for the lady? Don't tell me you didn't expect something dramatic? You know me better than that."

"I hope you know what you're doing."

"Have faith. Something will come to me. It usually does."

The carriage rolled through a tunnel of pungent eucalyptus trees, then along a steep, dirt lane past a manicured lawn. The sweet scent of roses wafted through the carriage as they moved past the rows of blooming yellow and red rose bushes. The driver pulled to a stop under the wide portico. Before they could step down, Genevieve rushed outside. "You're late. I was getting worried."

"We had a challenge this morning," Marinda said, glancing at Amalie, "but we're here and ready for a good time."

Mrs. Vellechamp swooped out on the porch. "What's the meaning of this, Genevieve?"

"Mother, I've invited Marinda and her sister to join us. Isn't it nice to have them here?"

Marinda backed into her at the older lady's glower. The matriarch shot Amalie a brief onceover before she set her attention back on her daughter. The woman's disdain set Amalie's nerves on edge.

"Oh, very well. They're here so they might as well come in and join us. We'll discuss this later, young lady." Mrs. Vellechamp turned around in a huff and strutted back inside the house.

Marinda grabbed Genevieve's arm. "Why didn't you tell your mother we were coming?"

"Nothing I do pleases her. Come in, you'll do fine."

"This is going to be pleasant," Amalie said under her breath. They stepped inside a large entry hall. A huge, five-tiered crystal chandelier hung overhead dwarfing everything else in the room. She followed Genevieve and Marinda's lead, but stopped to check out several oil paintings depicting the San Francisco area. The parlor, decorated in blue décor with a large bay window at the opposite end, hosted about a dozen elegantly dressed ladies.

Being in the same room as San Francisco's finest in their stiff-backed snobbery tensed every nerve she could still feel bound in the damnable corset. Mrs. Vellechamp had settled onto a chair resembling a throne with its gilded arms and royal blue and gold brocade.

Their hostess's impatient motion of her hand beckoning them to enter goaded Amalie into her Lily Fox persona. Amalie strolled across the thick blue carpet and made a slight curtsey. Appropriate she figured under the circumstances. "Hello, my name's Amalie Renard."

"Elizabeth Vellechamp," the haughty woman replied with a cool clip to her voice.

Amalie scanned the room. "I'd like to meet your friends, Betty."

"Bet-ty?" the society matron sputtered. "My name *is* Elizabeth, Mrs. Vellechamp to you."

"Whatever you wish, Ma'am." Amalie curtsied, and then inched her way around the semi-circle of ladies. "How do you do, Ma'am? I'm most pleased to meet you," she said to each woman as she grabbed their hand and pumped their arm vigorously. Their stiff response was humiliating, but Amalie wouldn't back down.

The introductions finished, she noted Genevieve and Marinda still standing at the edge of the room. Marinda had a quirk to her mouth. Amalie pursed her lips to keep from bursting out in laughter. The whole scene seemed dreamlike, but she'd dealt with snobbery before.

Marinda and Genevieve settled into a couple of chairs. She'd like to strangle Marinda for talking her into wearing her too snug clothes. The tightness around her chest kept her from sitting. She ignored the empty seat on the other side of Genevieve.

Mrs. Vellechamp rang a silver bell and snapped her fingers at two servants. While they pushed in teacarts with pots, cups, and small cakes, the matriarch turned her attention to Marinda.

"You seem to have outgrown your frumpiness, Mrs. Braddock. Being a doctor's wife agrees with you I see."

"Thank you. Ethan's a very successful physician in Paradise Pines. We're very happy."

"Do you have children?"

"Yes, we have a son, Benjamin."

"Hmmm."

Next she turned her gaze to Amalie. "Please, won't you sit?"

"Thank you, but I prefer to stand."

Amalie finally held Marinda's attention and nodded toward the door. Marinda shook her head and mouthed 'not yet' before she looked away.

Mrs. Vellechamp pointed to the chair next to Genevieve. "Sit, young woman! You're making me nervous."

Amalie locked eyes with Marinda again, glared at her, and sat on the appointed chair.

"That's much better." The matriarch waved a fan with a beautiful

Oriental design in front of her face. "Mrs. Renard, what is your husband's profession?"

Mrs. Vellechamp's condescending tone caused the hair on the back of Amalie's neck to stand on end. She could barely answer civilly. "I'm a widow."

"I see. Your deceased husband left you well off, I assume?"

"No, Ma'am, he did not." Disgust propelled her to her feet. "I'm a poker-playing saloon singer and am proud to say I make enough money to support myself in a fine manner."

Marinda and Genevieve both gasped. Mrs. Vellechamp grabbed her chest. The room erupted with cackles and shocked sighs.

Amalie returned to her seat with a jarring thud. Something gave way along her back, giving her some much appreciated breathing space. She relaxed, but only for a moment. The top three buttons on her bodice broke loose -- popped like they'd been shot off her clothes.

"Hells fire and damnation!" burst out of Amalie's mouth before she could stop herself. She glanced around at the horrified faces and shrugged. "I hate it when that happens, don't you?"

"Get the vulgar woman out of my house." Elizabeth Vellechamp shrieked.

Amalie accepted the white knit shawl Genevieve offered and wrapped it around her shoulders, tying the ends together in a knot. She plucked her small bag off the floor, snapped open the latch, and dropped the errant buttons inside. She tamped down her seething temper the best she could before strutting with the dignity of a queen toward the door.

"Guess I should have listened to Declan. He told me not to come here today."

"Wait one moment, young woman. Are you speaking of the scalawag, Declan Grainger?"

Amalie stopped midstride and slowly turned around, sending daggers at the rude woman. Sloughing off the insult to her was one thing, but she went rigid at Mrs. Vellechamp's slur against her man. "You sit on your high horse with your nose in the air and insult Declan Grainger? You're an insufferable, black-hearted woman with no inkling what qualities make a real man. He's the finest I've ever known."

Mrs. Vellechamp stood, shaking her finger at Amalie. "I should have known he'd end up with trash like you."

The reason for Declan's outburst against Mrs. Vellechamp's sharp tongue last night became more than clear now. She should have taken his advice and found something better to do.

"Did you dare call him scalawag to his face?"

"Of course I did. Somebody had to put such an upstart in his place."

Her blood churned hatred toward the self-absorbed bitch. She shot a fleeting look at Marinda, sending her brows in a questioning arch. Her sister shrugged, then nodded approval.

On the way back across the room, Amalie stopped at one of the teacarts and picked up a cut glass water pitcher. Her fingers wrapped around the handle, itching to drench the old bat.

The matriarch watched as she strutted along the blue carpet toward her. Mrs. Vellechamp's expression became taut, her face paled. Not one of her acquaintances tried to stop Amalie's forward advance. They sat frozen in their chairs.

When she reached the throne, Amalie recognized the woman for the pathetic, lonely person she was. Tossing water on her would do nothing but bring further humiliation onto herself. It scared her to think how easily she could have been a callous and uncaring bitch. Thankfully, Declan had taught her to love.

"My mother tried to raise me as a lady, but I rarely live up to her high expectations. I apologize for embarrassing your daughter after the kindnesses she has shown me and my sister. Before I met Declan Grainger I probably wouldn't have been offended by your vicious tongue and your disregard for those you think are beneath you, but now I am. He's shown me as well as the citizens of the community we live in the importance of being generous."

Elizabeth Vellechamp's mouth dropped open. She sputtered a few syllables, but stopped and moved her fan rapidly in front of her flushed face.

Amalie turned toward the center of the room. Not one of the ladies said a word, but the expressions spoke volumes. Doubtless they were shocked at her outburst, but as she passed each one they nodded and a couple ladies even dared smile. Following the example of kindheartedness Declan exemplified every day in Paradise Pines, she placed the pitcher back onto the teacart and left.

Marinda and Genevieve exited right behind her.

"You have my sincerest apologies, Genevieve."

Her new friend squeezed her fingers. "It was worth witnessing your performance to see my mother rendered speechless."

"Thank you." She grabbed Marinda's arm and walked out the front door into the fresh air, relieved to have Mrs. Vellechamp out of her life.

*****

Amalie peeked out the window and absorbed the spirit of the evening. Ahead of them carriage after carriage moved around Portsmouth Square toward the Jenny Lind Theatre. Each stopped in front of the well-lit entrance. Men dressed in dark blue uniforms aided the elegantly dressed passengers as they stepped onto the boardwalk. Her heart raced every time she noticed Declan's dimpled cheeks. His new appearance still took her breath away, not only because he looked so handsome, but because he exuded an undeniable air of self-confidence in his black evening coat and deep red cravat. The bushy, unkempt beard and shoulder length hair were gone, trimmed to accentuate his bold good looks.

He stepped to the boardwalk and reached for her hand. They strolled through the crowd of theatergoers. Amalie's pulse raced as they stepped inside the grand reception area. Several blue carpets were placed around the hardwood floor. Chandeliers illuminated the great room with light yellow walls, boasting of its history through photos of performers from past to present. A playbill with an attractive photo of Jenny perched near the staircase to the second floor. 'Final Performance' was printed on a ribbon running diagonally across the top right corner.

All eyes turned on her after Declan slipped the long, black cape off her shoulders. At first she thought it was their admiration for her beautiful new silk gown, but after hearing several loud comments, understood her actions earlier at Mrs. Vellechamp's tea now loosened their tongues.

Declan leaned close. "Is there something you want to tell me about this morning?"

She wondered how he would react if she admitted to her rude behavior.

"I know you're no coward, Amalie. I'd rather hear it from you than them." He nodded toward the gossipmongers.

"You're mistaken, Declan. They're admiring the handsome man at my side."

"You can flatter me all you want, my dear. It's not going to make this issue go away." His face beamed as his gaze rested on her. "Even as handsome as you say I am in these fancy clothes, I can't hold a candle to you dressed in your sensational gown."

She would not let that horrid woman ruin her great night. "I can explain."

He pointed toward the staircase to the right. "I look forward to your explanation. We can have privacy in John's loggia."

From the plush box Senator Bidwell so generously provided them,

Amalie could see straight down onto the stage. She surveyed their small area decked in dark blue, velvet wall drapes and four gilded chairs. Running her fingers over the blue velvet rail along the rim of the box, tears filled her eyes. "You have no idea how much this evening means to me. I have dreamed of being here most of my life."

He lifted her hand and placed a light kiss across her knuckles. "I'm delighted to please you, sweetheart. Now, stop stalling. I want to hear what caused the kind of reaction we received as we walked into the lobby."

One hand rested on her hip, the other moved furiously in front of her face as she worked herself into a rage remembering the events leading to her outburst. "The pompous woman insulted my sister and me from the moment we arrived at her house. The way she blatantly boasts of wealth from the outlandish furnishings to her condescending attitude toward her servants disgusted me. I couldn't help myself."

She stopped, glaring at his grinning face. "You're laughing at me."

"No, I'm appreciating your dramatics." He chuckled and shook his head. "Please go on. I can't wait to hear the rest."

"Well--" she leaned against the rail, "she insulted Marinda first and then verbally attacked me. I feel very justified in my actions."

"Uh huh. Don't keep me in suspense any longer. What actions did you take?"

"I told her I was a poker-playing saloon singer a moment before my--umm--certain undergarment ripped and the buttons burst off my bodice and--"

Declan roared with laughter. She couldn't help but laugh along with him as he pictured her disgrace.

"Come here." He pulled her into his arms. "I cannot imagine my life without you. I wish I could have been a fly on the wall. I assume she held court in what Genevieve refers to as the blue room?"

"Yes, the one with the throne." She turned serious. "There's one more thing. When she attacked your character, I might have overreacted a bit."

"You defended me? How did my name come into the conversation?"

"It's no matter. The important thing is, I've figured out what you're doing for the people in Paradise Pines. What I don't understand is why you're so secretive about it."

Chapter Seventeen

The deep blue velvet folds of the curtain eased open. The adored singer swept onto center stage. "*Jag heter Jenny Lind. Tack för att ni kom hit.* I am Jenny Lind. Thank you for your welcome."

The crowd stood, applauding. The evening started on a high moment. Finally everyone sat. Silence settled. Several wicker stands in a semi-circle behind her held white lilies and yellow roses. A dozen white candles placed in four golden candelabras lit an azure backdrop sprinkled with white stars.

Jenny nodded at the conductor. He raised his baton. Music floated from the orchestra pit, rising like a light mist over the audience. Jenny's voice, clear and sweet, captivated her listeners at once. Without exception, the entertainer knew how to delight her admirers.

Amalie slid her chair forward and rested her hands on the velvet rail. Declan delighted in watching his lady, so absorbed in Jenny's performance he feared she might forget to breathe. Her foot tapped, her head moved to the rhythm.

Her attitude at figuring out he was the Night Angel puzzled him. He'd expected at least some kind of outrage for stealing her jewelry. Maybe all his worry was for nothing.

Not one seat sat empty in the lavishly adorned auditorium tonight. Amalie deserved a comparable place to give her performances. Building a music hall equaling this grandeur wasn't a problem, but the remoteness of their area was. They needed a way to entice San Francisco's upper crust to Paradise Pines.

Jenny broke for intermission. Amalie's face glowed with happiness. "Isn't she remarkable, Declan? I mean, truly wonderful."

He marveled at her exuberance. No one could deny his lady's enthusiasm this evening. "Yes, she is. I'd say almost as talented as you, my dear."

"As me?" She placed her hand lightly on his arm. "I think you're a bit biased, but thank you for the compliment."

"Do you want to step outside with me for some fresh air?"

"I'd rather sit here and reflect on what I've experienced so far tonight. My mind's overflowing with a kaleidoscope of Jenny's songs and costumes."

Marinda also decided to stay in the loggia with Amalie. He

motioned Ethan to join him in the hall. He shut the door and faced his friend. "Did you tell Marinda about my Night Angel activities?"

"No, of course not."

Declan slumped against the wall. "Good. I'm not saying Marinda isn't trustworthy, but the fewer who know about my secret, the better. Amalie told me she knew what I was doing to help our townsfolk. I expected her to confront me about stealing her jewels. She didn't, so I have no idea what's on her mind."

"Why didn't you ask her while you had the chance?"

"I didn't want to raise more questions in case she might be referring to something else."

Ethan gripped his shoulder. "You've got to tell her, and soon. If Marinda found out I'd been lying to her, I know how she'd react. From my personal experience with the lady, Amalie's temperament's more volatile than my wife's."

He raked his hand through his hair. Ethan had a point. "I'll find a way once we get home." As vindictive as he'd been in stealing her jewels, it would serve him right if Amalie wouldn't have anything to do with him once she learned how he'd tricked her. He'd heard Angus's words of caution spoken many times in his youth. "Son, never worry about trouble until trouble comes a knocking." If ever those words hit home, it was now.

They stepped back inside the loggia and joined their ladies. After intermission, Jenny's choice of songs turned more poignant. The atmosphere in the auditorium changed from upbeat to somber near the end of her final performance.

A knock on the balcony room door caught Declan's attention. An usher handed him a note, stating Miss Fox must read it immediately.

He tapped Amalie on the shoulder.

She frowned. "Not now."

"You're to open this at once."

She took the envelope and gasped at the engraved name on the top left corner. Unsealing the flap, she read through the words quickly. Her eyes brimmed with tears. "Jenny's invited me to join her on stage. She wants me to sing."

He beamed at hearing his lady would perform tonight. This would be their draw, a way of introducing her talent to the elite. "She's giving you a remarkable opportunity."

"It's a dream come true. I'd ardently hoped, but never expected Jenny to be so generous."

"What's going on?" Marinda asked as Amalie stood.

"Jenny's invited me to sing on her stage tonight."

Marinda grabbed her hand, her eyes sparkled with pride. "I'm so happy for you. Go show them the Benjamin talent, sister."

"Thank you, I hope I do." She turned to Declan. "I'm to go to the stage entrance door. Mr. Stephens will let us inside."

"May I escort you, my dear?" He reached out to her. She placed her trembling hand into his palm. "Are you nervous?"

"Panicked would be the word I'd use." Big difference between the audience tonight and the drunken miners and millworkers she was used to entertaining. This crowd expected professionalism.

He studied her face. "What happened to the woman who marched into Reverend King's church not too long ago and stunned the man to say nothing of the congregation?"

"The church performance didn't matter. This one means more to me than I'd like to admit."

Uncertainty reflected from her eyes. Her laugh at best sounded shaky.

"This is my time to prove myself and I can't falter. I may never get another chance."

He ushered her into the hall and nodded toward the stairs leading to the stage. "Let's hurry along. You don't want to arrive late for your debut performance."

An elderly gent answered her knock. "Miss Fox?"

"Yes, Miss Lind--"

"Shhh, follow me," he said in a near whisper.

They made their way through an array of costumes and props. A strong fragrance of lilies and roses wafted through the air, mixed with the odor of kerosene from the many lanterns. At the edge of the stage, she grabbed Declan's arm. "Wish me luck?"

He brushed his lips against hers. "You're going to be fine. Give them a performance they'll never forget."

Jenny waved her onto the stage. "Lily, please won't you come join me?"

Amalie grabbed her courage and brushed the dampness from her hands along the sides of her gown. She entered the stage. Excitement welled up inside her. Standing next to the Swedish Nightingale with a sea of faces staring back at her wasn't what she expected. It was even better, more powerful.

"Ladies and gentlemen, I'd like to introduce, Lily Fox. She has agreed to perform for you this evening." Jenny squeezed her hand. "If you're ready, I'll turn the stage over to you for a solo. Have you a favorite?"

A quick glance at Declan earned her an extra boost of support. He mouthed Greensleeves.

She nodded and told Jenny her choice. The artist instructed the conductor and vacated the stage. Amalie's gaze roamed over San Francisco's elite. She *was* Lily Fox, confident thespian and chanteuse extraordinaire -- not ignored Amalie Benjamin anymore.

Strings and horns blended together in the first refrains of the sentimental love song. Since Amalie had experienced passion and contentment for the first time with Declan, the ballad touched a new, happier cord in her. After the first refrain, the nervous flutter in her stomach subsided. The song flowed strong and powerful as she gave the performance of her lifetime, drawing from a deep place in her heart.

Enthusiasm abounded throughout the theatre at the end of her performance. She bowed and blew a few kisses. The audience rose to their feet. Her face flushed with exhilaration during the full standing ovation lasting several minutes. She hadn't expected gratification would come along with reaching the pinnacle of her dreams.

Jenny strolled on stage and grabbed her hand. "You have an incredible voice, and by the sounds of the applause, I am not the only one who thinks so. I wish you well in the pursuit of your career, Amalie."

"Thank you--for everything." Amalie waved good night and exited the stage. She flew into Declan's arms. "I did it!"

He hugged her so tight she could barely breathe. "You knocked 'em dead, sweetheart. You were superb."

"My knees shook so badly. When the music started, I thought I might crumble to the floor. Once I caught my breath and gained my bearings though, I knew I was where I belonged. Did you hear the applause?"

"I did. I've never heard anything like it before. I'm so glad I could share in your success. Believe me, the stage is the right place for you."

"I certainly hope so." She turned to watch Jenny say her farewell. Declan wrapped his arms around her waist.

"*God kväll San Francisco.*" Jenny took a final bow. "Good night San Francisco."

Handclapping and stomping feet nearly raised the roof. Her audience stood and continued their appreciation for several minutes. Finally, the gas lights edging the stage flickered and went dark. She blew a kiss, stepped down the stairs lined with small white candles in clear glass holders and made her way through the center aisle, touching extended hands as she passed by them.

Along with her and Declan, a lot of dignitaries attended the reception in Jenny's room later that evening. By the end of the night Amalie's head spun from all the compliments on her performance and good wishes for her future. She overheard one conversation about her behavior at Mrs. Vellechamp's tea earlier in the day. She couldn't hold back a smile hearing they understood and appreciated her reason for putting the matriarch in her place.

She watched the reactions of the guests as Declan shared information on their upcoming music hall opening in Paradise Pines. If she read the crowd correctly, most of them would make the journey to the mountains to hear her sing again. The director of the Arts Council promised he'd post her scheduled performances in the San Francisco newspapers. Now the pressure was on Declan to get that music hall finished.

On their way back to the hotel, she snuggled against her man. "I'm so glad you were with me tonight, Declan. It made the experience so much more memorable."

He slipped his arm around her and pulled her as close to him as possible. "I'm sorry Mrs. Vellechamp snubbed you."

"You know what?" She gave him a quick smile. "I hardly noticed, but a lot of other guests did."

*****

Declan slid his key into the lock and shoved the suite door open. "Stay here a moment while I light a lamp." He moved around the dim room until he found matches in a drawer.

The soft yellow glow and the crook of his finger beckoned her to his side. His eyes, darkened with passion, raked over her in slow motion. Her lips parted and she responded to his kiss with complete abandon. Her body temperature soared. Quivers of hot and cold pulsated along her nerve endings.

"You sure know how to knock a girl off her feet, Mister Grainger." She swayed against him, lost her balance, and pulled him onto the settee over the top of her.

"You little devil," he said, "who's knocking who off their feet?" He struggled to untangle himself. Once he could support his body without pressing down on top of her, he leaned close to her mouth. "Now, kiss me you temptress."

"Wait." She pushed him back. "What if Ethan and Marinda find us like this?"

"You've nothing to worry about, my sweet." He kissed her again. "I threatened Ethan with buckshot if they come back before morning."

Pulling up on her elbows, she frowned. "You actually threatened to kill my sister and brother-in-law to seduce me on the sofa in your parlor?"

"Not exactly, but by the stunned expression on his face he got the hint." Declan cocked his head and grinned.

She fought the urge to giggle. "As proper as Ethan is, he must have been scandalized. I thought you were a gentleman."

"I am a gentleman." His lips captured hers in another searing kiss. "Wanting you turns me into a rogue."

"Declan?" A flicker of apprehension nipped at her heart.

"Hmmm?"

His lips ran alongside her neck, sending delicious prickles over her skin. "This isn't a dream, is it?"

He stopped kissing her and gazed into her eyes. "No, sweetheart, a dream come true."

"I've never imagined love like this was possible."

"You talk too much." He stood and slid his arms under her knees, sweeping her against his chest. She nuzzled her chin next to the smooth shaven part of his neck. She'd already given him her heart. Now she'd give him her trust, something she held dear.

Once he'd planted her feet firmly on the floor of his bedroom, he cupped her face. "If I'm not the man you want, now's the time to tell me. Because once we make love, it's forever for me."

She had no doubt he loved her. "Yes, I want you."

He unfastened the buttons down the back of her beautiful silk gown. She closed her eyes, giddy with anticipation, feeling virginal again. Pushing her gown over her hips to her feet, his warm fingertips moved against her hot skin.

She stepped out of the dress bunched at her feet.

Declan grabbed the shirttails of his fancy shirt and ripped the garment open.

She quirked her brow, questioning his sanity.

He shrugged with a quick rise of his shoulders. "It's much easier that way."

The need to get out of the rest of her clothes suddenly became urgent. Her fingers shook as she fought the ties of her undergarment.

"Let me help."

She grabbed his hands. "By tearing?"

"Trust me, my sweet." He took little nips and kisses along the back of her neck as he untied the laces row by row, driving her wild. By the time the corset fell away, her knees barely held her up.

She finally stood naked before him. A rush of heat washed over her at Declan's quick intake of breath. She melted against him. Her heart thumped erratically. Every rational thought perished as his hands gently held her face and their lips touched. He crushed her to him. The hunger of the kiss shattered the last of her hesitation.

He gathered her into his arms. His uneven breathing fanned against her neck as he strode the few steps to his bed. He gently eased her onto the feather mattress and positioned himself alongside her. She instinctively knew Declan's lovemaking would prove a joyous experience, not the selfish act Rupert had performed.

"I love you, Declan."

He tucked her against the warmth of his bare chest. Affection as she'd never experienced flowed through her like warm honey. A tingling of excitement raced along her skin as his fingertips explored the soft lines of her back, her waist, and her hips.

"Kiss me," Declan whispered in her ear.

She buried her fingers in his hair and pulled his lips against hers. His touch whispered a long awaited promise. He was giving her a great gift, one that strengthened her faith in the love he held for her. Each beat of her heart strengthened her trust in him.

"I love you, too, sweetheart," he whispered next to her ear.

She snuggled against his side, entwining their bodies. Declan's hand caressed the skin across her back, sending shivers along her thigh. He stirred her heightened passions, each level more exhilarating than the last. Amalie abandoned herself to whirls of sensation, absorbing one spark after another arcing through her body, nearly setting her on fire. An overpowering sensation of warmth and uncontrollable spasms resonated through her as he joined his body with hers, raising her craving for fulfillment until their passion exploded together. No words could describe the moment she reached her orgasm at the same time Declan groaned in fulfillment. He rolled to the side. She snuggled into his arms and laid her head on his chest. Her handsome Scot's lovemaking was much more than she'd ever dared dream. She'd reached an inner peace.

He gazed into her flushed face. "I didn't disappoint?"

"Hmmm, I'm not sure. I never knew the true act of making love until now."

"I can certainly do something to fix that." He chuckled and pressed his lips against hers.

In the morning she rolled over to nuzzle against her lover. Even thinking the word lover turned her body warm all over. His pillow was empty. She sat up and searched the room for him. "Declan?"

He didn't answer. Ice cold dread surged through her.

The door to his armoire stood ajar. She crawled out of the bed and pulled the door wide open.

"Damn!" Her hands ran across the empty hangers left on his side of the closet. Her heart dropped to the pit of her stomach. No! He couldn't have deserted her after last night. She'd believed him when he professed his love. She glanced to the corner where he'd kept his suitcase. Empty.

She wanted to curl up and die. Making love with a saloon-singing actress must not have lived up to Declan's expectations. She was used to being shunned, but hadn't seen this kind of heartbreaking betrayal coming. She was a damned fool for trusting him.

"Amalie?" Marinda knocked on her door. "There's someone here to see you."

Oh, thank God. She'd jumped to the wrong conclusion. Declan hadn't deserted her. She quickly splashed water on her face and cleaned up a little bit before snatching her wrap off the chair. She tied the sash around her waist and jerked the door open.

Jenny Lind stood in front of her instead of Declan. Utter dismay flooded through her. "What are you doing here?"

Jenny stared at her state of undress. "I'm sorry. Did I interrupt something?"

Amalie searched around the parlor behind Jenny, still hoping to see Declan. He wasn't there. She clenched her jaw so tight her teeth hurt. "Unfortunately not."

"I've got news. The Board of Directors of the Arts Council wants me to bring you to a meeting at the theatre this morning." Nearly bursting with excitement Jenny propelled Amalie onto the settee and sat next to her. "From what they explained, you have a good chance to take my place on tour." She grabbed Amalie's hands. "Isn't that wonderful news? You're getting your dream."

Shocked, Amalie couldn't move. "What are you saying?"

Jenny's bottom lip dropped into a pout. "Aren't you listening? I persuaded the Arts Council members to consider you as a replacement for me. You haven't changed your mind about wanting to sing on stages around the world have you?"

Amalie shot a glimpse at Marinda. She flinched at the thunderous expression clouding her sister's face.

"Don't look at me for approval," Marinda said.

"I need to see you in the bedroom." Amalie grabbed Marinda's arm and propelled her toward the room. "Please excuse us a moment, Jenny."

Marinda shut the door and rested against it. "What are you thinking?"

"I've waited my entire life for an opportunity to sing on tour. I've got to take the chance."

"Have you lost your mind? What about Declan? I thought you loved him."

"He's gone."

"What do you mean he's gone?"

She pointed to the empty side of the armoire. "All his clothes are missing along with his suitcase."

Marinda shoved the empty hangers along the rod. "Oh, honey, I'm sorry."

"What are you sorry for? I'd have thought you'd be happy I'm finally getting my comeuppance. The man who swore he'd love me forever just ran out on me. Go ahead and say it, I've had it coming after every miserable thing I've put all of you through."

"No, you've got it all wrong. I'm certain there's a logical explanation. Give Declan a chance to explain."

"I'm not going back to Paradise Pines. He said he loved me. He lied." Her chest ached with disillusionment. She pulled her suitcase out of the armoire and dumped it onto the crumpled quilt. "So much for trust."

"Find him, talk to him before you make such a life altering decision."

Amalie grabbed her clothes from the armoire and started stuffing them into the case. She noticed the blue gown she refused to wear to the Vellechamps' yesterday and tossed it onto the back of the chair.

"What are you doing?" Marinda squeezed her hand. "You're wrinkling your clothes. You can take your time after you get back from your meeting."

She ignored her sister and continued to cram her belongings on top of each other. How could he have done this to her? Amalie wanted to curl up in a ball in the corner and die.

She picked the gown off the chair back. She had to get out of here. "Help me get into this, please. I don't want to keep Jenny waiting."

"Stop it. You're running again instead of confronting Declan. I want to know why you're not going to give Declan a chance to explain, and I don't want some cockamamie excuse."

Marinda's contempt sent shards of fury through Amalie. "How I live is none of your business. Help me or get out."

Marinda pushed her onto the bed. "Not on your life, sister. You're not going to run and leave me to clean up your mess again. Never again. Do you understand me?"

*****

Declan opened the bag of gold eagles and counted out the sum he owed Jess and John for transporting the boxes to Paradise Pines. The last minute tasks lasted much longer than he'd anticipated.

His thoughts turned to Amalie. The passion they shared last night was more than he could ever have imagined possible. They'd be on their way home in a few hours and he'd urge her to marry him as soon as possible. Since he had no faith in the unethical Reverend King, he'd taken a chance the other day when he visited the orphans at the mission and spoken with the padre. As soon as Amalie was ready, he'll provide Padre Francesco transportation to Paradise Pines to perform their wedding ceremony.

Once the two transport wagons cleared the warehouse, he locked the doublewide doors and checked his pocket watch. Damn, it was much later than he realized. Luckily he'd thought ahead and stored his packed bag behind the check-in desk. He should have awakened Amalie and explained he might be late, but she looked so content in her slumber he didn't have the heart to disturb her. After last night, she probably hadn't budged from under the quilt yet. Leaving her in his bed had been damned difficult, but she'd understand once she read the note he left. If he hadn't headed out when he did, the wagons would never have pulled out in time for him to reach the steamship.

As he walked along the path to the hotel, he whistled a lively tune he couldn't get out of his mind. The day had dawned cool, but the warm sun had finally broken through the mist. It was definitely a good day for traveling home. He was in love. His heart was light. His mood playful.

"Amalie?" He called out, stepping into the suite. "Let's go home."

"Help me. I'm locked in."

"Marinda?"

"Let me out."

His bedroom door was shut, the key protruded from the bolt. "What the hell?" The moment he turned the lock's mechanism, Marinda burst past him mad as a wet hen.

"I'm going to strangle Amalie when I get my hands on her." Deep red stained her flushed cheeks. "My sister's selfishness is unbelievable."

He couldn't comprehend the bitterness in her voice. He grabbed her arm and spun her around to face him. "Where is she?"

Marinda shrugged off his grasp and dropped onto the settee. "We've been having a great time together. I thought she'd changed, but *no* she locks me in the bedroom so she can run off and leave me to make her explanations again."

Declan hovered over her. Marinda's babbling scared him. "My God, woman, calm down and tell me what's happened."

"My sister's done what she does best. She's run."

His heart skipped a beat before a burst of anger stole his breath away. He slammed his fist into the wall. "No!" This couldn't be happening. She loved him, he knew she did.

At Marinda's wide eyed stare, guilt washed over him for taking his displeasure out on her. "I'm sorry. I apologize for my bad temper. Amalie's erratic behavior isn't your fault."

"After the way we've gotten along lately, I never expected her to treat me like this again. She doesn't deserve you, you know."

His patience gone, he wanted to shake the information out of Marinda, but gripped his emotions. "Please calm yourself and tell me what happened."

"Amalie woke to an empty room and thought you'd abandoned her. Jenny Lind came by and told her the Arts Council members were considering her as a replacement for Jenny on the world tour."

"Dammit, I left her a note on the bedside stand." He stepped around the bed and glanced at the stand. It wasn't there. Bending down, he spied the corner edge of a white paper and pulled it off the floor. He shook his head. "She didn't see it."

He moved to the bay window. He knew Amalie's penchant for running and fear of trust. He stared at the hustle of Portsmouth Square below trying to make sense of the situation. What triggered her panic? After the affection they shared last night he thought--

"She loves you, Declan. I know she does."

He glanced at Marinda. "Just not enough to trust me."

"Her reaction this morning doesn't make sense. She was frantic to get out of here. Jenny's arrival with news of the tour offer was the escape she needed."

It made sense to him now. Amalie didn't know how to deal with trusting his feelings for her. She'd been betrayed all of her life and now doubts had surfaced again. He had to keep the faith she would trust her instincts and realize she belonged with him.

The clock sounded two bells. "It's time to leave for the steamship.

When's Ethan due back?"

"I am back," he said, walking through the door. "The carriage is out front. Are we ready to go?" He perused the room. "Where's Amalie?"

"She's won't be leaving with us. I need to speak with Colton. I'll meet you two in the lobby in a few moments."

The ride to the harbor became uncomfortable. Declan's gaze kept drifting to the empty space next to him. He noted Marinda's hand entwined with Ethan's. A stab of jealousy ran through him. He envied the deep bond of devotion the Braddocks shared. It's what he thought he had with Amalie.

"I'm sorry if I gave you some bad advice last night about the Night Angel," Ethan said.

Declan regarded Marinda first and then gave Ethan the I-don't-believe-you-said-that-look. "Marinda didn't tell you what happened?"

"No, she said it was up to you to tell me."

"This is a misunderstanding about trust, not about the Night Angel's activities, Ethan."

Marinda's gasp alerted him to the moment she figured out his alter ego. Her eyes grew wide with shock.

Chapter Eighteen

During their ride across Portsmouth Square, Amalie listened with great interest to Jenny's description of faraway places she'd visited. This unexpected job offer fulfilled her dream to sing in San Francisco and tour across Europe. If only Declan could share in her excitement. No, she couldn't think of him. She was about to start a new life, one she could control.

They stepped inside the darkened theatre and followed behind Jenny to the back conference room. Ladies and gentlemen she remembered meeting last night sat around a long table. Their enthusiastic greeting warmed her heart. Jenny pointed to two chairs near the front of the room.

"Miss Fox, I'm Bernard Oliver, one of the Arts Council's directors. I had the opportunity to speak with you and your gentleman friend at Miss Lind's party.

"Yes, I remember your kind words on my performance."

"We wait for one more associate to arrive and then we can start."

The board director's kindness put her at ease. Charlotte Dickson, a woman Marinda introduced her to at the theatre, served Jenny and her coffee. Before Amalie sipped the delicious smelling brew, Mrs. Vellechamp breezed into the room, filling it with her overbearing presence.

Stunned at seeing her adversary, Amalie set the cup down with a thud. The haughty woman took the empty seat at the head of the table. Amalie's previous air of confidence faded to frustration.

With complete indifference to her, Mrs. Vellechamp turned her back and gave undivided attention to Jenny. "Miss Lind, it's nice to see you again. I understand you must leave for the harbor in an hour, so we'd best get started."

Mrs. Vellechamp snapped her fingers. "Someone get me a cup of tea."

Damn the woman's arrogance. Amalie wished she'd drowned the bitch yesterday. Maybe she could make up for it now. She jumped up and stepped to the sidebar. "Cream and sugar, *Elizabeth*?"

The woman whipped around hearing her name on Amalie's lips. Amalie winced as each dagger from the lady's piercing glare hit its target. She set the tray on the table in front of Mrs. Vellechamp. "You're welcome, Ma'am. Anything else I can do for you? Sing, dance on the table, deal cards?"

Mrs. Vellechamp pursed her lips and glared at Mr. Oliver. "Bernard, I highly disagree with hiring this common saloon singer. She does not aspire to the high standards we demand from our performers. My vote is a definite nay."

Mr. Oliver sputtered. "Elizabeth, your statement is outrageous even for you. Did you hear Miss Fox sing last night? Her miraculous voice stole the heart of every patron in the auditorium. My God, the audience gave her performance a standing ovation."

"My decision is final." Her withering glare silenced the others.

Jenny pushed away from the table. "I was told earlier this morning the decision to hire Miss Fox had already been made. You embarrass me in front of my friend."

Amalie grabbed Jenny's hand and nodded she should return to her seat. "I will take care of this."

She leaned toward Mrs. Vellechamp. "You spiteful old woman. I understand you're angry about my rudeness yesterday, but to deny my ability to draw crowds and make money for the council is not only selfish on your part but ridiculous as well."

Mr. Oliver stared at her over the top of his wire-rimmed glasses. "Is Mrs. Vellechamp's accusation true? Are you a saloon singer?"

Amalie rose and strutted around the room making eye contact with each member as she spoke. "As a young widow I was forced to find a way to support myself. Being with child and no family I could turn to for help, I became desperate."

She noticed a softening in some of the panel member's expressions. She stopped in front of Mr. Oliver and gazed into his bespeckled eyes. "Certainly someone as considerate as you must sympathize with my plight. It's not easy to find proper work when you're all alone and in my condition. Then an unexpected opportunity to sing in a popular gaming hall in St. Louis was offered me. It was a chance I couldn't turn down under the circumstances. I had my baby to think about. What else could I have done?"

Elizabeth Vellechamp cleared her throat. "Don't let her play on your sympathy."

Amalie sighed, pulled her concentration back to promoting herself, and began again. "Mrs. Vellechamp is angry at me because I embarrassed her in her home yesterday. I know my actions were outrageous, but her unkindness to her servants pushed me to lose my perspective."

She stood tall and proud at the head of the table directly behind Betty Vellechamp's chair, and continued. "I am sorry for my rudeness to her guests, but not to her. She deserved my contempt then as she deserves it now. To put her personal prejudices against me before the welfare of this opera house should not be tolerated. I hope you will still consider me for the position. I promise I will not let you down."

"Won't it be difficult for you to leave your child if you go on tour?" a young woman across the table asked.

Tears formed in Amalie's eyes. She pulled a handkerchief from her sleeve and dabbed them away from her cheek. "My baby son, Benjamin, died when he was but two days old."

Mr. Oliver cleared his throat and stood. "Dear woman, if you will please step outside, we'll discuss the situation and let you know our decision."

"Thank you." Amalie grabbed the man's hand and gently squeezed his fingers before striding from the room with her chin up and a lead rock in the middle of her chest.

She sat at the back of the theatre. Busy workers cleaned the auditorium. A strong scent of lemon oil lingered in their aftermath. She stared at the closed stage curtain. The wide expanse of blue velvet blocked her view of the stage where she'd finally found the appreciation she'd craved her entire life. Singing last night and being loved by Declan brought her more happiness than she'd ever experienced.

Her heart weighed heavy. Her handsome Scot's gentle lovemaking touched something primeval, stirring her passions beyond a realm she'd never experienced. She would carry his tender touch in her memory forever.

Slumping against the back of the seat, doubts plagued her. Maybe Marinda was right. If Declan hadn't abandoned her this morning, he must despise her for running out on him. If her assumption was right, then Declan was a rogue of the worst kind like most of the men she'd known.

"Amalie?" Jenny poked her head into the theatre.

"I'm over here."

By Jenny's downcast expression, things had not gone her way.

"Good and bad news." Jenny sat next to her. "Because of the shrew, they won't let you sing in this auditorium again."

Waves of frustration enveloped her. So close, yet more disappointment. "I'm sure you did your best."

"Wait, there's still good news. Mr. Oliver's willing to send you on the tour I was contracted to take. He'll need about a week to arrange the details and then he'll contact you with the schedule."

"Thank you. I had my heart set on your theatre, but cannot complain about the tour. It's another dream I've had for years."

Jenny stood. "Come, we can discuss it on the way to the ship. My driver will be happy to deliver you to your hotel after he drops me at the harbor."

My hotel? She rummaged through her bag. Why hadn't she thought to grab some coins before she left this morning? Her bright future dimmed with each passing moment of this horrific day. She no longer had a room at Browns Hotel. She was broke and destitute, something she had sworn would never happen again.

She sat across from Jenny in the comfortable carriage twenty minutes later and tried to concentrate on what her friend said.

"The tour will probably be back east first, then once all the proper paperwork's taken care of you'll sail to England."

Her heart sank as another door slammed shut. "By back east do you mean New York?"

"I'm certain New York will be one of the stops. If it's the way they set up my schedule before, you'll go as far west as St. Louis."

She wanted to scream at the injustice of it all. "I can't go to St. Louis."

"If you want to go on tour, you go where they send you. You have no choice in the matter."

The driver pulled to a stop on the dock in front of the tall sailing ship carrying Jenny back to her fiancé and Sweden.

Jenny leaned over and hugged her before she grasped the driver's hand and stepped out of the carriage. "Don't worry, Amalie, with your great talent you'll have a successful career. If you ever get to Stockholm, be sure to let me know and I will show you my favorite city." Jenny waved as she stepped up the gangplank. "I'm sure everything will work out well. Bye."

Amalie pasted a smile on her face and waved back. No, everything would not be alright, not ever again. Her world crumbled around her feet so quickly she had no idea how to deal with any of it. She needed to take immediate action. On the way to Browns Hotel, she devised a new plan. She'd pick up her luggage and find a cheap place to stay. The first thing she needed was a job to pay for food and lodging.

The clerk who'd stored her suitcase wasn't behind the counter. The man on duty returned from the storage area empty handed. "I'm sorry, Ma'am. I didn't find nothin'."

"What?" She pushed past him and checked every nook and space in the cramped room, but he was right, none of the cases were hers. "When does the other clerk come back? He must know where my bag is."

"You're going to have to return tomorrow mornin'."

She started to panic. She needed her suitcase.

"Is Declan Grainger still here?"

"No, Ma'am. He and his friends left a half hour ago."

She dropped onto the bench near the lobby entrance. A couple of dapper gentlemen tipped their heads on the way out of the hotel. Gamblers. She doubted Colton Brown would ever let a woman sit at a poker table, but he might consider her as a singer. She strode back to the check-at the counter with a spark of hope. "Excuse me."

The clerk rolled his eyes, but approached her none-the-less. "I still haven't found your suitcase, Ma'am."

"I'd like to talk to Colton Brown."

"Mr. Brown is out."

Her heart dropped to her toes. "When's he expected back?"

"I don't know, lady. He was gone when I came on duty."

Amalie turned on her heel and strode out of the lobby onto the boardwalk. She gazed up and down the street, not knowing where to turn next. Eventually she strolled in a daze along the walkway. She passed the street vendor where Declan bought her pearl. Why hadn't she put it around her neck this morning? Now the necklace was gone along with all of her other possessions.

Her head throbbed. She was hungry and tired, and exhausted after not sleeping much the night before. Spices wafted on the air -- what was it? Sausages. The German restaurant. She ran up the stairs and jiggled the door handle. It was locked, dammit. She banged until Otto swung it open.

"Fraulein, we're closed."

She hurried past him into the empty dining room and settled on one of the chairs before he could turn her away. "Please, I have nowhere else to go." The weight of the world bore down on her shoulders. If they turned her out, she'd simply die.

"Greta!"

The older woman hurried into the room and gasped. "Fraulein, what has happened to you?" She glanced around the room. "Where's Declan?"

Amalie stared at Greta, barely coherent. In a quick moment she was on her feet being pushed toward the kitchen.

"Sit." The German woman motioned to the table where she'd shared a meal with Declan two nights before. "When did you eat last?"

Amalie could no longer form logical thoughts. "I don't know, maybe supper last night."

She couldn't understand the string of words Greta let out. A steaming bowl of noodles topped with beef and gravy was immediately set in front of her. Amalie picked up a fork and dug into the food like a starving street urchin.

Otto entered with a mug of beer. "Do you feel better?"

She covered a yawn with the back of her hand and nodded. "I've never tasted food better than this."

"*Gut.* My wife's an excellent cook."

As she sipped the ale, Greta hustled around the kitchen preparing the restaurant's evening meal. The stout woman stopped and picked up her empty plate. "Did you have enough to eat, Fraulein?"

"Yes, more than enough. I'm so full I can hardly move."

Greta pulled over a chair and sat at the table with her. "Where's Declan? Why is our boy not with you?"

Amalie's face fell. She couldn't hide the pain tearing her apart. "He's gone, and I have nowhere to go."

"What do you mean?"

Amalie set her elbow on the table and rested her forehead in the palm of her hand. "I don't know anything anymore." Her eyelids drooped.

Strong hands shook her. She opened her eyes and gazed at Greta's concerned face.

"*Meine arme, kleine.*"

"What?"

"My poor little girl. You come with me."

She followed the German lady along the hallway and entered a bedroom at the end. Greta rummaged through the top drawer of a dresser. She pulled out a cotton nightdress and handed it to her. "Put this on and get into bed. We'll talk in the morning after you've had some sleep."

The next morning she opened her eyes to bright rays of sunlight filtering through lace curtains. Amalie gazed around the small, but tidy room. Where was she? A small print of a castle on the wall caught her attention and stirred her memory.

She slipped out of the borrowed nightgown and pulled the rumpled, dark blue gown over her head and did up the buttons. Voices drifted down the hall from the kitchen along with the most heavenly fragrances of breakfast cooking.

"Good morning." She stepped into the warm room and took the seat

Otto pulled out for her.

"Morning, Fraulein." Greta handed her a cup of coffee. "Sleep well?"

Amalie sipped the strong brew gratefully. "I don't think I moved all night. You were so kind to let me stay here."

Otto grabbed a shopping list off the table and slipped out of the room.

"You seemed quite troubled yesterday." Greta put a plate of bacon, eggs, and toast on the table. She pulled utensils from a large cabinet in the corner and placed them with a napkin next to the plate. "You have argument with my boy?"

"Declan abandoned me, snuck out of the bedroom in the night while I slept."

Outrage sparked in her eyes. "You lie."

*****

Declan kicked at the burned timbers of Amalie's music hall. He picked up a charred piece of wood and turned it over in his hand. Outrage swept through him. "What the hell happened, Patrick?"

"I dunno. Joe stepped out back to toss trash last night about ten o'clock and smelled smoke." Patrick shoved his hands into his pockets and rocked on his heels. "We were lucky. Saloon patrons kept the damage to a minimum until the fire brigade arrived."

"Trick's damaged?"

"No. The rock walls saved us. From what I could see after a quick appraisal, most of the damage occurred in this front section of your building."

Declan offered his hand. "Thanks, I appreciate you saving as much of the structure as you did. I'll do a more thorough evaluation in the morning when I have a clear head."

"Don't thank me. *Lily's* admirers did this for her. Joe rushed inside and alerted everyone her music hall was on fire. Not one of them hesitated to help put the blaze out."

"She's stolen the heart of most men in town I'd wager." Declan moved back and assessed the overall damage. "Maybe it's a good thing Amalie didn't come back with me to see this mess."

"Where is she?" Patrick was quick to ask.

Irritated by the prying tone of Patrick's voice, he tamped down his urge to tell him it was none of his business. He had no intention of feeding the man's curiosity, not now, not when bitterness clouded his every thought of Amalie. "She's found a better offer."

"Sonuvabitch!" Patrick ripped off his hat and slapped the brim alongside his leg. "I told you she was trouble."

Unwilling to discuss Amalie with Patrick, he walked away.

Patrick jogged alongside him. "What are ya going to do with the building now?"

"Nothing has changed. We proceed as previously planned." He had no choice if he was to convince Amalie he never doubted she'd come home. If she came home, that is.

"If she's not coming back--"

"She knows I'm the one funding the theatre."

Patrick grabbed his arm to keep him from walking away. "Everything?"

He pushed away from Patrick. "Yes."

"How'd she find out? I can't figure you'd have told her."

"Life's circumstances." Declan gripped Patrick's shoulder. "I've had a long day. I'm going back to the hotel. Talk to you later."

"Right." Patrick finally caught on he was in no mood to chitchat and returned inside the saloon.

Declan almost tripped over Bunny on his way through the lobby. He knelt, rubbing his pet's head. "Ye miss me, boy?" Bunny's tail wagged a mile a minute. Declan affectionately tolerated the slobbering tongue along the side of his face. "I missed you, too."

He opened the supply cabinet door and grabbed his violin case. He patted the side of his leg. "Come, Bunny, let's go for a walk."

Walking through the cemetery entrance, serenity, peace, and quiet greeted him. His broken spirit vacillated between despair and rage. The fragrant daffodil blooms were gone now. Weeds and dried grass replaced the bright blooms, reminding him of his own miserable life.

He leaned the violin case against a gnarly apple tree now bursting with ripened fruit. Bunny took off across the graves in pursuit of a jackrabbit. He dropped onto his knees in front of Judith and Angus's grave markers and removed dead blooms from around them.

"My grand plans have turned to dust." He tossed the weeds across the way by the tree. "Maybe I should say 'turned to ash' instead." He set back on his heels and gazed at what was left of his family. Brushing the ground in front of their markers reminded him he needed to plant some summer flowers up here. Judith always loved daisies. "I'll find some daisies and plant them for you, Mama." *Oh God, what am I doing?* He grabbed his head and rocked back and forth. The huge hole in his heart hurt like hell. "I'm so lonely. I have nowhere else but here to turn for comfort."

He dropped his chin to his chest, wishing his foster parents could provide him with a way to find relief. For someone who'd been so blessed in his life, he now felt cursed.

"Call me fool, Mother, but I want her back. I love Amalie and she knows it, but yet she ran at the weakest excuse. If I thought it would do any good, I'd go after her and drag her home. I've come to realize if we're to survive, she has to decide on her own to return to me. I'd never know for sure she'd stay otherwise."

He stretched out on his back between the two graves and watched clouds move across the orange-touched sky as evening approached. Where was she? Did Amalie regret leaving without giving him a chance to explain? The uncertainty made him crazed with worry. As far as he knew, she had no money when she left the suite with Jenny Lind. Colton assured him he would take care of her if she swallowed her pride and went to him for help.

Bunny's frantic barking grew louder. He rolled over to see a skunk on the run straight toward him. Bunny nipped at its heels. He jumped to his feet. Swinging his hands and stomping his boots, he managed to veer the skunk off its track. What else would go wrong today? The day just kept getting worse.

"Get over here, you crazy hound."

Bunny dropped across Angus's plot.

He ran his fingers through the dog's matted fur. "Are you telling me my attitude stinks, you wily beast?" He gazed at his violin. "Alright, you win."

He leaned against the tree and tuned his instrument. The shrill sound of the cicadas blended with diligent bees buzzing about the sweet fruit overhead. A haunting melody flowed off his bow, circling around the silent grave markers. Bunny's snores added a bit of bass. He smiled, and then chuckled at his makeshift orchestra. Not bad. He'd asked for a lifting of his morale, lightening of his heart. Judith and Angus's spirits answered him one more time. Music would always be his salvation.

He tucked his violin in its case and stood, waking Bunny in the process. "Come on you lazy mutt. We've got work to do."

On the trek into town he contemplated the preacher's betrayal to his townsfolk. The fire starting so soon after his encounter with King may be a coincidence, but doubts ran rampant in his head. Amalie stood up to the reverend, hurt his pride, but he didn't think she'd pushed him to the degree of burning down her music hall. He'd eaten supper at the man's table a few Sundays a month the last couple of years and never noticed King's attitude as belligerent. If he confirmed his fears King burned the hall as a warning to Amalie to leave town, he'd take immediate action to protect her.

"Hey, Declan." Ethan waved as he left the boardwalk and crossed the dirt road. "Have you got a minute?"

"Sure. What's the problem?"

"Maude's had an accident and I'm worried about her."

"Let's grab a bite to eat and you can tell me about it." He opened the door to the Bell Tower Cafe and ushered the doctor inside. Ethan ordered a cup of coffee, but Declan's stomach nagged him, reminding him he hadn't eaten all day. "Will you bring me my regular, Anna?"

The waitress paused and pointed to the menu posted on the wall. "Are you sure you don't want something besides meatloaf, Declan?"

"Absolutely not, and bring a big piece of warm apple pie with that meal, will you? It should be illegal for anything to smell so good."

Once the waitress left, he turned to Ethan. "What's going on? Is that dear old lady seriously hurt?"

"Maude tripped down the stairs. She has lots of bruises but thankfully only a sprained wrist. It's enough to keep her down for a while. I'm amazed she didn't break her neck."

"When did this happen?"

"Last night. Claire wrapped her wrist and stayed with her until I could get to the boarding house today. The banister needs repair for one thing and she's going to need help around the place. Can you suggest anyone who might assist her?"

"I'll speak to Harold Eriksen tomorrow about fixing that banister." He thought a moment. "Widow Russell might be interested in the job. It would be ideal. She could take her children with her."

Anna set his meal in front of him and refilled his coffee cup. The aroma of meatloaf and gravy made his mouth water. He picked up his fork and dug in. Being home around what he held dear, including Mrs. Clayton's meatloaf, is where he wanted to remain.

"There's something else." Ethan put a half teaspoon of sugar in his cup and stirred.

Declan stopped eating at the hesitation in Ethan's voice. "What is it?"

"I'm so sorry for letting your secret out to my wife. I thought--well, I didn't think is the trouble."

"Don't worry about it, Ethan. Maybe it's time for me to make some changes. We'll see what happens the next few days."

"I know Amalie hurt you, and I'm sorry. You've been an astonishing influence on the woman."

"I've not given up on her yet. How's Marinda dealing with this situation? Her anger hit the boiling point by the time I found her locked in my bedroom."

"I'm sure deep down inside my wife's sad to have lost the special bond the two of them built, but right now she won't talk about it. She had such hopes her sister changed, but I fear not."

Chapter Nineteen

Greta's hostility bewildered Amalie. "What else am I to believe? In the morning I woke to an empty bed. He'd gone and taken his belongings."

"My heart aches for you, Fraulein. You are such a foolish young woman. My boy would never treat a lady in such a manner."

She flinched at Greta's sharp criticism. She'd survived many disappointments in her life, but Declan's thoughtlessness caught her off guard, sorely stinging her pride, and breaking her heart in the process. Now this woman burdened her with guilt for criticizing him?

"Are you going to eat your breakfast?"

How could she eat with her stomach tied in knots? She pushed the plate away. "I'm not hungry anymore."

Greta gathered the dishes and carried them to the sink. She lifted one of the lids off the stove and dropped more wood inside. The cuckoo clock chirped nine times.

"We need to get started on tonight's meal." Greta hefted a pot off the stove and poured hot water into the sink.

"You don't want me to leave?"

"You said you have no other place to stay. You lie about that, too?"

"No."

"Then you work until you leave."

"I wouldn't be much help in the kitchen."

Greta wiped her wet hands on her large white apron. "I have rules. Those who don't help don't eat. You do chores until we find you proper job," she said. "Start with these dishes."

"I have to retrieve my suitcase at Browns Hotel this morning. Maybe when I get back I can give you a hand."

"Nonsense. Otto soon returns with supplies. He can fetch your case while we cook."

The critical comments she'd made earlier against Declan certainly put her on Greta's wrong side. Caught in an uncomfortable situation, she grabbed a washcloth. The least she could do was help with a few chores.

The mess seemed daunting, but one by one she emptied the sink of dishes, utensils and pots. The hot water burned her hands while sweat dripped off the end of her nose. She wiped the errant strands of hair off her forehead and pushed on.

Once she restored all the clean kitchenware in their proper cabinets, she pulled out a chair and sat at the table. Greta dropped three dripping wet, headless chickens in front of her with a thud. "I need these plucked clean."

Amalie's stomach reeled at the thick gamey stench. "You can't be serious? I'm not touching those -- those things." Blood seeped across the table toward her. She grabbed her stomach and bolted out the back door and retched into tall weeds. Afterwards, she leaned against the outside wall trying to compose herself.

She returned to the kitchen on unsteady legs. Greta shoved a glass of cool water at her. "You look pale. Are you alright?"

She sucked in a couple more deep breaths and nodded.

"*Gut*, I need them chickens done in an hour, Fraulein."

Amalie drew an inner strength and faced the mess on the table. Greta had wiped the blood away, making the task at least tolerable. Half an hour later she slumped back in the chair, wishing she could run out the front door, but massaged her aching fingers instead. She couldn't go anywhere until she found her baggage.

"Sorry Fraulein, no suitcase," Otto said, joining them in the kitchen. "If your belongings don't show up in a week, the boy at the front desk said they'll give you money."

"A week? I can't wait a week. What a ridiculous policy." She wiped her hands on a towel and pushed away from the table. "I'm going to take care of this right now."

Greta scowled at her. "Fraulein, you have chickens to finish first."

Amalie appreciated Otto's understanding glance. He rolled up his sleeves and joined her at the table.

"Thank you," she mouthed silently as soon as his wife returned to peeling apples. Amalie pushed wisps of hair out of her eyes, grabbed the last bird and started ripping feathers.

Grateful for Otto's help, Amalie hummed an upbeat tune. His foot tapped to the rhythm. The diversion helped pass the time. Soon he bagged the feathers and carried them to the garbage container out back.

Amalie cleaned the mess from the table and joined her hosts. She accepted a cup of coffee and relaxed as the room filled with the aroma of baking apples.

"I've an idea where you might borrow clothes until your suitcase is found," Greta said, sipping from her cup. "The nuns at the mission keep donations for the needy. It might be better if you let them help you for a while."

The barbed suggestion infuriated Amalie. After she'd worked her fingers to the bone all morning, the woman still disliked her. Her dress reeked of sweat and fowl. She needed something clean and tidy to wear. Amalie thanked them both for their hospitality and, after cleaning up, left with written directions to the mission clutched in her hand.

A stroll through three blocks in an uphill residential area brought her to the sprawling whitewashed Mission Dolores tucked off a main road. Children's voices raised in laughter came from behind a high fence. She lifted the latch of a large wooden gate and entered a tidy enclosure. Flower gardens graced the walkway along the way to the chapel entry. At the first door she encountered, Amalie passed through a two-foot thick adobe wall into a dim room. Religious statues adorned the far wall. Her gaze settled on the large cross between them.

"Ma'am?"

She whirled around and stared at an older man garbed in a brown robe tied with a rope. "I'm sorry. If I'm intruding, please forgive me. This is my first visit to a mission."

He pointed to a crudely carved wooden bench. "I am Padre Francesco. Please, won't you have a seat and tell me how I can be of help."

"Thank you, Padre. My name's Amalie Renard. I--" The humiliating words caught in the back of her throat. "I'm a proud woman who's always paid her own way until now. I am so embarrassed asking for a handout, but I'm stranded without clothes or money. I spent last night with the couple at the German restaurant, but can't intrude on them any longer."

His eyes clouded. "If I might ask, are you in trouble with the law?"

"The law? No," she shook her head. "My family and I were staying with the owner of the Browns Hotel, but they've all returned home and my luggage has been misplaced."

"Do you speak of Declan Grainger?"

"You know him?"

His face lit up. "I most certainly do. A friend of Declan Grainger's is most welcome here." He stood and held his hand out to her. "Please, won't you come with me?"

He led her out into the bright sunlight. She shaded her eyes as she glanced around a large courtyard framed by a huge vegetable garden on one side and a long building on the other. The older children played ball in the yard. The padre excused himself a moment. He had a few words with a couple of nuns who kept watch over the younger ones.

"We have many orphans who live within our sanctuary." He pointed to a long building to his left. "This is a dormitory for our younger children."

She followed him inside a tidy room filled with about two dozen beds covered in multi-colored quilts. A wooden cross hung over each bed, tacked onto the brown adobe walls by a golden chain.

She admired the coziness of the dormitory. "This is a wonderful place for the children."

"A friend who was an orphan himself donated everything the children needed."

"Declan did this?" She surveyed the room a second time, appreciating his benevolence.

"Declan Grainger's a very generous patron. Each month we receive money for their care."

How many lives has Declan touched? She picked a book off a miniature table surrounded by several chairs and glanced through brightly colored pages. The padre spoke of him as the orphans' guardian angel. She'd heard the same kind of comment in Paradise Pines about the Night Angel. Could he possibly be both? She shook her head. *Now you're being ridiculous, Amalie.*

"Is there something wrong, Ma'am?"

"Declan isn't the type of man who'd abandon a woman without telling her he was leaving, is he?"

The padre frowned. "I have no idea what you refer to, miss, but I've known the lad since he was a boy searching to find his way. He would never abandon anyone, especially a woman as lovely as you."

His words struck a note of truth. "Do you have time for me? I'd like to ask for your advice."

"Come." They stepped outside. He pointed to a table under a large shade tree. "We can sit over there."

He motioned to one of the nuns. In a few moments, a young woman carried a tray of lemonade, glasses, and a plate of cookies to the table.

"Thank you, Elspeth. I'd be delighted if you'd fill the glasses for me."

The girl nodded, and after she'd finished her task returned inside another smaller building.

"What I don't understand is why you didn't stay to see if Declan returned?" the padre asked after she explained her predicament.

"I was scared."

"Of Declan?"

"No, of trusting my feelings for him. I believed his tender words." She fought the urge to cry. "I still do."

"Giving trust is never a guarantee it'll be reciprocated. Acting in haste has brought you here. Quite often we make it impossible for people to live up to our expectations. He's a man who may only be guilty of an error in judgment. You should have kept an open mind until you knew the facts."

The more she thought about her assumption yesterday morning, the clearer it became she'd made a terrible mistake. If only she'd listened to Marinda.

The padre patted the top of her hand. "Declan holds his emotions close to his chest. If he told you he loves you, I would take him at his word."

"How can you speak with such certainty?"

"Declan told me Saturday while he was here."

"Declan told you he loves me?"

"He inferred he'd finally found the kind of happiness Judith wished for him and then asked me to journey to his mountain town to perform a marriage ceremony."

"His marriage?"

"I'm assuming so. You don't happen to have an angelic singing voice, do you?"

"He keeps telling me I do." She couldn't help but smile. *He does love me, or at least he used to before I made an ass of myself.* "Thank you for your advice."

"You're welcome." He motioned for a young girl with a handful of clothes to join them. "This is Ruth. She's found several gowns for you to choose from. May God go with you, young lady."

Amalie accepted the garments and followed Ruth into a small bedroom. She tossed one ugly dress after another across the narrow bed in disgust. One gown came close to fitting, but it needed a cinch around the waist. *Beggars can't be choosers,* she reminded herself.

There was no mirror in the room. She would have to keep the faith nobody would laugh at her drab, dark brown attire. Since no one was around to thank again after she'd changed clothes, she slipped out of the mission and headed back to Portsmouth Square and Browns Hotel.

After yesterday's confrontation, she had no patience left to deal with the rude clerk. He actually rolled his eyes again as she approached the desk. She wanted to jump across the counter and scratch his eyes out. "I want my belongings now."

"How many times do I have to explain, we don't have your bag, Mrs. Renard?"

Colton Brown approached with rapid strides. "Amalie, what's the problem?"

"This idiotic man lost my suitcase and I want it back."

He gazed at the clerk. "Is this true?"

The young man stammered at the inquisition. "Yes, sir."

"Why didn't you come to me, Amalie? I need to talk to you anyway."

She was angry enough to spit. "Why would we have anything to talk about?"

He gripped her arm and pointed toward the stairs. "Calm down. We've a lot more to discuss than you realize."

They strode up one flight of stairs where he ushered her inside his office. She sat in front of his massive oak desk and picked a piece of peppermint candy from a pottery dish. Her breathing slowed, somewhat calming her ire.

He hunkered down at a large safe and spun the dial. "Before he left, Declan asked me to give you the key to his suite."

Struck speechless by Declan's generosity, she didn't know what to say.

Colton swung the heavy door open. "You're welcome to use the suite until you go on tour." He handed her the key and a bag of coins. "If you need more money, ask one of my employees to get hold of me."

She stared at the large, silver key. "This is so unexpected."

Colton leaned against the edge of his desk and crossed his arms over his chest. "I've known Declan for years and consider him a close friend. He's being quite generous with you, but you're his business not mine."

"I suppose you're feeling a bit protective of a partner, but at the time I left I was taking care of myself the best way I knew how."

Colton settled back into his leather chair. "If I've made you feel uncomfortable, I owe you an apology."

"No, you don't owe me anything." She stood.

"Wait. Please don't leave in a huff. Declan expected better of me or he'd not asked for my help. You are a guest in this hotel and I am at your service."

"I'm not his responsibility anymore. Why do either of you care what happens to me?"

Colton threw his hands up. "How can two such intelligent people act so damned stupid?" He moved around his desk and gripped her arm before she could reach the door.

"Let me go."

"Not until you listen to me." He spun her around to face him. "Declan packed his suitcase and left it behind the counter downstairs so he'd be ready to leave once the supplies for the theatre were packed into the wagons. He feared last minute tasks might cut his time short and didn't want to miss the boat."

Each word slammed against her. "Are you sure?"

"Yes, I'm sure. He stood where you stand right now and told me."

She sank back onto the chair. "Why didn't he leave me a note or wake me?"

"I thought he did. It's something you can ask when you see him." He pulled an envelope from the safe. "I assume you'll return to Paradise Pines and straighten out this mess?"

She covered her burning cheeks with her hands. "Yes, I believe I will."

"Then I'm to give you this."

She opened the flap of the envelope and found a steamship ticket inside with a note attached. "Hurry" was written in Declan's bold handwriting.

She slumped back in the chair. Declan still wanted her. The note cinched it. Tears streamed down her cheeks. "Do you have a clean handkerchief I can use?"

He nodded and pulled one from his shirt pocket.

"I can't believe how dumb I've been." She wiped the dampness away and blew her nose.

"Don't be too hard on yourself, Amalie. I'm sure you can work your differences out."

She relaxed now the tension had eased. "I hope you're right."

"Do you suppose we can be friends after getting off to a bad start?"

He'd been patient with her and seemed genuine. She laid her hand in his, accepting the offered truce. "Yes, I'd appreciate your friendship."

"How about having supper with me tonight? It'll give me a chance to apologize for butting into your personal business."

She ran her hands along the sides of her unstylish gown. "Thank you, but without my suitcase I have no clothes or anything else I need to make myself presentable."

He walked to the door and called someone named Gil. "Have a carriage brought out front for Mrs. Renard immediately."

"Certainly, sir."

Colton motioned for her to go with his employee. "Have Madame LaCroix provide enough clothing to get you back to Paradise Pines. I'll cover the cost."

"I don't need your charity, Colton." She held up the bag he'd given her from the safe. "I can pay for my own clothes with the money Declan left for me."

"Our employee's negligence is my responsibility. I always make sure our guests are treated with the highest standard of care. I insist on replacing your belongings."

He escorted her from his office. "I'm assuming you'll be ready to leave right away."

She grimaced. "Yes, I've some kowtowing to do. I'm sure Declan thinks the worst of me."

*****

"My God, Mrs. Renard, what's happened to you?" Madame LaCroix ushered her into the back room. "Get out of the horrid rag and toss it into the trash."

Amalie smiled at the whirlwind Madame LaCroix caused as she stormed out of the room, cursing in something Amalie presumed was irate French. She stripped the dress off and kicked it out of her way.

Two women struggled through the door with a large copper tub. Several younger women followed behind with pots of steaming water. "Madame thought you needed the laundry water more than the pile of dirty clothes."

Even with all their irritating chatter regarding the state of her appearance, Amalie wanted to hug the girls. Once they left, she removed her undergarments and slipped into the heavenly warm water, savoring the lilac bar of soap.

Alone, she leaned against the back of the tub thinking about Declan's unexpected kindness. He was a good man, probably too good for her. She closed her eyes wondering what kind of reaction she'd receive when she got home. Home. She'd never thought of any place as home before. Her beautiful pink and white room in the hotel beckoned her. Sleeping in her own bed seemed a corner of heaven. Maybe feathers did have their place -- as long as she didn't have to pluck anything to get them there.

Madame LaCroix poked her head through the doorway. "Are you alright, Mrs. Renard?"

"Yes, and please call me Amalie."

One of the girls entered with a large, white cotton towel and clean undergarments while Madame LaCroix slipped a hanger holding a light green dress onto a hook. "This gown will fit. If you like the dress, you can wear it back to the hotel this afternoon."

"Thank you. You have no idea how much I appreciate something pretty and clean to wear again. Colton Brown will cover the cost of my clothes today. His clerk lost my suitcase."

Madame LaCroix winked. "In that case, I'll see what else I can find in your size."

By the time she dried off and slipped the new gown over her head, Madame strolled into the room with several more dresses. The nightmare ended at last.

Amalie rode back to Browns Hotel with a satchel containing several days' worth of clothes and another pair of shoes resting on the seat next to her.

The vacant suite's quiet stifled her. She opened the heavy drapes and swung the window open wide, letting in the last rays of sunlight and fresh sea air. The magic of San Francisco had dimmed, but she'd love to visit again. Next time she'd insist Declan spend time with her. She wanted him to show her places he loved and share childhood memories with her.

She picked up the settee pillow and brushed her nose against the soft fabric, breathing in Declan's spicy cologne. What a fool she'd been for doubting his promises. She hurt the man who'd been so generous with her. It amazed her Declan still loved her in spite of her selfish ways. She hoped his support continued after she encountered him again. Somehow she'd find a way to convince him to forgive her.

With her wardrobe replenished, Amalie could dress with care. Colton warned her they'd dine at a fancy restaurant overlooking the ocean. The carriage stopped in front of a single story building located high on a cliff. The elegance of the place stole her breath. One entire wall consisted of glass, the others boasted murals of ocean scenes. Their table overlooked white, foaming waves breaking against treacherous rocks.

Plates of battered fish and several kinds of crustaceans arrived after a short wait. She appreciated the variety of seafood Colton chose for her. Their waiter filled glasses with a rich red wine. He raised his to her. "I wish you and Declan much happiness."

He sipped his wine. "You are quite attractive tonight in your new gown, Amalie."

"You have no idea how much I appreciate something clean and beautiful to wear again."

"Miss Fox?"

Hearing Mr. Oliver's voice, she turned. The Arts Council director's approach caught her by surprise.

"Pardon me for interrupting your supper, but I have good news which might give you cause for celebration."

"Do you know Mr. Oliver, Colton?"

He nodded at the interloper. "How are you this evening, Bernard? I haven't seen you at the gaming tables lately."

"That's because I've been setting up Miss Fox's tour. It's worked out much better than I expected. You leave in three days' time and travel east, stopping at several cities on your way to New York City. You'll join the European troupe three weeks after you arrive in New York. Arrangements are being made for you to perform for a minimum of six months across the European continent."

"How have you arranged this so quickly? Jenny Lind said it would take a week or so."

"As luck would have it, one of the organizers hadn't left town yet. He's traveling back east and is delighted he can escort you himself. Plans couldn't have worked better."

She stood. "Could you excuse us for a moment, Colton?"

A look of surprise crossed her dining partner's face, but he nodded.

Amalie returned after her discussion with Mr. Oliver, sat, and picked up her fork, ignoring the questioning glance Colton sent her. She dipped the piece of white fish into a tangy sauce. "This is delicious. Do you come here often?"

When he didn't answer, she noticed he had a deep frown.

"Is something wrong?"

He set his fork down. "I don't know. Why don't you tell me?"

"I can't think of a thing. I sent a very disappointed Mr. Oliver on his way. Tomorrow I'm going home where I belong."

Colton picked up his wineglass. "Here's to a lady who has made a great decision and the lucky man who's waiting for her."

*****

A golden sunset settled over the community Amalie considered home as Lucas drove the stagecoach into town two long days later. A few people strolled along the boardwalks at the supper hour. Lucas drove past the music hall. She stared in horror at the burned timbers. She stuck her head out the window, but missed catching another look before he drove around a parked wagon.

She couldn't get out of the coach fast enough. As soon as Lucas pulled to a stop in front of Chaumers Hotel and helped her alight, she entered the lobby only to find the registration desk empty. She left her satchel behind the counter and rushed along the boardwalk, ignoring the people who greeted her. She was frantic to reach the music hall.

It's burned. Her heart sank. How could this happen?

Night Angel

A lantern sat on a barrel of nails inside the charred entrance. She lit the wick and entered the dark interior. Each step widened the crack in her heart. The faint illumination didn't give her much view of the destruction, just enough to send her spirits spiraling into despair. Then she noticed the stage -- her stage. It wasn't damaged. She moved around the burned section of floor until she could run her fingers along the edge where Mr. Eriksen created his beautiful carvings of flowers. Tears welled in her eyes. She sank against the edge trying to bring her emotions under control.

A noise alerted her she was no longer alone. She blew out the wick and stood as still as possible in the darkness.

Someone moved toward her with a lantern in his hand. Shadows kept her from determining his identity. A couple of feet from the stage he set the lamp on the floor and cocked a rifle. "Step into the light."

She let out the breath she'd been holding. Declan's voice stirred her senses. She searched his face, noticing his eyes held a sadness which hadn't been there before she ran away. His beard had grown thicker over the past four days and wisps of hair stuck out from underneath the brim of his hat. Even so, he was still the most handsome man she'd ever known and she wanted him back.

"Step out now and show yourself, or I'll shoot and ask questions later."

She moved into the lantern's glow. The attraction between them charged the air. "Are you going to shoot me, or can I come home now?"

Chapter Twenty

Amalie held her hands above her head and sauntered toward him. The subtle swing of her hips shot his blood pressure through the top of his head. A trickle of sweat ran down the side of his neck. She had him hot all over. He'd never wanted her more than he did at this moment.

The little temptress knew exactly how to play him. Her very essence charged the air around them. He leaned the rifle against the stage and wrapped his hands around her tiny waist. His lips claimed hers in a deep, penetrating kiss. He wanted to devour her, keep her tied to his side so she'd never disappear again. Her soft, sweet moans drove him to near insanity. Breathless when he released her, he rested his forehead against hers. "What took you so long?"

"Why didn't you wake me before you left?"

The slight tilt to her chin alerted him she wasn't as sure of herself as she wanted him to believe. He cupped her stubborn chin. "I thought you understood I was showing you the depth of my devotion when we made love. You have to trust me to do what's right. I've never been a husband before, so how about you giving me a wee bit of leeway until I perfect my skills." His lips claimed hers once more.

He pulled away and searched her face. "I'm not your father or dead husband, Amalie. They were fools not to appreciate the amazing woman you are."

She wound her arms around his chest and pressed her cheek against his heart. "I'm sorry, Declan. I've never been in love before so maybe I need a wee bit of leeway, too."

He couldn't move, couldn't unfurl her embrace. He wanted to believe her. Resting his cheek against her soft curls, he inhaled the sweet fragrance of lilacs. "For how long?"

"Until forever."

The depth of emotion in her voice as she spoke the words he'd waited to hear took his breath away. Trusting them to be true was another matter. He searched her eyes for an answer. The deep sapphire acted as an aphrodisiac. "You don't know how much I want to believe you. These last three nights have been the loneliest of my life." He ran his thumb over her lips. "I want you in my bed, in my life now and always."

Her eyes widened, a hint of guilt reflected back at him. "I panicked. I feared somehow I'd make a mess of things and you wouldn't love me anymore."

"Do you still feel that way?"

"I know what love is now, and have no intention of living without you. I'm not going anywhere," she answered without hesitation. "Those days I spent alone in San Francisco forced me to face some facts. I'd rather be here with you than anywhere else, including stages in foreign places."

His instincts told him to take the chance and trust her. He had to or let go, and letting go was impossible. She'd become as important to him as breathing. He could not imagine his life without this tempestuous woman. "I wouldn't survive if you left me again, sweetheart. Tell me now if I'm not who you want to spend the rest of your life with, because if you're not going to stay--"

She pressed kisses over his face, along his neck. "I want you, Declan," she whispered in his ear. "You have every right to be leery of my past actions, but I've changed. Please, trust me."

An angry growl erupted from her stomach. She tried to stifle a giggle. "Talk about bad timing."

"How true. Come on, let's head over to the Bell Tower Cafe and feed you." He grasped her hand, picked up the lantern, and led her outside.

"What happened here, Declan?" she asked, watching him board up the front of the music hall.

"I wish I knew. It's strange the fire happened Sunday night when town's the quietest."

"Yes, the same day the preacher expected me to stand in front of his congregation and profess my servitude to him."

He glanced over his shoulder at her. The determined jut to her chin didn't bode well. "What are you thinking?"

"There's one person I can think of who'd take pleasure in forcing me out of town." She glimpsed the rifle propped against the blackened timber.

"Don't be ridiculous, Amalie. You're not going after the preacher. We'll tell Matt our suspicions and let him handle the problem."

Her back went rigid. "Either you or that gun comes with me."

There was no use arguing with his lady in her mood. He grabbed the rifle and nodded toward the church on the hill. "I'm right behind you."

The darkened church on a Wednesday evening puzzled him. A stab of apprehension for what they might find made him cautious. "Stay close and follow me."

He peeked through a side window, but nothing, not even the glow of a candle flickered inside. He motioned her to follow close behind him. They slipped through the hidden door in back and headed through the storage room into the parish office. Everything appeared in good order.

"This looks very suspicious. I've never known him not to be here on a weeknight. I want you to wait for me at the restaurant while I get the sheriff. When I confront King, I'd feel better if Matt was with me."

Her hands went to her hips, and her foot began an annoying tap. "After only three days your bossy ways are back? Do I have to retrain you every time I leave town? You should know me well enough by now to realize I won't be dictated to."

He wanted to strangle her pretty neck. Why'd she always have to fight him? "Until I know what's going on, you will not go anywhere near Reverend King. Do you understand me?"

Tension raised a wall between them. "You didn't treat me as a child in the music hall a while ago. What am I, a woman to be taken seriously, or a child to be spoken to in such an audacious manner?"

"Don't push me too far." He caught a trace of mischief in her eyes and stopped. He took a deep breath. "I prefer to deal with Amalie, not Lily."

He rested his hands on her slender shoulders and gazed deep into her eyes. "I'd like it better if you're somewhere I don't have to worry about you. Please, Amalie, will you grab a bit of food and wait until I find out if there's a problem or not?"

"Now, was that so difficult?"

"Depends on whether you're going to--"

She placed her hand against his mouth. "Stop while you're ahead, honey."

*****

At Matt's knock, Preacher King jerked the door open. "Get the hell off my property."

The man's ashen face heightened Declan's concern. Weeping resonated from the back of the house. He shoved the preacher out of his way. At an opened bedroom door, he stopped and called out to Mrs. King. Slumped over in a wooden rocking chair positioned next to the bed, she either didn't hear him or ignored his presence.

A soft glow from a bedside lamp reflected across Phoebe still as death. A gasp tore from his throat. Not believing his eyes, he stepped up to the foot of the bed and stared. Her flesh, charred beyond recognition, made his skin crawl. "Dear God, what happened?"

Mrs. King jumped to her feet. "Get out you devil's spawn." She pummeled her fists against his chest.

Declan grabbed her hands and held them at her sides. The overwrought woman crumpled against him. He carefully helped her back onto the chair and wrapped an afghan around her shoulders.

"What's going on in here, Declan?" Matt asked, entering the darkened room.

Declan nodded toward Phoebe lying in the bed and hurried out. He returned to the parlor and sat next to the preacher. The man had aged drastically since he'd seen him last week. "What happened? Did your daughter try to stop you from burning the music hall?"

The preacher sat tight lipped and defiant.

Matt entered the room, disgust lining his brow. "Quit stalling, King. Answer the man's question."

King threw his hands up. "Alright, give me a chance. Halfway to the church Sunday night I remembered I'd forgotten my glasses. On my way back home I noticed Phoebe pass under the street lamp with my large lantern in her hand." He stopped and caught his breath before he continued. His gaze locked with the sheriff's. "I called out, but she ignored me and tossed the oil lamp against the front of the building. Some of the fuel must have splattered onto her clothes. By the time I reached her, fire consumed her. I wrapped my coat around her to put out the flames, but not soon enough." He brushed his sleeve against his eyes.

The turn of events shocked Declan. "Why didn't you get her proper medical care?"

King shook his head. "Ethan was out of town. I found the herbalist I'd heard about in the Chinese camp. He's put a poultice on the burned skin every few hours since the accident happened."

"I'll get Ethan, Matt. She needs proper medical attention immediately."

The sheriff followed him outside. "Let me handle the situation, Declan. Your presence here will only make matters worse."

"You're certain?"

"It's for the best under the circumstances."

"Why do I feel responsible for what's happened?"

"Don't let King's grief flow over onto you. He hurts like hell right now and is out of his head with heartache and guilt. Go be with your lady."

On the way to meet Amalie at the restaurant, he worried about how she would take the news. He stepped inside and strode around a few tables. Her worried expression indicated she'd figured out something terrible happened.

She wrapped her fingers around his and squeezed. "Declan, what's wrong? Did King confess?"

He shook his head. "It's bad. Phoebe accidentally set herself on fire while burning the music hall. I don't think she'll live through the night."

"What?" she stammered.

What he'd witnessed at the King house must have disturbed him more than he'd thought. Several quick shocks ran the length of his body. A chill surged through him. How could the situation have gotten so out of control? Until now, he'd always been a good judge of character. "I should have noticed Phoebe was as unstable as her father. Matt tried to convince me I'm not responsible, but I don't know. I set her misguided action into play."

"No," Amalie blurted out. "Matt's right, you're not to blame. It was her decision to start the fire. Her own carelessness put her in a deathbed. Not you."

Amalie's words held merit, but he couldn't shake off the reproachful look in Mrs. King's eyes when she'd attacked him. He studied his lady and noticed her tight lips. "What else is going on in your head?"

"Phoebe burned the music hall, not the hotel. It was me she wanted to hurt, not you. I know you cared for her, and I'm sorry she might die, but I don't feel guilty. Her jealousy drove her to do it."

He rested back in the chair contemplating her comments. "You might be right."

"Did the preacher blame you, too, or does he have enough moral fiber to place the responsibility where it belongs -- on himself?"

"The man's so weighed down with grief he isn't thinking straight. I fear what actions he'll take and against whom when he has to face the loss of his only child."

He rose and held his hand out. "Let's go home."

*****

Declan lit the lamp on her vanity. "My suitcase," Amalie shrieked. She searched through her possessions. "How'd the case get into my room?"

He set the satchel she'd left downstairs earlier in the day on the floor next to the bed. "George probably brought it up when you arrived."

"No, it's been misplaced since I left it behind the check-in desk at Browns Hotel Sunday morning."

"Ethan or Marinda must have had your bag loaded onto the buggy with mine before we left for the steamship. I had my suitcase stored behind the counter, too."

"Enough about suitcases," he pulled her against his rock solid chest. "Are you going to talk all night or kiss me?"

"Hmmm. Sometimes your bossy ways aren't as annoying as others."

She pressed her soft lips against his. He couldn't get enough. Starved for her the last several days, worried he'd never possess Amalie again, he hungrily ran his fingertips over her flushed body. He pressed her against the sheets. A soft, yellow glow from the bedside candle flickered across her face. "I'm worth taking a gamble on, sweetheart."

"Yes, my king of hearts."

He had the rest of their lives to love her, but tonight he needed to prove to himself she was indeed his.

*****

Sunrays filtered through the window waking Amalie early the next morning. Her hand touched an empty pillow. She jerked up.

"Take it easy, sweetheart, I'm here."

She wrapped the sheet around her naked body. "Why are you on the floor?"

"Along with looking for my boot, I'm searching for a bride. Do you know where I might find one?"

She sent him an impish grin. "Certainly not under my bed, Mr. Grainger."

He chuckled, a deep sensual sound bringing every nerve ending she had to life. His intense green eyes softened.

"Are you available?"

She shrugged, enjoying their banter. "Maybe, but you've not proposed. A girl could shrivel up and die an old maid waiting for you to ask properly."

He got up, slipped his second boot on and grabbed her dressing gown off the vanity chair. "I refuse to do this if you're not clothed."

She frowned.

"Too hard to concentrate," he said with a grin.

"Oh." She slipped her arms into the sleeves, wrapped the ties around her waist and knotted them. He was being so wonderful about proposing properly.

Taking both her hands, he knelt on one knee. "Sweetheart, from the moment you put your hand into mine the day you arrived in Paradise

Pines my life has never been the same. You've turned my world upside down, and I cannot imagine life without you. It would be my greatest honor if you'd become my wife."

His voice, full of deep emotion, spoke directly to her heart. "Dearest Declan, yes, I want to be your wife. God help us both, I'll marry you."

He cupped her face and pressed his lips against hers. Hungry for more kisses, she slipped her hands around his neck and pulled him closer. The rapid beat of his heart pounded in anxious harmony with hers.

Their gazes locked. "You're certain about this, aren't you?" Declan pushed an errant tuft of hair off her cheek.

"Very."

He pulled her back against him and kissed her long and in a most satisfying way.

Declan opened the balcony door. Fresh mountain air filled the room. The warmth of the morning promised another beautiful day. "I must get to work. There's a hotel to run and a music hall to rebuild."

She crawled back under the covers and watched him dress. To think he belonged to her warmed her all over. She prayed she wouldn't do something stupid and ruin her chances this time.

He pulled on his shirt and tucked the tails into the waistband. He slipped the red suspenders over his shoulders and grabbed his hat off the bedpost. "I'll be in the hotel until breakfast is over and then you can find me at the music hall."

"Thank you for keeping me informed."

He dropped down on the edge of the bed and grabbed her hand. "You have no idea how terrible I feel for the pain my thoughtless action caused. I know how vulnerable you are when it comes to trust and should have awakened you instead of leaving a note."

"You left a note? I didn't find one."

"When Marinda explained what happened, I feared you'd not seen it. I found the piece of paper on the floor by the bedside table." He looked deep into her eyes. "Am I forgiven?"

She pulled his lips against hers. "We both made bad choices, but it's over now. No more misunderstandings. From now on I promise I'll give you the benefit of the doubt if you'll do the same for me."

"Deal. Now I gotta go or I will never get out of here. You are much too much of a temptress dressed in your flimsy wrap." He blew her a kiss on the way out the door.

Content as a kitten she snuggled deeper under the blankets until a loud knock roused her. Pulled from a deep slumber she sat up, orienting herself. After she stumbled to the door and opened it, Mama Claire waltzed into the room.

"About time you got yourself home, lass." The heavy set woman sat on the vanity chair and surveyed her. "Speak ta me."

Amalie crawled back into the bed. "I missed you and your tender ways, Claire."

"Are you staying with the lad or not?"

"Are you good enough with a needle to make a wedding dress?"

Claire's eyes lit up. "He proposed?"

"Yes, and I accepted."

Claire made the sign of the cross. "Thank you, dear Lord. I was worried about me boy." She moved around the room picking up scattered clothes. "When he came home without you, the lad was hurtin' bad."

She looked away, not wanting Claire to criticize her, too. She'd had more than enough admonishment about her bad judgment from Greta.

"What type of bride dress are you goin' ta be wanting?"

"I don't know yet. I've been engaged--umm, what time is it?" She glanced behind Claire at the clock and shrieked. "Noon? Declan will never let me hear the end of this."

She climbed off the bed and searched through the armoire. "As I was saying, I've been engaged four hours and slept through them. I need to discuss plans with Declan first. I'll need your help."

"You might ask your sisters for help as you make plans."

She grimaced at the thought of Marinda. "I don't know yet. One of my sister's is probably not speaking to me. Until I fix the damage, it'll be you and me."

She handed Claire the lustrous, pink pearl necklace. "I want to wear this on my wedding day. It's the first gift Declan's given me."

Claire gasped, taking it from Amalie. "It's beautiful."

"Hide it for me, please. I don't want the Night Angel taking this piece from me, too."

"Most puzzling the way the man has taken a fancy to your jewelry." Claire wrapped the necklace in a handkerchief and slipped it into her skirt pocket.

Amalie tossed a white lace bodice and dark blue skirt on the bed. "I've some business with Patrick I must take care of before I continue with my list of candidates. The sooner I catch the thief, the happier I'll be."

Close to an hour later she strolled inside Trick's with her tablet and pencil stashed in her bag. Deep in conversation with the bartender,

Patrick didn't notice her enter. It gave her a chance to study him. Did he agree to front the music hall for notoriety or greed? Whatever the reason, she knew he'd been instrumental in giving her a chance at her dream.

"Patrick?"

His scornful glance irritated her, but she held her tongue.

"What brought you back, Amalie? I thought you had bigger places to go?"

"Can we talk? I have a few things to say."

He pointed to a table in the back of the room. "You want some coffee or a whiskey?"

"Coffee would be fine."

She accepted the cup and sipped the potent brew. "I know you fronted the music hall for Declan. I don't know why, but--thank you."

His jaw dropped. "What?"

"Thank you for the chance to change my life. I know how you feel about me so I'm a bit surprised."

"Jesus, I can't believe you just thanked me." He sipped at his coffee, contemplating her. "Don't fool yourself. I didn't do it for you. I did it for the money."

"I thought money was probably your motivation, but appreciate your honesty at last. You didn't have to save the building from the fire Sunday night. I guess I have you to thank."

"What's going on? This isn't like you. Are you backing out of our deal to perform at Trick's or what?"

"No, I want to settle some debts before I start my new life." She rose and leaned close to his ear. "Declan has asked me to marry him. See you tonight." With that said, she moseyed over to confront two patrons dressed in black.

Satisfied none of the men at the table fit the mold of the Night Angel she stuffed the list back inside her bag and strode outside onto the boardwalk.

"There you are," Declan said. "Won't you please come on a picnic with me right now?"

"Sorry, but my Night Angel list has priority today."

"The list can wait. I can use some quiet time with my lady this afternoon. What do you say?"

*****

He pulled the buggy to a stop at the end of a long, dusty road. "You are now at my favorite spot along this section of the American River." He wrapped his hands around her waist and helped her to the ground, not passing up a chance to capture her lips in a long, sultry kiss. "This marriage situation might work out better than I imagined." He snickered as he handed her the fishing pole and grabbed the basket.

The golden brown grass snapped under their feet. A slight breeze rustled the leaves of birch and oak trees growing along the bank. He led her along a narrow path through some shrubs to a wide spot in the river.

She took a seat on a large rock and slipped her boots and stockings off. The sand eased through her toes, tickling her feet while she watched Declan assemble his fishing gear.

"Now, observe the master."

His cocky grin and quick wink caused her heart to skip a beat. *Lord, he's a beautiful man.*

Declan pulled cheese from the basket and rolled a small ball in some crushed green stuff.

"What are you doing?"

"This is the herb anise. For some reason it draws fish to its licorice taste. I learned the trick from an old miner who stayed at the hotel a couple of years back."

"You're cheating."

He ruffled her curls. "Wait until after you taste the fish I cook for you, you'll soon change your mind. Trust me?"

She touched his arm. "Always."

He nodded and stepped across a couple of large rocks until he was about midstream. She'd watched a few moments before he yelped.

"Grab the creel and come get this trout." He held a trophy of a fish in his hand.

She bent over, grasped the back hem of her skirt, and pulled it forward, tucking the end inside her waistband. With her legs bare to the knees, she could easily maneuver through the water.

He unhooked the fish and dropped it into captivity. "You want to try your luck?"

She shook her head.

"Coward."

She grabbed the pole from his hands and swung the line mimicking his style. The hook went wild and caught on a birch tree. "If you laugh, I swear I'll swipe the smug grin off your face."

With more patience than she could imagine, he wrapped his arms around her shoulders and demonstrated how she could cast the line into a pool where he'd caught the first fish.

Contentment stole over her. Now, more than ever, she was thankful she'd returned to Paradise Pines. Jenny Lind had been right. It would have been a treat to travel around the world for a while, but long nights without Declan would have taken away the pleasure.

A tug on the line sent her into action. "I've got a fish." She jerked the pole back, swung the dangling trout out of the water, and spun her catch around her head. Declan rushed to help her get the fish off the hook and inside the creel.

She beamed at him. "I caught a trout."

He scratched his head. "I must say it's the strangest way I've ever seen a fish landed."

Her chin jutted. "I have my own unique way of doing things."

An easy smile tugged at the corners of his mouth. "Really? I never would have guessed."

She broke into a rapture of giggles. "I suppose you'll exaggerate the tale when you tell about my skills."

He tipped her nose with his wet finger. "I'm sorry, honey, but it's too tempting a technique not to share." He handed her the pole and picked up the creel. "Let's eat. I'm hungry as a big old grizzly bear."

While he cleaned their catch, she pulled slices of cheese and biscuits from the basket.

He placed the fish into a hot cast iron pan. "For a girl, you're not bad at fishing, just very entertaining."

She snapped her head around. "Are you asking for trouble, or is this an attempt at humor?"

"Just teasing," he said with a mocking grin. "From where I sit, I'd say everything you do as a girl is quite appealing."

She poked her finger into his chest. "I promise you this, *Mister* Grainger. Your life with me will never be dull. I'm full of surprises."

His raucous roar cleared the trees of birds. "I look forward to living on the edge of uncertainty, my dear."

After they'd eaten, he returned their equipment to the basket. "About time you meet Angus and Judith."

"What?"

"When we get there, you'll understand." They strolled back to the buggy hand in hand. He stored the fishing gear and basket in the rear compartment before helping Amalie settle onto the seat. He joined her and headed the horse toward the edge of town.

The cemetery appeared remarkably well maintained. Declan grasped her hand and pointed to a fruit laden apple tree. She dropped to her knees in front of two beautifully carved wooden markers and rubbed her fingers over the top of the one with Angus carved across the front and then the other one bearing Judith's name. The sight of the two of them together brought forth unexpected emotions.

He knelt next to her and slipped his arm around her shoulders. "Why the tears, sweetheart?"

"I hope someday someone will stand in front of our graves and say 'these two loved in life and now sleep next to each other for eternity.'"

Declan brushed a curl from her cheek. "Let's get married as soon as we can make the arrangements."

He pulled a diamond ring from his shirt pocket. The breath caught in her throat as he slipped it onto her finger.

"The night Judith died I promised I'd give this ring to the woman I chose as my wife."

The diamonds, cast in the shape of a blooming rose, sparked bright blue, red, yellow, and white in the sunlight. "Judith was such a beautiful, dignified woman. I wonder how she'd feel about you marrying me, a sassy, poker-playing, saloon singer."

"Dignified?" He snorted. "You have Judith wrong. She and Angus were down-to-earth, simple people who grew up dirt poor in the Scottish Highlands. True, my foster mother loved beautiful things around her. I mean, she kept me, didn't she?"

"You do have a point."

"Would you honor me and wear Judith's ring? Angus had it made special for their twenty-fifth wedding anniversary. I don't want you to feel pressured if you'd prefer another one or a band instead."

She laid her hand over his arm. "The thought as well as the beautiful design are so amazingly lovely, how could I not accept?" She smiled at him. "As long as you come with it, I'd wrap a piece of wire around my finger."

Secure in his love and in his embrace, she snuggled against him. "To think I almost missed all of this."

"You're here now is what matters."

The cock of a rifle snapped behind them so suddenly Amalie flinched.

"Jezebel!"

She sat up and stared over Declan's shoulder. A scream froze in her throat.

Chapter Twenty-One

Declan snatched the knife from his boot and propelled his head into King's rotund belly. The rifle flew from the preacher's hands, exploding wildly into the air. The stout man hit the hard surface. A palpable thud shook the ground.

With his temper barely held intact, Declan pressed one knee against King's chest. He ran the tip of his knife across his adversary's neck and drew a slight trickle of blood. "You force me to protect what's mine."

The stocky, German gravedigger trudged up the slight hill. "Dammit, Grainger." Gustav pushed his wide-brimmed straw hat off his forehead and jammed the tip of his shovel into the soil. "The preacher's here to pick a gravesite. Leave him to his grief."

Declan pulled back and returned the blade to his boot. "The grave's not the only reason he's here, Gustav. The bastard tried to kill Amalie." He got to his feet and brushed the dirt off his britches. "Go fetch the sheriff."

He grabbed King's rifle from between two grave markers and checked on Amalie. "Are you alright, sweetheart?"

She nodded. "I'm fine now." Her eyes grew wide. "Look," she pointed across the cemetery, "King is getting away."

"You stay here." Declan shoved the rifle into her hand and chased the preacher through the cemetery, but didn't reach him before the man took off on his horse.

Amalie caught up with him at the gate. "Let him go. We've all had enough."

He wrapped his arms around her in a secure hug. "Calm yourself. I'm not going anywhere. I'd never catch him with the buggy."

Unease washed through him as he watched King disappear. From now on he'd keep an eye out for the unstable man. His sense of the man's emotional state fed his fear for Amalie's safety.

Later at Trick's Declan leaned against the wall while Amalie entertained the patrons. He looked forward to the time her nights in the saloon ended. Possessiveness was new to him. Jealousy raised its ugly head whenever another man ogled her strutting across the temporary stage. She would fight him to the end if he asked her to quit.

Amalie stepped off the bar and sauntered toward him in the startling beautiful blue gown. "You ready to take me home?"

He ran his finger along the soft skin of her cheek. "I'm more than ready, my love." They strolled from the smoky bar into the energized night air. He inhaled a deep breath. "The heady scent of sawn lumber is in the air."

"Yes, Paradise Pines has its own special fragrance. I missed the mountain's bouquet while we were in San Francisco."

She stumbled on the boardwalk. He slipped his hand protectively around her waist. "I don't know why you insist on wearing those ridiculous boots. You'll be lucky to get back to the hotel without a broken ankle."

"Madame LaCroix insisted higher, smaller heels will soon be the height of style in San Francisco."

"I'll never understand women's fashions."

She chuckled. "It's a conspiracy. We keep changing them so you won't learn our secrets."

He could barely see her smile in the soft steady glow of the street light, but knew it was there mocking him.

Reverend King stepped out of the alley and stood under the streetlight, blocking their way. "I've got a gun."

The maniacal tone of King's voice caused the hair on the back of Declan's neck to stand on end. The preacher placed the gun against Amalie's head and motioned for them to step into the alley.

Declan's gaze focused on King's finger pressed against the trigger. One slip and the gun would go off. A fear so great it almost strangled him rose in his throat. "Let her go, you bastard."

"My daughter's dead because of this strumpet."

Declan glared daggers at the man before spouting a string of expletives.

Amalie didn't hold back her anger either. "Your daughter *is dead* because she tried to burn down my music hall. Don't shift the blame on me, you ass."

Declan gazed at Amalie in dismay. Was she trying to get shot?

"Go ahead and curse me, Jezebel. I'll have my revenge."

Declan feared the preacher might carry out his threat one way or another. He worried the man might be carrying an explosive device in the pouch strapped over his chest. He must disarm the unstable man. "Calm down, Preacher. A man of God forgives."

"Shut your deceitful mouth. Your false promises and lies lured my beautiful Phoebe from my teachings." He ripped open the cumbersome pouch. A stash of Chinese fireworks filled the leather bag. "Now I take from you as you took from me."

Fear for Amalie's safety rose to new heights. Declan had witnessed firsthand the kind of damage black powder caused. "Lots of people could get hurt if those explosives go off."

"I deliver justice for my daughter."

"You bastard!" Without another thought, he lurched toward King.

King grabbed a fist of Amalie's hair, snapping her head back. "Step away and get rid of your gun, Grainger."

Declan didn't move.

"Now!" King pulled the hammer back a click.

"Don't hurt her." He chucked his weapon the length of the alley and held up empty hands. "I did as you said, now let her go."

"Don't Declan. Lily Fox never begs."

"Stay out of this, woman. This is man's business."

"Not when the problem concerns me, it isn't." She struggled to break loose from King's grasp. "This supposed man of God tried to seduce me in his own church. He has no morals."

"Shut up," King snapped.

Amalie's exceptionally loud, high pitched shriek reverberated into the otherwise peaceful night. She shoved her elbow into King's midriff, and at the same time slammed the sharp heel of her boot into his instep.

"You bitch." King knocked the pistol butt against her head and thrust her to the ground in a fit of fury.

Horrified, Declan glanced at her curled in a heap a split second before his right hook connected with the preacher's jaw. King spun around and fell off kilter against a pile of trash stacked inside the alley. Fireworks scattered out of the satchel across the ground. A moment later, the determined man pulled wooden matches from his shirt pocket.

"You damned fool, King." Declan hunkered down next to Amalie's still body. A soft moan escaped her lips. It was the most beautiful sound he could possibly imagine.

The first of the explosions rattled the walls of the buildings lining the alley. Fire already consumed the street entrance. His heart pounded even harder as each new blast threatened his chances of seeing Amalie to safety.

He scooped his lady off the ground, held her tight against his chest and ran as best he could across the alley toward a tunnel entrance wedged between the Wells Fargo building and a wall of solid granite. The tip of his boot slid under the lid's edge enabling him to slide the plank aside. He adjusted Amalie's slight frame across his shoulder. Once she felt secure, he negotiated the ladder rungs downward until he could lay her on the ground.

"Grainger!" King yelled.

Declan groped around the dark floor until he gathered a handful of rocks. Halfway up the ladder he spied King near the entrance. He lobbed the stones across the alley into the rubbish.

King emptied the pistol into the crates where the stones landed.

The distraction gave Declan a perfect opportunity to slide the lid back over the entry. His knife wedged against the edge of the plank provided a temporary lock.

The narrow passage was near impossible to maneuver with a torch plus the dead weight of Amalie's unconscious body. Each step increased his unease.

A loud explosion overhead rattled a few rocks loose from the tunnel's low ceiling. Another blast vibrated the ground beneath his feet. His steps quickened. Fear of being trapped heightened his already out-of-control claustrophobia. In a short distance they'd be out of this auxiliary tunnel and into the larger, main channel which would lead them to safety in the cavern. He wiped the sweat from his brow with the back of his sleeve before continuing.

Amalie moaned. Her eyes opened wide in shock. "Oh, God." Frantic, she glanced around the rock walls.

He wrapped his arm tight around her flailing hands. Her feet dropped to the rock floor, knocking him off balance. He fell back and cracked his head hard enough to see stars.

"It's me." He grabbed the torch from the ground and illuminated his face. "It's me, Declan."

Her body shook. "Where are we? I'm cold. I thought hell would be hot."

"You're not dead. You're with me in an abandoned mine tunnel. You're safe, sweetheart."

Another explosion erupted above them, his arm banded around her waist. "Can you walk?"

After a couple of steps, she agreed to try. He led her deeper underground until they reached the grand cavern, stockroom, and haven for the Night Angel.

He lit several lanterns. The illumination chased the demons from the large chamber.

"What is this place?" She rubbed her arms.

He pulled a blanket from a cabinet and wrapped it around her shoulders. "Miners used this natural cavern for storage. Over there's a prehistoric river. Now it's a creek with fresh water."

She glanced where he pointed. "The mine still looks occupied." She sat on an overturned ore cart. "How'd you uncover the cave?"

"Angus found a tunnel during the hotel remodel. I'm not too keen on dark places so avoided the mine until after his death."

Letting out an exhaustive sigh, she scooted back and relaxed against the stone wall. "What happened after I fell?"

"King lit those damnable fireworks. By the time I got us to safety, the street was ablaze. I've heard several blasts since which leads me to believe there's a fire above."

He knelt in front of her and touched the bump on her head. "That's a nasty knot. How do you feel?"

"I'm a little dizzy, but I don't think it's serious."

Amalie leaned forward. She ran her fingers through his tangled hair until she touched a tender spot.

He flinched.

"You've got a deep gouge on your head. Take my seat." She slipped from the blanket. "I'll find something to remove the blood."

He shrugged off her concern. "Don't worry. My head's so hard I hadn't noticed."

She ignored his comment and rummaged around in a barrel where he'd tossed bits and pieces of his costume. He held his breath. She could find something which could give his night jaunts away. When she picked up a discarded mask, he winced. He sure as hell didn't want to explain his alter ego under these circumstances.

"This rag should do."

She didn't seem to notice anything peculiar about the cloth. He let out his breath at the good fortune and said a silent prayer of thanks.

She sidled around the large pile of firewood he'd stored. At the creek's edge, she knelt and soaked the mask before returning. Her breasts rubbed against his shoulder while she cleansed his wound. When he could no longer repress his mounting desire, he wrapped his hands around her waist and pulled her tight against his chest.

"Stop flirting with the nurse." She grinned, but didn't hesitate to plant a kiss on his puckered lips.

Another blast reminded him where they were and what forced them into the tunnels. He leaned his head against hers. "One of the traits I admire the most about you is your indomitable spirit, but goading King with his pistol pushed against your head was an insane action to take."

"It worked, didn't it?"

"You could've been killed for God's sake."

"Don't raise your voice to me. I remember mentioning life as my husband would never be dull."

"I can't say I've not been warned." His gaze searched her face with the resiliency of a man given another chance. He prayed it was the last, and from now on their life wouldn't be an uphill push. "Can we go home now?"

She pushed a stray curl off his brow. "The scrape doesn't look as bad as I first thought." Amalie eased away. "I'll be right back."

He tried to grab her hand, but she was too quick for him. "Where you goin'?"

"I need to rinse the cloth and my hands. You know how I feel about the sight of blood."

This time his luck didn't hold. She lifted the dark material and stared at the mask. He knew the moment she figured out what she held. Her entire body went rigid. Mad as hell, she strutted toward him in those ridiculous boots.

"Is this--this thing yours?"

"Yes." He caught the mask she threw at his head.

A deep frown crossed her brow. "You have nothing else to say?"

He stepped within two inches of her. "Wait just one damn minute. I'm not the only one at fault here, sweetheart."

"Ooh," she stomped her foot, "don't you 'sweetheart' me you--you cold hearted beast. I want to know why you stole my jewelry and annoyed the hell out of me."

She didn't give him a chance to answer. Amalie paced, mumbling. "Of all the low handed, mean tricks anyone has ever played on me, this takes the prize. You're nothing but a common thief and--and--" Her toe tapped madly. "What do you have to say for yourself, and you'd better make it good, Mister Grainger?"

He couldn't even begin to comprehend the quicksilver turnabout of her emotions. Tired and out of patience, he dropped his hands over her shoulders. "I kept telling you to consider me as the Night Angel. How many times did you refuse to put my name on your ridiculous list?"

"You know I didn't take you seriously. You could have been more adamant about the Night Angel's identity."

"Would you have believed me? You closed your mind for various reasons, none of which had anything to do with common sense."

"Such as?"

"My eyes weren't the right color. I wasn't tall enough. My shoulders weren't broad enough. Shall I go on?"

Her toe stopped tapping and her jaw dropped. "I can't believe you were jealous of your own self, Declan."

"I'm not proud to admit I've been jealous of any man who draws your attention away from me."

"Now who's being ridiculous?" She failed miserably to hide a grin. "If only I'd listened to my heart."

He started to relax. "What do you mean?"

"Every time the Night Angel taunted me, my throat got dry, my heart beat erratically."

"You were frightened. It's understandable."

"No. Like I told you..." Her eyes grew wide. "Oh no, the things I confided in you about my feelings for the Night Angel." She dropped her head into her hands. "I am so embarrassed."

He chuckled, enjoying this unexpected turn of events.

"Amalie, look at me." He raised her chin. "Your jewels are safe. I took them to protect you."

"Why? The one person I needed protection from was you."

"You conveniently forget the man in St. Louis who recognized his sister's ring."

"That doesn't explain why you stole my jewels."

"I figured if I took the jewels piece by piece, you'd run out of jewelry eventually and wear the damned ring."

"Why didn't you ask me for it, explain your motives?"

"I was waiting for you to trust me enough to ask for help."

Her body slumped as Amalie took in what he'd told her. "I ran you a merry chase, didn't I?"

He nodded.

The woeful expression in Declan's eyes stirred Amalie's heart. She figured it was a ploy to win her over, but she didn't care. He really loved her. "I'm sorry it took me such a long time to trust in you, my brave champion." She rose on her toes and kissed him. "We can go home now."

Declan guided her along another dank tunnel. The lantern illuminated their way with a wider arch than the torch. Finally they reached a tall ladder. He handed her the lamp before edging up the rungs. She couldn't see what blocked their way, but took comfort he'd probably done the same procedure many times since he'd discovered the tunnel.

He called her name. She ventured up the ladder until he took the lantern and grasped her hand. He pulled her into the room a second before explosions drew them to the window. Smoke filled the air. Loud voices sounded and people rushed past the hotel.

"I hope nobody got hurt."

He grabbed his gun belt and buckled it around his waist. "I'd prefer you to remain here in my bedroom until I find out what's happening on the street. Until we know where King is, you're not safe. Will you stay here until I return, please?"

She nodded. "Be careful."

She surveyed a clean and tidy room, noticing the sparseness with the exception of a wicker chair, cabinet, and floor to ceiling bookshelf.

He replaced the cover over the tunnel entrance and pushed the bed back into place. "Have a seat in the lobby."

She sat on the large chair in the corner. "This is quite different from what you have at Browns Hotel."

"I don't spend much time in here, so it's never mattered." He brushed a kiss on her cheek and walked out the door. A moment later he popped his head back inside. "I love you."

Her heart warmed. He was gone before she could answer back.

While she waited for his return, she paced the length of the lobby. The clock struck twice. What's taking so long? She'd never forgive herself if something happened to him.

Thirty minutes later Declan walked through the door covered in soot. She rushed to him, but he held his hands up. "Don't touch me, or you'll get filthy."

"The fire? Preacher King?"

"Slow down, sweetheart. A small section of the Wells Fargo building's roof is damaged. A portion of the News and Novelty Store needs to be replaced, but the coffee shop is gone, burned to the ground."

She didn't care if he was dirty. She sagged against him. "I'm glad there isn't more damage. What of King?"

"He can't hurt you anymore. Black powder shows no mercy."

"He's dead?"

"Yes, like his daughter, he didn't heed the danger of being careless with fire." He held her away and touched the tip of her nose and both cheeks. "Now look at you. You and your clothes need a good wash up."

Amalie pinched his cheek. "You think you're so cute, don't you?"

Marinda entered the hotel.

"What brings you out this late?"

"Ethan is checking out a couple of men who tried to put out one of the fires. He'll be in to check on the bump on your head as soon as he can."

"I'm perfectly fine. Just a few scrapes and bruises." She pointed to the chairs. "Let's sit while we wait."

It was only a few moments until Ethan joined them. He looked into her eyes and fingered the lump along her hairline. "If any of the dizziness Declan says you experienced returns, I want to see you right away."

Amalie thanked Ethan before turning to her sister. "I want to apologize for locking you inside the bedroom in San Francisco. I must have been out of my mind. I'm sorry."

"You're apologizing? I never thought..." Marinda grabbed her in a hug and squeezed. "Nobody could find either of you after the fire started. We assumed the worst." Tears trickled down Marinda's cheeks. "I guess I do love you."

"I'm glad because I'm going to need both yours and Darrah's help with the preparations." She held up her hand and showed Marinda the beautiful engagement ring.

Marinda squealed. "It's about time. I'm so happy for you both. We'll have such fun making plans for your wedding."

Ethan grabbed Declan's hand. "Congratulations. Guess this means we're to be brothers."

"So it seems." Declan shook Ethan's hand.

Declan motioned Amalie toward his bedroom.

"Wait, I need something from my room first."

Amalie returned in a few moments with the hatbox. She set it in the middle of his bed and shut the bedroom door. "Before we start our future, I need to face my past honestly."

She opened the lid and lifted the false bottom. The emerald and diamond ring rested in the folds of the blue velvet bottom. She picked it up and placed the damning piece of jewelry in his palm. "Will you help me return this to Virginia's brother?"

Declan stared at the ring for a long moment. "If the gambler hadn't recognized this trinket, you wouldn't have run all the way to Paradise Pines in fear of being arrested for murder. I owe the man a lot more than the ring. I owe him for my life with you."

She wrapped her arms around his waist and rested her head against his heart. "I never thought something so wonderful would come from Rupert's evil." She pulled away. "I've more." She dumped the rest of the hidden stash of jewelry onto the coverlet. The diamonds and other gems sparkled in the lamplight. "I don't need the security of these items Rupert stole any longer. Since I can't return them, will you find a way we can help people who've been victims of vicious crimes? Giving them to the padre at Mission Dolores might be nice. He can sell them and maybe put the money toward educating the children."

"I'm certain the padre will be delighted. Helping the less fortunate without expectation of receiving anything in return is a good way to live." He reached for his mother's keepsake on the top library shelf. With a flick of his finger, the snap on the back panel gave way. "I believe these are yours."

She stared at the ill-gotten jewelry. "I don't want these either. They never were really mine. You've shown me I'm important for who I am, not what I have." She grabbed the jewels and placed them on top of the stash.

"Why'd you take on the Night Angel persona? You have to admit it's an unusual way to help people."

He sat in the chair and pulled her onto his lap. "Elizabeth Vellechamp's rude comments about me being a worthless orphan gave me the idea. Once the pretext started, I couldn't stop. If my foster parents hadn't been so generous after my father passed away, I'd have died an urchin on the streets of New York City. When they left me a fortune, I decided to return their generosity by helping others. Paradise Pines townsfolk are proud people. I needed to find a way of helping without them feeling beholden to me."

She snuggled against him secure in his love. "I'm ready to join you in that bed now."

*****

During the next three weeks, Paradise Pines buzzed with activity. The Mitchell brothers arrived with the two wagonloads of equipment and furniture for the music hall. Seamstresses, carpenters, painters, and printers were hired. No longer under Preacher King's oppressive control, the citizens' spirits brightened, attitudes changed.

Amalie stayed cosseted at the church most days with rehearsals. The choir and musicians showed promise and couldn't wait to join her on stage.

The music hall finished, Declan sat in the back row of red velvet seats and admired the results. He was amazed at how fast the reconstruction work progressed. The room was now restored to Amalie's specifications. She'd been right about the curved stage being lit with a semicircle of oil lamps placed around the edge. The red, velvet curtains pulled back with golden rope ties created an appropriate frame for her artistic performances.

"There you are. Admiring your handiwork?" Amalie appeared happy, her cheeks rosy from the exhilarating walk from the church.

He smiled and nodded. "How'd rehearsal go today? Are the musicians going to be ready for the grand opening tomorrow?"

She sighed. "If you believe in miracles, I'd say yes. Some haven't played music in years, but they're excited to be involved with my performances. I've heard several comments about the song you asked them to learn. You should tell them you wrote it."

"Only if it turns out as good as I hope."

"I don't think there's any doubt." Amalie planted a kiss on his cheek and sat in the comfortable seat next to him. "Please tell me where you found such a grand assortment of musical instruments."

"The Lord moves in mysterious ways, my dear."

She tapped her toe and glared.

"Alright, I can see you won't quit nagging until I tell you. Joey had them sent to you. When a beautiful woman is involved, he can be very resourceful."

"Joe Crandall, the steamship captain? Why?"

"He'll be here tomorrow night. You can ask him then."

"I want to know now."

He hated to give in so easily, but when she pouted her bottom lip, he became distracted and couldn't help himself. Nor could he keep something as tantalizing as this a secret any longer. "Elizabeth Vellechamp donated them."

Amalie flew off the seat. "That woman would never help me with anything except a coach out of town."

"Joey asked Genevieve's parents for her hand in marriage. The old bitty was so eager to rid him from their life she offered him a bribe of the instruments. Sound familiar?" Declan let out a raucous laugh. "I wonder how Elizabeth Vellechamp would react if she knew she'd helped make one of your dreams come true after all?"

Amalie frowned. "What about Genevieve? She must have been heartbroken being abandoned by Captain Crandall."

He took her hand and kissed the back of it. "You've turned into quite a tender heart, haven't you?"

"Genevieve introduced me to Jenny Lind. I adore her."

"Your friend's not hurt. Joey and I met her when we were kids. They've secretly been friends ever since. It was actually her idea to trick her mother into helping with your music hall. She convinced Madame LaCroix to ship them with your new wardrobe. You might even see Genevieve up here with Joey tomorrow."

A loud bang sounded from the front of the building. He bolted from his seat and rushed out the exit with Amalie close behind him.

An appreciative crowd greeted him. "What's going on?" He noticed a mischievous grin on Amalie's face. "Do you have something to do with this?"

She grabbed him by the shoulders and turned him around. The new marquee across the front of the building read 'Carnegie Hall' with 'dedicated to Angus and Judith Carnegie' painted across the bottom in smaller letters. A picture of Amalie as Lily Fox posed in a dance position graced the middle. He could barely believe his eyes.

"Are you pleased?" Amalie asked.

"Pleased?" He wrapped his arm around her as he continued admiring the sign. "By honoring my foster parents, you honor yourself as well." He leaned down and kissed her. "Thank you."

*****

Amalie finished her encore song. The audience stood with a loud and appreciative ovation. She raised her hands, quieting them. A moment later breathtaking music flowed from a violin in the dark recesses of the stage behind her. Chills covered her flesh. Declan? It had to be. She recognized the song he'd asked the musicians to learn. The Night Angel stepped from behind the velvet curtains, violin resting under his chin, bow gliding with ease over the strings. The orchestra enhanced his spellbinding performance.

Each note brushed over her with a soft kiss. He was making love to her with his music. Note by note, Declan devoured her heart. He sauntered to her side. Similar to the first time he'd kissed her on the very same spot, her knees turned to jelly. She grabbed his arm for support at the end of his song.

The audience clapped with enthusiasm. He stood straight and tall taking in their praise. Moisture glistened in his eyes. He handed her the violin and bow, then his black hat. Her eyes misted in anticipation of what he was about to do. He untied the mask and pulled it from his head. A loud gasp resounded.

"My friends, you don't need the Night Angel anymore. Over the past couple of weeks, I've seen a miraculous change come over this community. The oppression of Preacher King is gone. You have purpose again and can live the dream of why you came to this country. The proof is in this splendid music hall you sit in today."

He clasped her hand. Devotion radiated from his eyes, speaking to her heart. "I won't be spending my nights in those damnable tunnels anymore."

The residents of Paradise Pines jumped to their feet, wild with their applause. Amalie smiled and lifted the violin to hand it back to him. Declan reached for the special piece, but griped her wrist instead. With a squeal of surprised delight, she found herself bent backward over Declan's strong forearm, his lips warm and tender against hers.

The cheers and whistles grew louder as she kissed him back. Love filled her heart. She wrapped her arms around the strong column of his neck, overwhelmed with joy and feeling for the first time in her life she truly belonged to someone.

The band began to serenade them. Declan lifted his head. His expression filled with tenderness and his smile curved with the promise of unending passion to come.

Lost in Declan's eyes, she realized there was no stage or audience to compare with the miracle of a lifetime with this amazing man.

She claimed his lips in another soft kiss and the roar of the crowed faded into silence as Amalie drowned in the security of Declan's love.

Don't miss a story in the Paradise Pines series.

Marriage Bargain

About Paisley Kirkpatrick

Dusty bearded men in miner's boots and faded shirts, gamblers in fancy vests and frock coats, a ghost or two tossed in for good measure -- these are the characters who come to life on my pages. Mix them with strong, independent women of the Gold Rush era who delight and tempt their heroes to take a chance on love and, voila, it's romance.

My husband of 43 years and I are fortunate enough to live in the Sierra Mountain Range of California where this colorful time in history took place. Exploring gold mines, inspecting the stately historic homes, and traveling through tunnels zigzagging underground stirs my imagination and brings reality to my stories.

To write and create has always been my dream. Joining Romance Writers of America twelve years ago opened the door to achieving what I was born to do.

http://www.paisleykirkpatrick.com/

CPSIA information can be obtained at www.ICGtesting.com
Printed in the USA
LVOW11s0921231016

509928LV00002B/349/P